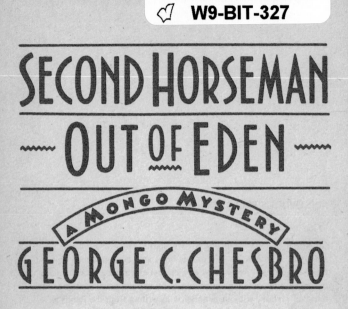

SECOND HORSEMAN
~ OUT OF EDEN ~

A MONGO MYSTERY

GEORGE C. CHESBRO

THE MYSTERIOUS PRESS

New York • London
Tokyo • Sweden • Milan

1.

SANTA Claus was long overdue, and if I didn't hear sleigh bells in another hour I was going to start calling the hospitals.

Santa couldn't be drunk, because my brother no longer drank—not since he'd emerged from the drug-induced madness that had transmogrified him into a de facto, reluctant religious guru to millions, and the subsequent events that had caused the deaths of thousands of people and almost killed the two of us. Garth kept a well-stocked bar in his apartment for drinking friends and his imbibing sibling, but at the moment he was out of Scotch—the imbibing sibling's drink of choice. Consequently, I went up a flight to my own spacious apartment on the fourth floor of the renovated brownstone on West Fifty-sixth Street that we'd recently purchased, and which now served as our respective homes as well as the richly appointed offices of the recently founded investigative firm of Frederickson and Frederickson, Incorporated. As founder and senior partner I had, of course, insisted that my name be listed first.

I didn't really want a drink and could think of no reason why Garth would call my apartment when he was supposed to meet me in his own. But I poured myself a drink anyway and checked my answering machine; there were messages from three former colleagues at the university who had called to wish me a Merry Christmas and tell me how much I was missed in the halls of academe. Nice. I put on a heavy cardigan, slid open the glass door at one end of my living room, and went out onto my frozen rooftop patio and garden to look down into the street for some sign of jolly old Garth, whom I desperately wanted to see stay jolly. The possibility that something could happen to conjure up my brother's sleeping demons was a constant haunt.

It was four days before Christmas, not quite two years since my brother had emerged from his long illness and subsequently burned all his professional, and most of his personal, bridges behind him. Not that there had been that many bridges left standing for either of us to raze, but I'd at least had my somewhat problematic career as a private investigator to which I could return.

Almost ten years before we had become involved with one of your mad scientist types, definitely not of any garden variety. Dr. Siegmund Loge had had two abiding obsessions: the music of Richard Wagner, specifically the *Ring,* and saving humankind from what he was convinced was its impending self-imposed extinction. All he'd needed to indulge his passion for Wagner was a good sound system, but it had turned out that his second obsession required the cooperation, however obtained, of Garth and me, of all people. Lucky us. Siegmund Loge had come within a Frederickson brother or two of loosing upon the world a plague that could have conceivably altered the makeup of every living thing on the planet, and forever changed, perhaps canceled, human history. Finding a way to stop him had nearly cost us first our sanity, and then our lives. And, as far as I was concerned, Garth's sanity was still a tenuous thing, to be jealously guarded and tenderly nurtured.

It was a situation for which, perhaps, I had myself to blame, and I would probably never know if certain key decisions I had made concerning my brother's health had been the correct ones.

When Garth had gone into a coma induced by a mysterious substance called nitrophenylpentadienal, I had intentionally, by using Richard Wagner's *Ring* Cycle, endeavored to reach into his deep mind to stir nightmare memories of Siegmund Loge and his Valhalla Project that had nearly swallowed up the two of us. The musical ploy had gotten Garth out of bed, all right, but it had also gotten me, not to mention the governments of the United States and Russia, and a few million people around the world, considerably more than I'd bargained for.

As a result of my well-meaning ministrations, Garth had emerged from his coma with what might modestly be described as an altered consciousness. He was a gaping emotional wound, an almost total empath who literally suffered with all the wronged, helpless, and injured of the world, while at the same time appearing as a kind of stony automaton to people—including me—who were more or less able to keep on trucking through the big and little travails of everyday life.

Garth had been . . . well, scary.

He'd come out of that more or less on his own, when the effects of the nitrophenylpentadienal poisoning had finally worn off. Or I'd thought—hoped—he'd come out of it. In fact, I now accepted the fact that, in some subtle and other not-so-subtle ways, he had been changed forever. Which didn't mean that he couldn't act like his old self, sometimes for prolonged periods of time, and that was how he had been for nearly two years. It was this sense of well-being that I felt, for no discernible reason aside from the fact that Garth was late, was somehow hanging in the balance this night, and

I couldn't shake a suffocating sense of foreboding. As far as I was concerned, there could be no more sojourns into harm's way for the Frederickson brothers. It was not myself that I was worried about, but Garth. I did not want to lose my brother again, for if I did I feared I would lose him forever into some terrible sinkhole of the soul.

Jingle bells, indeed. Where was he?

The poison had worn off, Garth had resigned from the NYPD, from which he'd been on an extended leave of absence. Eventually he had become my partner, and we had formed a corporation.

Well.

Much to our collective amazement, virtually overnight we became the "hot" investigative firm, not only in New York City but in Washington—to which we now commuted by shuttle three or four times a month to oversee a small satellite office and team of staff investigators we maintained there. There is often, it seems, a fine line between notoriety and celebrity, and apparently we—or I, at least—had crossed it, and found riches on the other side. We'd hardly had time to advertise our new corporate headquarters and list our telephone number before a score of *Fortune* 500 companies were lining up to offer us the most ridiculously easy assignments, for the most outlandish fees. Our more adventurous days now seemed part of a distant past, as we spent virtually all of our time doing things like background checks on prospective CEOs, coordinating industrial espionage investigations, working for congressional committees, or performing mostly cut-and-dried investigations for high-priced law firms. We were on permanent retainer to fifteen major corporations, and were rarely called upon to do anything to earn the fat fees these companies seemed all too happy to pay to Frederickson and Frederickson.

Good-bye, murderous minions of the C.I.A. and K.G.B; good-bye, mad scientists, witch covens, assorted thugs and assassins; and good-bye to all the other garden variety loonies I felt as if I'd spent most of my life dealing with. Hello, fat city.

Whether or not Kevin Shannon, president of the United States, was subtly steering business our way was difficult to tell. Shannon certainly knew that our attitude toward him was decidedly ambiguous, but that didn't seem to matter. The fact that the president had publicly acknowledged the "nation's debt" to us for our role in unmasking a very dangerous K.G.B. operative and had then awarded us the nation's highest medal for civilians—at a ceremony which Garth and I hadn't bothered to attend, for decidedly personal reasons— had apparently been enough to convince corporate America that Garth and I were "connected," and we saw no reason to disabuse our clients of such a notion. It seemed we were in imminent danger of becoming fat, lazy, and wealthy, and we loved it. Both my brother and I had struggled hard, each in our own way and for our own reasons, most of our lives, and we had been very close to death not a few times. We owed each other our lives many times over. Only when we had finally escaped from the bizarre ripples and vicious undertow of the Valhalla Project, which had haunted, threatened, and consumed us for the better part of a decade, had we come to realize that physically, emotionally, and spiritually we had both spent the better parts of our lives clenched like fists. You could say that we were trying to learn to relax; money might not be everything, but we were discovering that it can certainly be a powerful tranquilizer.

A lot of the work for which we were being so well paid could be done by our staff investigators, or with a few telephone calls; a lot of the work for which we were being so well paid was also crushingly boring—but that was fine with us. Garth and I had zestfully agreed that we would be happy to be crushingly bored with our work at least into the next century, at which point we might take the time to reevaluate our attitude.

Good-bye, bullets, knives, mind-altering drugs, broken bones, and squashed souls.

And, at least on my more optimistic days, it had seemed to me that Garth was healing. There had been lots of sports, including membership on a championship softball team with Garth as the star slugger and me as a second baseman who set a league record for most walks in a season, lots of concerts, lots of time with friends, especially loving women friends, lots of good food, and—perhaps best and most important of all—lots of good talk. Once again Garth had learned to laugh without shedding tears for those in the world who would never know joy or find anything in their lives funny, love without suffering pangs of sorrow for those who were alone, dine without feeling the hunger pangs of the starving, tell a joke without rage at the legions of manipulators who made other people's lives a joke. Sometimes it was all enough to make me believe that my brother was completely recovered.

Silent Night. Oh Come All Ye Faithful. Come home, Garth.

We did a lot of *pro bono* work, which we enjoyed—mostly investigations for attorneys who were themselves doing *pro bono* work for poor clients—and we made regular contributions to our favorite charities.

And, as always, we looked forward to Christmas.

From the time we arrived in New York, we had, along with thousands of other New Yorkers, taken great delight in observing one particular tradition. Each year, during the Christmas season, tens of thousands of letters addressed to Santa Claus are mailed in the greater New York metropolitan area, and they all end up at the General Post Office on West 33rd Street in Manhattan. Here, the children's letters are placed in cardboard boxes, which in turn are placed on the block-long marble counter inside the main lobby. Anyone is free to come in, browse through the letters, and select up to five to which he or she may wish to respond with gifts or services, or whatever.

Yes, Virginia . . .

Garth and I always spent a good deal of time each year doing our Santa Claus number. On our appointed day or days we would go to the GPO, start at opposite ends of the counter and work our way toward the center, poring over the letters in each box, searching for the ones which it would please us the most to "answer." Each year, as a result of this search, ten children—usually from poor and obviously needy families, but not necessarily—received brightly wrapped packages on Christmas Eve, delivered by special messenger and directly dispatched by Santa Claus at the North Pole.

We normally began our selection process early in December, as soon as the first boxfuls of letters would begin to appear, but this year Christmas had caught up with us. Late November and early December had been uncharacteristically hectic, with a heavy workload that had demanded our personal attention, and we'd just returned from an exhausting two-week stint in the Middle East, where we'd been attending to the needs of one of our corporate clients, an oil company. It had been necessary to prepare a report hurriedly, which then had to be presented orally before the corporation's board of directors. With Santa-time quickly running out on us, Garth and I had flipped a coin; I'd gotten to deliver the report, and he'd gotten to spend the day at the post office doing a letter search for both of us. Delivering the report, and then answering a host of detailed questions, had taken me all of the morning and most of the afternoon, and then I'd eagerly rushed back to the brownstone to see what, if any, treasures Garth had been able to excavate from what had to be, by now, a severely depleted trove of interesting or worthy Christmas wishes. Garth hadn't been in our offices, and I hadn't found him in either his apartment or mine. There had been no note, no phone message. I was still waiting for him, or for some word from him. It was 10 P.M.

Huddled inside my bulky cardigan and sipping at my Scotch, I stood at the three-foot-high brick balustrade at the edge of the roof and peered up at the sky as light snow began to fall, dusting my eyelashes, the brick patio, and the dormant, burlap-swaddled plants in my garden. Within minutes the snow began to fall more heavily, filtering and diffusing the bright city lights, creating a kind of milky glow around the illuminated tops of the Chrysler and Empire State buildings. It was growing colder—or perhaps it was only the chill that had been steadily growing inside me, and which had nothing to do with the weather.

Where the hell was Garth?

Enough, I thought as I drained off the rest of my Scotch, flung the ice into my garden, and headed back inside. I'd already waited too long.

I had a list of the telephone numbers for all the hospital emergency rooms in the five boroughs taped inside the front cover of my Manhattan directory, and that's what I turned to as I picked up the telephone in my oak-paneled, leathery library-study. I was just starting to dial the first number when I heard my front door open and close. I slammed down the receiver, hurried out of the study, across the living room, and around a large Chinese silk screen into the foyer, where I stopped suddenly and sucked in my breath, shocked by what I saw.

Garth was still tough-minded, to be sure, and in some ways even more tough-minded—some would say callous—than he had been during the years when he had been a county sheriff in Nebraska, and then a much-decorated NYPD detective. In fact he wasn't callous at all, but he no longer had any time for cant, hypocrisy, or any of the sundry nonsense that flows through and around most of us during the ordinary course of our everyday lives; Garth just ignored all that. To some, this attitude made him seem emotionally flat, but this was far from the mark. The one characteristic he had retained from his poison-induced change of consciousness was a profound sense of caring, or near-pure empathy, for people truly in need. His experience had rounded off some rough edges, making him even more sensitive to other people's pain, and caused certain other rough edges to become even more pronounced—if you happened to be the cause of other people's pain, it was best seriously to consider avoiding my brother. Even his appearance had changed, inasmuch as he now wore a full beard—much more liberally streaked with gray than his long, thinning, wheat-colored hair—in order to shield himself from the curious who might otherwise recognize him as the disgraced and discredited former leader of "Garth's People." I was told by women friends that the beard made him look very sexy; I thought it made him look most imposing, what with his six-foot-three-inch solidly built body and piercing, light brown eyes.

Right now Garth didn't look very imposing at all; he appeared almost shrunken, with red-rimmed eyes and the kind of pallor that comes not from poor diet or lack of sunshine, but from the kind of intense, unrelieved stress that can suck at a man's guts until he's turned inside out. He looked truly haunted, as if something horrible had followed him home and was lurking, waiting for both of us, just outside the door.

"Garth!" I managed to say when I had recovered from my initial shock at his appearance. "Jesus Christ. I was just outside, and I didn't see you coming down the street."

"I came down Fifty-seventh and up the back way," Garth said in a tight voice that was oddly distant, as though he could not get his mind off whatever it was that was bothering him. "I figured you'd be up here waiting for me."

"I was just about to start calling the hospitals, for Christ's sake! Are you all right?"

"I'm all right," my brother replied in the same distant tone.

"Nothing happened to you?"

"No. Nothing happened to me."

There were times, I thought, when Garth could make the Sphinx seem like a loquacious party animal. I laughed with equal parts nervousness, relief, and annoyance. "Then where the *hell* have you been? One of your reindeer throw a shoe? Where the hell are my five letters?"

Garth's response was to reach into the pocket of his gray, snow-speckled overcoat and remove an envelope, which he held out to me. "I think this one letter is about all you and I are going to be able to handle this Christmas. Read it and see what you think."

The first thing I did was examine the business-size envelope, front and back; the paper was cream-colored, textured, heavy bond—the expensive kind of stationery that usually has a personal or corporate name and address tastefully embossed in the upper left-hand corner, or on the back. This envelope was unadorned, the stamp standard post office issue. The postmark was New York City, and the envelope was addressed to Santa Claus at the North Pole. The handwriting was a child's light, uncertain scrawl.

The folded letter inside was of a matching heavy bond, with no return address. There were a number of dark smudges on the paper, and in the creases of the envelope were tiny specks of what appeared to be dirt. The letter was written in the same child's handwriting. It read:

> Dear Santa,
>
> Please bring me a puppy to keep me company because it is very lonely in here and Mommy and Daddy won't let me go out and other kids can't come in because it is a secret place but I know you will be able to find me because you know where every boy and girl in the world lives. I would like a girl puppy but a boy puppy will be all right if that is all you have.
>
> Also please bring me something real nice I can give to Reverend Billy so he will stop hurting me between my legs and sticking his big thing in my mouth and behind. Reverend Billy says God will not let me into heaven with Mommy and Daddy if I tell them and sometimes he hurts me very much and I bleed.
>
> I have been a good girl Santa.
>
> I love you.
>
>   Vicky Brown
>
> P.S. If you do bring me a puppy I promise to take very good care of her and before I go to heaven

with Mommy and Daddy I promise I will find her
a good home where she can stay until the demons
come and Dear Jesus and Satan fight and the world
ends. I think Jesus will win.

With something approaching disbelief I reread the letter a
second and then a third time, and felt within me a great
upwelling of sadness, rage, and frustration. With tears filling
my eyes, I slowly refolded the letter and replaced it in the
envelope. I looked up to find Garth gazing steadily at me.
His brown eyes gleamed with resolve, and the hard set of his
features belied the softness of his voice.

"Agreed, Mongo?"

"Oh Jesus, Garth. Agreed."

With Vicky Brown's words throbbing in my head and
heart, I suddenly felt slightly dizzy and nauseous. With Garth
following behind me, I turned and walked back into the
living room. I sat down at a chess table set up next to a
window and stared out into the snow, trying to calm down so
that I could think. Garth went to my bar and, to my surprise,
poured himself a drink—straight bourbon. He downed that,
then poured himself another before coming over and sitting
down across from me.

"You've been all this time trying to track down the letter,
haven't you?" I asked the king on the chessboard in front of me.

"You want me to get you a drink?"

I looked up, shook my head. "I've had enough. Could you
find out anything?"

Garth absently sipped his bourbon, then set the glass down
at the side of the board. "You noticed that there's no return
address." It was not a question.

"I noticed. New York City postmark, though."

Garth sighed; it was a soft, sibilant sound that was in total
contrast to the tension clearly etched in his face and the
stiffness with which he sat in his chair. "Christ, Mongo, that
postmark covers upwards of eight million people in the five
boroughs—and that may not be all; a lot of letters to Santa

that are mailed in Yonkers, Rockland, and Westchester end up here.''

"With a New York City postmark?"

"I'm told it can happen; sometimes Santa letters are grouped together and handled differently. I didn't even bother looking in the phone book, since there are probably hundreds of Browns in Manhattan alone."

"And not one of them would be likely to admit knowing—if they did know—that their daughter was being sexually abused."

"Right."

"Whatever you've been up to, Garth, you should have called me. I'd have given you a hand."

Garth shrugged his broad shoulders. "I didn't know how long you'd be tied up in meetings, and by the time the sun started to go down I was pretty much into what I was doing. It was a one-man job, anyway. But I should have checked in. I'm sorry I caused you to worry."

"Yeah. The sexual abuse is clear. I assume you notified the various social service agencies?"

"Sure, but that's a dead end too. There are lots of people named Brown on the welfare rolls, and lots of girls named Vicky. Welfare has no record of any Vicky Brown being reported as sexually abused—and there's no way of knowing if the family of this Vicky Brown is on welfare to begin with. Finally, even if some agency did have an address for a family that seemed like likely candidates, the child probably wouldn't be there."

"Because she's in a secret place," I said quietly.

"Yes."

"I assume you've been to the police. What did your former colleagues have to say?"

"Considering the lack of information and the fact that there's been no formal complaint, there's not much they can do, Mongo," Garth replied in a flat tone. "At least not officially. They said they'd take note of it."

"You'd have done more than that when you were a cop, Garth."

My brother slowly shook his head. "No, Mongo. I'd have been upset, just as I am now; I'd have worried, and I'd have taken note of the information—but there wouldn't have been a whole hell of a lot more I could have done, at least not on city time. The NYPD has a lot more to do than to investigate suspicious letters to Santa Claus."

"They could have checked out known sexual offenders."

"They did that for me. There are dozens with the first name Billy, or William, but no Reverends in the bunch."

Deciding that I wanted another drink after all, I rose from the chess table and went to the wet bar across the room. I put ice in a clean tumbler, splashed in some Scotch, swirled it around. "I can think of a certain Reverend, first name William, who's displayed some perverse sexual behavior in the past," I said, peering into the amber fluid as I held my tumbler up to the light over the bar. "I don't recall his being accused of child abuse, but I wouldn't put it past him. He's one crazy son-of-a bitch, and history teaches that a lot of people who believe they have divine inspiration also tend to believe they have divine permission to do just about anything they want."

I turned to find Garth staring at me intently; it seemed I'd sparked his interest. "Kenecky?" he asked quietly.

"Just a thought. They still haven't found the lousy, neo-Nazi prick. Nobody's suggested that he's dead, so he's still out there someplace. But your guess is as good as mine."

"Not always, brother; you can be a hell of a good guesser. I hadn't even thought of Wild Bill Kenecky, and I should have. It would tie in with that demon and end-of-the-world business in the girl's letter."

The gentleman we were so fondly discussing was one Reverend Doctor William Kenecky, the holder of a Doctor of Divinity degree issued by a mail-order "university" of his own devising and founder of a religious cable television broadcasting network that, before the plug was pulled, had come to dwarf the electronic resources of all the other boob-tube preachers combined. Like most televangelists, Kenecky

was a Christian Fundamentalist, a so-called Charismatic of
the sort who give the impression that they can't wait to go to
bed at night because they hope to wake in the morning to find
the world ending, and a warrior-Jesus returned to smite the
forces of Satan—meaning, apparently, sundry demons popping up from hell, all non-Christians, all non-Fundamentalist
Christians, and all non-Fundamentalist Christians who had not
sent money to Kenecky. Garth and I had found the Reverend
Doctor William Kenecky a howl even before it came out,
after he disappeared, that he had, for years, been associated
with a particularly perverse group of wacko neo-Nazis whose
"religious" ideology, labeled Jesus White Christian, included
the curious tenet that *Mein Kampf* was a missing book of
the Bible.

Garth and I had never understood the appeal and success of
any of the televangelists, with their obvious—to us, anyway—
chicanery, overt appeal to ignorance and bigotry of all kinds,
and blatant mismanagement of the dollars sent to them by
people who surely needed the money more than these owners
of Rolls-Royces and multimillion-dollar mansions. We'd agreed
that it would take a team of anthropologists to try to make
sense of this peculiarly American phenomenon of television
preachers, but the appeal of William Kenecky had always been
the biggest mystery of all. We had often watched his show
for entertainment, much like kids watching the Saturday
morning cartoons, whooping and hollering along with him as
he "healed" people by smacking them on the forehead, and
trying to anticipate his most outrageous—and oft-repeated—
lines. But we certainly never sent him money, and were in
full agreement that Wild Bill Kenecky was not a man any
self-respecting God would choose as a mouthpiece; we considered him a spiritual thug, albeit a skinny one. He'd always
worn black suits, and this gave his thin, slightly stooped
figure the appearance of a half-finished scarecrow. We'd read
somewhere that he was forty-one years old, and we'd been
shocked. We'd thought that he was at least a decade older;
hate, always shining clearly, in living color, in his jet black

eyes, has a distinctly aging effect. We'd considered him the funniest thing on television, and had always made arrangements to tape his five-days-a-week show when we knew we were going to miss it.

But then, nobody had ever accused either Garth or me of paddling in the mainstream of American religious or cultural thought. For millions of Americans, Reverend William Kenecky's talk of Armageddon, the Rapture, and the ultimate destruction of everyone in the world who didn't believe exactly as he did, seemed just the ticket in a world filled with wars America was losing, women's rights, curse words in the movies, and satanic music played on the radio. To Garth and me, Kenecky's paranoid fantasies were incredible and highly amusing, his show a kind of window into the open psychiatric ward that was a part of the collective American psyche. But those same millions of Americans shared his beliefs, and they'd sent him money—lots and lots of money. And, Kenecky would explain, since Armageddon was just around the corner, there was no reason for him to stint on spending that money—and he hadn't. He'd owned a luxury car for every day of the week, mansions in the mountains and at the seashore. Palpable evidence of God's grace, he'd called it.

And then Wild Bill had pulled his own plug, even before his secret links with the neo-Nazis and Jesus White Christian were exposed. Charismatic, apocalypse-oriented, Fundamentalist Christians—at least the ones who supported Kenecky's extravagant life-style—take a dim view of sex in general, and an even dimmer view of sex outside marriage or sex in any of what are, in their view, its perverse forms. When an enterprising reporter uncovered the fact that Wild Bill had, for years, been trading promises of salvation for sexual favors from both men and women, it was the end of him—or at least the end of his television empire. The exposure of his many sexual escapades, the variety of his tastes, and the voraciousness of his appetite hadn't gone down well with his Tribulation, Rapture, and Armageddon crowd.

Contributions had dried up, and—despite his feverish pleas and assurances that God had forgiven him—his member stations had dropped off one by one.

Then, as surely as pestilence will follow drought and famine, the well-dressed, truly fearsome minions of that greatest Satan of all, the I.R.S., had come knocking at his already badly battered door, descending on him and his operations like some biblical plague.

Thoroughly disgraced, his financial holdings seized, under indictment for tax evasion, and facing the very real possibility of a long jail term, William Kenecky had somehow engineered his own personal Rapture; he'd promptly disappeared. For six months no one had heard a peep, apocalyptic or otherwise, from him.

Now it seemed possible that we had heard from him—in the form of a cry for help from a new and totally helpless victim; it seemed to me not at all unlikely that Kenecky was holed up somewhere and whiling away his time while waiting for the world to end by sexually abusing a little girl.

"It's a bitch, Garth." It seemed like such a trivial, inappropriate thing to say that I repeated it. "It's a real bitch."

"And we have to do something about it."

I nodded. "What we have to do is find the girl, and then I assume the proper authorities will investigate any possible sexual abuse. And if it does turn out that 'Reverend Billy' is none other than William Kenecky, we might even spend a couple of quarters to telephone the F.B.I. and I.R.S."

"Uh-huh," Garth said absently as he stared at the chessboard in front of him. "The authorities here in the city are already on notice; the police and Social Services are waiting to hear from us." He paused, looked up at me. "What's our business status right now? Are we finished with the Middle East assignment?"

"Yeah, but we're still busy beavers—or we will be if we try to handle all our other business while we search for the girl. I suggest we farm out everything our staff people can't handle; if any of our clients object, we'll explain the situation and ask to be released from our contract. I think most of them will understand. If they don't—tough. Money certainly isn't a problem for us at the moment.''

"Okay," Garth said in the same distant tone as he sipped at his bourbon. "Good idea."

"Garth?"

"Huh?"

"So now we're going to look for Vicky Brown, and when we find her we'll turn over any information we've gathered to the police and welfare people. But all we've got to work on is a letter with no return address, a name that's as common as rain, references to some right-wing religious gobbledygook, and a child abuser who may or may not be a fugitive from justice. Even if the child and her abuser weren't in some 'secret place,' they'd still be lost souls in one of the largest cities in the world. Sorry if I sound pessimistic. I may be a hell of a guesser, but I have to tell you that I haven't a clue where to begin.''

Garth turned in his chair and favored me with one of his faint, enigmatic smiles. "What are you trying to say to me, brother? Are you suggesting that this may be a difficult case?''

"Yeah, I think I was trying to say something like that."

Garth drained off his bourbon, then sat back in his chair and cupped the empty glass in both hands. His smile had vanished. "Did you notice the smudges on the letter and the dirt in the creases of the envelope?''

Suddenly my heart began to beat more rapidly. "Son-of-a-bitch! You had it analyzed!''

Again, the faint, fleeting smile. "I pulled a few strings, appealed to old ties that bind, called in some IOUs, and got the people in the police labs to do some quick work for us—which turned out not to be so quick. I just came from there, and they'd been working on those soil samples since three thirty this afternoon. By the way, Frederickson and Frederickson is going to be getting some hefty telephone bills for a few very expensive computer linkups.''

"But they were able to analyze it?! The dirt can tell us something?!"

"It can tell us something, all right—but I'm not sure it's going to do us any good. For one thing, that soil is teeming with all sorts of microbes which, according to the technicians, are quite exotic."

"So what?!" I snapped, making no effort to hide my impatience. "Could they tell you where it came from?"

"Oh, yes," Garth replied dryly, rolling the empty tumbler between his palms. "Finally. According to the experts we talked to over those phone and computer linkups, there's only one place on the face of the earth where you'd find that particular variety of soil, and that place is the floor of the Amazon rain forest."

2.

THE New York Botanical Garden, located next to the Bronx Zoo, occupies two hundred and fifty acres along the banks of the Bronx River. That was where we were headed, hoping that our cabdriver could find a way through and around the traffic tieup on the Harlem River Drive so that we'd be on time for our two o'clock appointment with one Dr. Samuel Zelaskowich, the Botanical Garden's top expert on tropical soils and plants.

It had taken the better part of the morning to take care of our business—which in our case had meant giving it away, assigning some to our staff and farming out the rest to people in other agencies with whom we had worked well in the past, and whom we trusted to do a good job. None of our clients had been too pleased to have anyone but Frederickson and Frederickson handling their account, but all had eventually agreed to the arrangement after we'd explained the situation. Three of the corporations had offered money or services to help us in our search for Vicky Brown; we'd declined the money, told them we'd be in touch if there was any other way they could help. We were leaving in our wake clean desks and a number of very happy competitors.

Driving us on were the haunting images of a little girl being repeatedly brutalized and sodomized in some "secret place" which we had to find, a secret place where a child played in dirt from the floor of the Amazon rain forest.

It was rough going all through upper Manhattan, but our driver made some fancy detours once we reached the Bronx, and we arrived at the Botanical Garden with minutes to spare. We paid the driver, gave him a fat tip, then made our way through an eerie, improbable, snow-covered jungle of shrubbery and trees to the main administration building.

We found Dr. Zelaskowich in his office—a cramped cubicle not much bigger than a walk-in closet—with his broad back and shoulders hunched forward as he bent over and peered at a computer terminal. The walls of the office were papered with an odd mixture of graphs and charts, family photographs and what appeared to be personal memorabilia. I had a sense that the big man did not feel comfortable here, and that his discomfort did not have anything to do with the confined space.

He was a big, rangy man with a high dome of a forehead which was particularly pronounced when viewed in profile. He had a receding hairline, and a wispy, light brown beard. The thick-lensed eyeglasses he had propped up on his forehead kept slipping down over the bridge of his nose, and he kept pushing them back up as he peered intently at the symbol-filled monitor above the computer keyboard. He wore a white lab coat covered with dirt smudges, and there was dirt under his thick fingernails. I put him in his early thirties, and I thought he looked rather young for the hotshot expert he was supposed to be—but then, I'd met more than my share of young-genius types during my aborted career as a university professor.

"Be right with you," Zelaskowich called over his shoulder when I knocked on his open office door. "Please find a place for yourselves to sit."

We stepped into the tiny office and, at my insistence, Garth sat down on the only chair in the room—a high metal stool which looked as if it might have been appropriated from some ice cream parlor. I leaned against the wall by the door and watched Zelaskowich punch a button on the computer keyboard with one of his thick fingers, activating a printer which began to clatter and spew out paper. The man punched a few more buttons, and a fresh set of symbols appeared on the screen of the monitor.

"I really hate these damn things," the man continued good-naturedly, darting us a quick glance and revealing a boyish grin. "Botanists aren't supposed to work on computers; we're supposed to be down on our hands and knees in the dirt. But a few months ago our board of directors got the bright idea that we should take a census of everything we have growing here, and put it all in a computer. It's a bear, let me tell you."

Garth and I glanced at each other. "You people don't know what you have growing here?" I asked Zelaskowich.

The botanist's glasses had once again slipped down over his nose. He pushed them back up, looked at me, and shrugged. "Oh, no, Dr. Frederickson," he said with great gravity. "I imagine you must find that surprising, since this *is* the New York Botanical Garden, but the problem of identifying everything that's here is much more complex than you might think. It's not a matter of simply looking in the records to see what's been planted over the years, but of determining precisely what's growing there *now*. This census is going to take years, with dozens of us working on our hands and knees—and *then* we may miss a lot. You see, sometimes an entirely new genus can spring up without anyone noticing. I mean, we have more than five hundred types of *hemerocallis* alone; we're not certain, but it's possible that we may have more than two hundred and fifty thousand varieties of plants here. You see the problem, of course.''

''Uh . . . I'm not sure we do, Doctor.''

''Well, let's take an example. Let's say you plant a *dryopteris clintoniana* next to a *dryopteris goldiana*; before you know it—maybe in a year or two—you may very well have an entirely new plant growing between them, a sterile hybrid we call a *dryopteris clintoniana x goldiana*. Now, this isn't a separate species, but for the purpose of our census it is considered a different type of plant from either of its parents. Multiply that example by the thousands of plants we have here, and you begin to see the problem we're up against.''

''You're right,'' Garth said dryly. ''It does sound like a bear.''

Zelaskowich tapped a key firmly with his index finger, and the printer ceased its clatter; another tap, and the monitor screen went blank. He spun around on his stool, a satisfied grin on his face. ''There!'' he exclaimed. ''Now I can get back to where I belong—with my plants. At least for a little while.'' He rose, shook Garth's hand, then mine. ''I'm sorry to have kept you waiting, but I really did have to finish that little bit of mechanical business while the mood was on me. I must say that it's quite a thrill to meet the famous Frederickson brothers, and I'm flattered that you should be coming to see me; botanists rarely get to meet real-life private detectives, especially such distinguished ones, and I must say that it's quite exciting. Now, how can I help you?''

''We appreciate your time, Dr. Zelaskowich,'' Garth said as he rose from the stool, reached into his jacket pocket, and drew out the police lab report. He handed the paper to the young botanist. ''This is an analysis of a soil sample. Can you punch that up on your computer?''

Zelaskowich adjusted his glasses on the bridge of his nose, held the computer printout at arm's length as he studied the columns of chemical symbols, grunted. ''I don't need the

computer for this," he said. "This is incredibly rich soil,
teeming with microbial life. It's certain that you didn't pick
up this soil sample in New York—not the city, and not the
state. In fact, I can't think offhand of any site in the United
States where you'd find soil like this."

Garth said, "The technicians in the police lab who did that
analysis tell me there's only one place in the world where
that kind of soil is found: the Amazon rain forest. But we
found the traces of soil that were used for the analysis in an
envelope, and that envelope had been dropped into a mailbox
somewhere in the greater New York metropolitan region.
We're a long way from Brazil, Doctor, and it occurred to
Mongo and me that there might be one other place where that
kind of soil might be found—right here, at the Botanical
Garden. We were hoping you might know if there's soil like
that here; and, if so, who might be working with the plants
that are growing in it."

Zelaskowich pushed his glasses back up on his forehead,
pursed his lips, then shook his head. "No, Mr. Frederickson,"
he said after a few moments. "I would say not."

"Are you sure, Doctor?" I asked. "It's very important. If
that didn't come from here, Garth and I don't have the
slightest idea where to start looking next. We've checked
with some florists, but they tell us that there's virtually no
chance that a tropical plant sold here would have been potted
in its native soil. This is the only place we could think of that
might use it. You yourself said that you don't know how many
plants you have here. Isn't it possible that there's some rain
forest soil dumped someplace and you don't know about it?"

Again, the botanist shook his head. "If tropical plants
potted in soil like this were left out in the open, they wouldn't
survive; and there is no soil in any of our terrariums that
resembles this. You see, we just have no need for this kind of
soil—and, if we did, we would have a good deal of trouble
obtaining it."

"Why?" I persisted. "Why couldn't you just have someone over there dig up a barrel or two of the stuff and ship it

to you? I can't imagine that there's a shortage of dirt in Brazil.''

"Indeed not, but the very high microbial count would present a problem. The Customs Service would frown on the importation of such soil in even relatively small amounts. In fact, that's just about what happened a few months ago."

"What happened a few months ago, Doctor?" Garth asked, his sudden excitement and tension clearly evident in his voice even as I felt my own heart begin to beat more rapidly.

Samuel Zelaskowich shrugged his broad shoulders. "Well, you see, for some years a number of our staff members have served as consultants to a company called Nuvironment, Incorporated."

I asked, "Is that normal procedure for you people to do outside consulting work?"

"Actually, it's rather unusual. But this is a rather special circumstance. Nuvironment happens to be owned by a very rich—and, I'm told, very eccentric—man by the name of Henry Blaisdel. I'm sure you've both heard of him."

I'd heard of him, all right—as had anybody who even occasionally scanned the business pages of any newspaper or magazine, or read the kinds of tabloids that specialize in fantastic stories, virtually all of them made up, about bizarre personalities. According to *Fortune* magazine's last compilation, Henry Blaisdel ranked in the top ten of the world's billionaires, having just been nudged out of the top five by a couple of members of the Saudi royal family. Blaisdel owned lots of things—corporations, land, and people—all over the world, including a sixty-eight-story skyscraper, the Blaisdel Building, on the primest real estate in America, Fifth Avenue in midtown Manhattan. The building, among other things, was the corporate headquarters of the Blaisdel Holding Corporation, an umbrella company that coordinated Blaisdel's global operations. The fact that he hadn't been seen in public for almost a decade only increased the legendary aura that had grown up around him. His aversion to the public obviously hadn't affected his business acumen; his holdings, his fortune, just kept growing.

"Nuvironment, apparently, is Henry Blaisdel's pet company," Zelaskowich continued. "It would certainly have to be, considering the tens of millions of dollars he's poured into it over the years."

"You seem very well informed about the company, Doctor," Garth said in a neutral tone.

"Well, that's because Nuvironment has been using various members of the staff here as consultants since the company's founding—which was before I got here, but I'm well aware of the importance our board places on cooperating with the Nuvironment people. Henry Blaisdel is our biggest benefactor —as he is for many of the large cultural and scientific institutions in the city. In any case, about six or seven months ago we were asked to allow them to import one hundred tons or more of that particular type of soil under our aegis—using our contacts and knowledge, that sort of thing."

I asked, "Why couldn't they just import it themselves?"

"Soil is considered an agricultural commodity, or component, and special clearances and permits would be required for a shipment of that quantity. In effect, we were asked to serve as importing agent for the shipment, the reasoning being that our stature would make it easier to get the various permits required. Well, it just couldn't be done, even under our aegis. The Customs Service frowns on the importation, in large quantities, of any foreign soil, and the high microbial count in this particular soil led to adamant objections. Nuvironment dropped its request." Zelaskowich paused, raised his thin eyebrows slightly. "That makes this analysis you've brought me most curious. You're absolutely certain it was obtained from a sample found in this country?"

"Yes," Garth replied.

"Then it appears that the Customs Service must have relented and given Nuvironment itself the permits, and they used a different purchasing and shipping agent."

"What if they just went ahead and imported it without the Customs Service even knowing about it?" I asked. "Blaisdel certainly has the resources—probably including his own piece of jungle—to do it himself, without ever going outside Blaisdel Holding Company."

Zelaskowich pursed his lips and grimaced slightly, as if I had said something that wasn't fit to be heard by decent company. "That's certainly true, Dr. Frederickson, but Nuvironment is an outstanding company, with an impeccable reputation. They just wouldn't do something like that."

It was clear that Samuel Zelaskowich had spent a lot more time on his hands and knees in the dirt than he ever had in the business community, but I decided not to tarnish his illusions. "Maybe some other company imported the soil."

The botanist tentatively scratched his left temple, shrugged. "I suppose anything is possible, but if that's the case I'm afraid I can't be of much help to you. Nuvironment is the only concern I know of that would have any possible use for that type of soil in such large quantities."

I glanced at Garth, who seemed to be only half listening. My brother had taken Vicky Brown's letter out of his pocket and was rereading it yet again. I wished he would stop; I didn't think it was good for him.

"What did Nuvironment plan to do with the soil, Dr. Zelaskowich?"

"Please, call me Samuel."

"All right, Samuel. I'm Mongo, and my brother's name is Garth. What use would Nuvironment have for soil from the Amazon?"

"Nuvironment is not a profit-making corporation, Mongo; indeed, I suspect that it must draw financing from other Blaisdel holdings—lots of financing—in order to maintain its operations. It exists for the sole purpose of researching—and one day, hopefully, building—biospheres."

"Biospheres?" It was Garth; it seemed my brother was paying attention after all.

"Yes," Samuel Zelaskowich replied. "Biospheres are totally self-contained, self-sustaining environments—small worlds, really, that regulate themselves much as the earth does, producing and recycling everything from oxygen, food, and water, to waste. Someday, Nuvironment hopes to be able to produce such biospheres on a massive scale, each one encompassing many acres. It's theoretically possible to construct such a facility, which would be enclosed under a giant plastic dome that would let in only sunlight, if you had all the necessary components in exactly the right proportions. You see, a very delicate balance would have to be maintained if one cycle was not to eventually overwhelm the others—production of waste overwhelming the system's capacity to biodegrade, for example, or an incorrect ratio of air-breathing, carbon-dioxide-producing animals to plants that would absorb the carbon dioxide and produce oxygen. Nutrients would have to be able to sustain life inside the biosphere, while at the same time there must be resources—microbes, for example—available to biodegrade and recycle those things that die. It's a very complex problem, this finding of just the right balance, especially when you plan to maintain human life inside the biosphere. Fruit bats and hummingbirds would be natural choices to pollinate various plants, but you would need more than three thousand blooming plants just to supply the nectar needed to sustain a single pair of hummingbirds. And you can't use just any species of hummingbird; your hummingbirds would have to be low fliers, so that they wouldn't bump into the top of the dome and injure themselves. Even termites, which you would need for the proper balance of life forms, could pose special problems; certain species might develop a taste for the epoxy compound which would be needed for properly sealing the various plastic and glass panels to each other and to a steel supporting structure."

"So the soil would be used to degrade waste products?" I asked.

"Yes. But there's more to it. In theory, you would also need the rain forest itself, albeit on a very small scale, to produce both sufficient oxygen and rain."

"Rain?"

Zelaskowich nodded. "Yes; produced by condensing coils mounted in the top of the dome, over your rain forest. Naturally, this rain forest would produce a great deal of organic waste, and that particular type of soil, with its high microbial count, would be required to break down the waste."

"You're saying this company planned to build a jungle under glass?" Garth asked, making no effort to mask his skepticism.

"Or plastic. Yes, Garth. And not only a rain forest, but also a desert, an ocean, a freshwater lake, and saltwater marshes as well; all of these things would be needed if they hoped to maintain a proper ecological balance inside the biosphere."

"To what end? What would be the point?"

"One day—and that day could be far in the future— Nuvironment hopes to be the sole supplier of such biospheres to the world's space agencies. Such a biosphere would enable humans to live on and colonize not only, say, the moon, but other planets as well. If and when that day comes, Henry Blaisdel's long-term investment will, of course, be repaid many times over. But I don't really think he worries about what Nuvironment is costing him, or future profits; after all, he'll be dead for years, perhaps centuries, before biospheres could be in use throughout the solar system—if that day ever comes. Blaisdel is a philanthropist, with an apparently highly developed social consciousness. In my opinion, he sees Nuvironment, with its sole function of finding a way to build biospheres, as his bid for immortality. After all, there are lots of billionaires in the world, so that simply amassing great sums of money is not sufficient to guarantee that you will even be remembered, much less honored. For example, Howard Hughes is remembered by most people for his eccentricities, not his accomplishments. I suspect Henry Blaisdel doesn't want to make the same mistake—although that's only my opinion, as I say."

Garth and I exchanged glances, and then Garth stepped up

to the botanist and shook his hand. "Thank you, Samuel. You've been very helpful, and I can't tell you how much Mongo and I appreciate your taking the time to share this information with us."

Zelaskowich looked back and forth between us, a puzzled expression on his face. "But I haven't been able to tell you where the soil sample could have come from."

"You've shown us where to look next," I said.

"Oh dear," the botanist said, and he flushed slightly. "Are you going to question the people at Nuvironment?"

"Is that a problem?"

Samuel Zelaskowich took off his glasses and began to fumble with them; he looked decidedly uncomfortable. "It's just that . . . well, I'm afraid they tend to be very secretive about their research activities; they want outsiders to know as little as possible about what they're doing. In my enthusiasm to share my knowledge with you, I may have been indiscreet. Actually, I rather doubt that anyone there will even agree to talk to you, and the fact that I've leaked—that's the word they'll surely think of—information to you could reflect badly on the . . . Botanical Garden." He paused, flushed again, put his glasses back on and pulled himself up straight. "What I really mean is that it could cause me some personal difficulties if you talk to the people at Nuvironment."

"Don't worry, Samuel. Neither Garth nor I will say where we got our information; your name won't be mentioned."

"But they will most definitely speak to us," Garth murmured in a low, flat voice that was almost inaudible.

"Thank you," Zelaskowich said, visibly relieved. "Uh, may I inquire as to just why it is that this information is so important to you?"

"We're trying to find a little girl who's in danger," Garth replied simply as he headed for the door. "Merry Christmas," he called over his shoulder.

"Merry Christmas, Samuel," I said, and headed after Garth.

Zelaskowich caught up with us just as we were leaving the

building. He'd been running. "Excuse me," he said, red-faced and panting. "Can you wait just a minute? I may have something else for you."

"What is it, Samuel?" I asked.

The botanist took a deep breath, slowly let it out. "Garth, you said there's a little girl in danger?"

"A great deal of danger," my brother replied evenly. "And she's hurting very badly. Mongo and I have to find her in order to stop that hurting."

"Oh, my," the moon-faced man said as he made a birdlike motion with his hands that seemed surprisingly delicate for such a big man. "That's terrible."

"Yes," Garth said in the same flat tone. "That's terrible."

"And you think that soil sample is a key to finding her?"

I nodded. "We're certain of it, Samuel."

"In that case, you don't have to concern yourselves with keeping my name out of any discussions you may have. I wanted you to know that. And I'll be happy to do whatever else I can to help, if you need me."

"You've already helped, Samuel. Garth and I will have no need to mention your name. But thanks for the offer."

"I thank you, but what I'm most concerned about right now is the possibility that nobody at Nuvironment will agree to talk to you. Perhaps I should call them and try to do something to pave the way."

Garth shook his head. "The people at Nuvironment will be our concern, Samuel."

"Well, there is somebody else who might know something about that soil sample."

My brother glanced quickly at me, grunted slightly. "And who would that be, Samuel?"

"Craig Valley; Dr. Craig Valley."

"Does Valley work here?"

"Craig used to, but I'm afraid he was fired about three months ago. He was our curator of orchids. As I mentioned, many staff members here have done consulting work for Nuvironment at one time or another, but Craig was the

primary liaison between the company and the Botanical
Garden. Indeed, more than a few of us suspected that Craig
considered his efforts on behalf of Nuvironment more important than his regular duties. All requests from Nuvironment
came through him, and he doled out the consulting assignments
—which could be quite lucrative. It was Craig who received
the initial request from Nuvironment for the rain forest soil;
indeed, he'd already made preliminary shipping arrangements
when the Customs Service intervened and stopped him. He
took it personally; he was quite upset. I'm thinking that it's
possible Craig may have continued to work for Nuvironment
after he left here, and that he may have finally persuaded the
Customs Service to give him the required permits. In any
case, he may have information that could prove useful to
you." Zelaskowich paused, looked down at the floor, continued quietly, "Craig is a rather . . . uh, strange man. He can
be very difficult to talk to, but I don't see how he could
refuse to cooperate with you on a matter of this importance,
something that concerns the well-being of a child."

"We'll see," I said.

"The personnel department may have his address and
phone number, and I'd be happy to check it out for you. I
seem to recall that he lives in a town house on the East Side
of Manhattan, somewhere in the sixties or seventies."

"We'll find him."

Garth asked, "Why did Valley get fired?"

Again, the botanist lowered his gaze. "I don't like to
gossip, Garth. Do you really need to know that?"

"At the moment it's difficult for us to be certain just what
it is we'll need to know in order to find the girl," I answered. "Knowing something about Craig Valley before we
go to talk to him might be helpful to us in ways we can't
anticipate now. You described him as a 'strange man.' Why?
In what way is he 'strange'?"

Zelaskowich sighed, then shoved his large hands into the
pockets of his lab coat. "Well, in my opinion it was his
religious zealotry that got him fired—although that wasn't the

official reason given; after all, the city and the Botanical Garden wouldn't want to be charged with religious discrimination.''

"He was fired for religious reasons?''

"He was fired for incompetence and inattention to his duties.''

"But you said that the real reason may have been his religious zealotry.''

Zelaskowich shrugged. "I think it was a factor that, in the end, weighed against him. It wasn't so much his religious beliefs in themselves so much as the way he tried to foist them on others. His behavior could make Craig . . . well, obnoxious on occasion. I believe he was one of those . . . what do you call them? Charismatics? Pentecostals? Whatever he is, I believe it's much more fanatic than simple Christian Fundamentalism; that's just my opinion, though, and I don't claim to know that much about any religion. Craig was always warning us that we were going to be sent to hell very soon if we didn't accept Jesus Christ as our savior and if we weren't, as he put it, 'born again.' It seemed to me very odd behavior for an educated man. There are a number of Jews on the staff here, and a few Muslims. I'm a humanist, myself. At first, we used to dismiss Craig—condescend to him, and laugh among ourselves behind his back. I'm afraid that didn't stop him from trying to 'save us,' if you will. I really believe that the man thinks the world is going to end soon, within our lifetimes, and that all sorts of demons are going to pop up out of the ground to make mischief. Then, it seems, Jesus Christ is going to descend from heaven to defeat the demons and start a new world in which only people who believe like Craig will be allowed to live. I know it sounds absolutely lunatic, but I think the man actually believes these things.''

"Did Dr. Valley ever mention somebody named William Kenecky to you?" I asked, catching Garth's curt nod of approval out of the corner of my eye.

"Kenecky? You mean the crazy television preacher who's on the run from the tax people?''

"That's him."

Zelaskowich thought about it, shook his head. "No, Craig never mentioned him to me. But now that you bring it up, it occurs to me that a lot of the nonsense Craig used to spout sounds like the nonsense Kenecky spouted. Maybe that's where Craig got his silly notions from. I still can't understand how somebody who's been to college—and earned a doctorate, no less—could believe such ignorant, vicious stuff. It's very sad."

But not nearly as sad as what somebody—maybe William Kenecky—was doing to a little girl named Vicky Brown. "Was Valley really incompetent as well as obnoxious?"

"He became so, yes. I think his belief that the world was going to end about the day after tomorrow finally sort of infected his brain. Obviously, he's one of the world's leading experts on orchids; if he weren't, he wouldn't have been our curator. However, in the last few months he simply let his work go. In fact, he was warned about it; and he was so bold—or stupid—as to say that it didn't matter if all his orchids died because Jesus was on His way. Can you imagine?"

"Religious zealotry can do strange things to people," I said as I glanced at Garth, who smiled thinly and raised his eyebrows ever so slightly.

Zelaskowich nodded. "Indeed. In any case, Craig had been steadily neglecting his work for some time, but in somewhat subtle ways. However, after the Customs Service interfered with the importation of the rain forest soil, he became positively unhinged. Then the administration had to let him go. You'd have expected him to be upset, but he really wasn't. In fact, he told me that it was almost a relief not to be distracted by work while he was waiting for Jesus to come, and that now we'd see he was right about the imminent end of the world and the rising of demons." The botanist paused, shook his head sadly. "Poor Craig. On his last day I came across him in one of the gardens. He was down on his hands and knees, rocking back and forth, babbling absolute nonsense in a very loud voice. He seemed almost hysterical. In fact, I think there's a name for that sort of thing."

"There is," I said. "It's called glossolalia—'speaking in tongues.' "

3.

DR. Craig Valley's three-story town house was on East Sixty-third Street, half a block away from one of the shifting, ephemeral boundaries so common to New York City, where architecture, patterns of street activity, planted things, and commercial activity abruptly changed to become an entirely different "neighborhood." The neighborhood in the next block was considerably seedier, with dirtier buildings plastered with advertisements for rock concerts, no trees, and dirtier sidewalks. Judging from the condition of Valley's town house, with the flaking paint on its window frames and its facade of crumbling brick, it looked as if this onetime curator of orchids at the New York Botanical Garden was existing on the borderline in more ways than one.

The man who answered the door was five feet five or six and overweight—except for his face, which had a pinched look about it, with a narrow nose flanked by watery, pale gray eyes that glinted with suspicion, and thin, pursed lips. His red hair was thinning, and there was a rash on his chin and cheeks, as if he might recently have shaved off a beard.

"What is it?" he asked in a high-pitched voice laced with equal parts of hostility and suspicion.

Made slightly uneasy by my brother's stony expression, which would certainly have made me hostile and suspicious, I flashed my most disarming, winning smile. "Dr. Valley?"

"Who are you? What do you want?"

"Our names are Frederickson, Dr. Valley. We're private investigators working on a matter of considerable urgency, and we'd very much appreciate a few moments of your time."

Valley exercised his neck muscles by first looking down at me, then up at Garth, then down to me again. "I've heard of you two," he said in a voice that was close to a hiss. Back up to Garth. "You were the false messiah—the leader of that pitiable cult who called themselves Garth's People."

"I wasn't any messiah, Dr. Valley, false or otherwise," my brother said in a flat voice that betrayed no emotion. "Like my brother said, we'd like to ask you a few questions, and then we'll be on our way."

"What is it you want to know? I can't imagine how anything I know could be of any use to private investigators."

The lack of emotion in my brother's expression and tone told me that he was, in fact, feeling more than a tad impatient, and was in no mood for small talk; naturally, that would have to be my department. Still smiling, I said: "We'd like to ask you a few questions about a company called Nuvironment. We understand that you used to do some consulting work for them."

Valley frowned, and his thin lips pinched together even more. "Who told you that?"

"May we come in?"

"Certainly not, Frederickson. My time is very valuable, and even if I wished to give you some of it, I wouldn't speak to you about my professional contacts or activities."

"Then we'll get right to the point," I said curtly, dispensing with my smile, which had been starting to hurt me anyway. "Did you arrange to import one hundred tons of Amazon rain forest soil for Nuvironment?"

The pale gray eyes went wide with shock, and the thin lips parted as his jaw dropped slightly to reveal uneven, gray teeth that looked as if they might have been color coordinated with his eyes. He recovered, quickly stepped back and started to close the door—only to find his effort frustrated by Garth's very large right foot. Garth casually put his hand on the door and pushed, effortlessly forcing Craig Valley back into what turned out to be a wood-paneled vestibule decorated with what I considered to be rather tacky religious art. I stepped in first and Garth followed, closing the door behind him.

"You have no right to come in here!" Valley squeaked, continuing to back away until he banged up against the side of the archway that framed the entrance to his living room. His face was deeply flushed, making the rash on his chin and cheeks stand out like chalk dust. "I'll call the police!"

"A good idea," Garth said brusquely as he brushed past the cringing Craig Valley and entered the living room.

I walked up to stand in the archway beside Valley, watched as Garth picked up the receiver of a telephone on a small desk across the room, held it out.

"You want me to dial them for you, Valley?" Garth continued casually.

"What is *wrong* with you people?!" Valley shouted near my left ear. His voice was growing even higher pitched, and was now close to soprano range.

"You mentioned something about calling the police," I said, stepping away and rubbing my left ear. "Garth is just trying to oblige you. When they arrive, we can all sit down and chat about a possibly illegal shipment of an agricultural commodity that you arranged for Nuvironment. I certainly hope you acquired the necessary permits, Valley. I also hope you have whatever money was promised to you, because my bet is that your bosses are going to be very unhappy to be caught with dirty hands, if you will. Now, Garth and I really don't give a damn about all that dirt, or the bugs in it, so you might be better off just answering our questions. What do you think, Dr. Valley?"

The blood slowly drained from the botanist's face, leaving his flesh with a pasty, grayish hue. His mouth kept opening and closing, but no sound came out, and his head kept swiveling back and forth between Garth and me, his watery eyes wide with shock—and, I was certain, fear.

"How could you know?" he finally managed to say in a small voice that cracked. "How on earth could you possibly know?"

I motioned for Garth to put down the phone, and he did; then I motioned for Valley to sit down on the sagging couch in his living room, and he did. His movements were stiff and awkward, as if he were drunk.

"We're really not interested in getting you into trouble, Dr. Valley," I said as I went into the living room and sat down on a footstool in front of the couch. I glanced over my shoulder at Garth, who had moved to the fireplace and was leaning on the mantel. His face was impassive, but he was gazing intently into the red-haired botanist's face. "All we want is some information, and we have a very good and important reason for wanting it. Nobody will be told that we got the information from you." I paused as Valley suddenly leaned forward, clasped his hands together, and bowed his head. At first I thought he might be sick, and it was a few moments before I realized that he was praying. "Are you all right, Dr. Valley?"

There was no reply. I again glanced at Garth, who simply nodded as an indication that I should go on.

"We already know that Nuvironment's sole business is conducting research into the feasibility of constructing self-contained environments called biospheres," I continued quietly, speaking to the top of the man's head. "Bringing in that soil means that they're ready to construct at least an experimental prototype, most probably on a site somewhere around here. I repeat: we're not interested in getting you into trouble. But we already know that you tried to get the soil for them while you were working at the Botanical Garden; we know all about how the Customs Service stopped the plan, and about the personal and professional difficulties you suffered soon afterward; we know that the soil is now in this country. Before, Garth and I weren't sure that you'd been involved in importing it; after your little outburst in the foyer, we are sure. Now, sir, we need to know where that soil was dumped, and we need to know right now—this minute. The truth of the matter is—''

Suddenly Craig Valley's head snapped up and his right arm shot out so that his trembling index finger was only inches from my chest. The veins and cords in his neck stood out and writhed like worms beneath his skin, and his watery gray eyes gleamed with rage, hatred—and madness.

"You'll know the truth before long, nonbeliever!'' he shrieked at the top of his lungs, thoroughly startling me so that I almost fell backward off the footstool. '' *'And there went out another horse that was red!'* Soon you and your brother will see the second beast!''

I braced myself on the stool and waited for more, but Valley had apparently finished saying his piece. He glared at me for a few moments with his madness-glazed eyes, then abruptly slumped into a corner of the sofa, covered his face with his hands, and began to tremble violently. And then he began to pray again—or chant, or something; his voice was steadily rising in pitch and volume, but I couldn't make out anything he was saying.

Garth abruptly strode across the room, grabbed a handful of Valley's shirt, and pulled him up into a sitting position. End of prayer. Valley gasped, then made a mewling sound deep in his throat, like the cry of a startled animal.

"Pull yourself together and do your praying later,'' my brother said in a low, even voice. "The reason we need to know where the soil was dumped is because there's a little girl somewhere around there who's being sexually abused. Considering the fact that some guy could be giving her a bad time at this very moment, Mongo and I really don't have any time for you and your bullshit.'' Garth paused, and smiled thinly without any warmth whatsoever. "It's almost Christmas, pal, so how about getting into the spirit of the season and giving a little kid a break? I'll take it as a nice gesture if you do, and then I'll refrain from breaking your arm. If you don't want to be opening presents with one hand, the next words out of your mouth had better be in a language Mongo and I can understand. Now where the fuck is Nuvironment storing that dirt?''

Garth had certainly gotten Valley's attention; the man's pale gray eyes were wide—but they now mirrored as much shock as alarm or madness. ''What you say is impossible,'' he said to Garth in a hoarse, croaking voice. ''It's impossible.''

''What's impossible?'' I asked. ''Are you saying Nuvironment doesn't have the dirt, or are you denying that you helped them bring it into this country?''

Valley's response was to wag his head repeatedly. His mouth with its thin lips opened and closed, but the only sound he managed to produce was a kind of whimper. He resembled nothing so much as a very ugly beached fish that had been brought up from some very deep, lightless layer of a poisonous ocean.

''No, I don't think that's what he means,'' Garth said, his voice soft and oddly distant. My brother's matter-of-fact tone and lack of visible expression were beginning to make me feel decidedly uneasy. I'd learned that with Garth, since his poisoning with nitrophenylpentadienal and his eventual recovery, it was best to read his emotional and behavioral traffic signals in reverse from the way they would be read with most other people. ''I do think he means that what I said was happening to the girl is impossible.'' He paused, tightened his grip on the botanist's shirt ever so slightly. ''If you don't want to talk about one kind of dirt, pal, then we'll talk about another. Tell us where the good Reverend William Kenecky is holed up.''

Craig Valley finally found his voice—and it sounded haunted. ''It's impossible. The reverend is a man of God; he would never do such a thing.''

Garth yanked Valley to his feet, ripping the man's shirt. My brother let go of the tattered fabric, wrapped his fingers around the other man's throat. ''He's repeatedly raping a girl by the name of Vicky Brown, Valley—and I assume you know who she is too. Jesus Christ, man, if you care anything about children, or even just this child, tell us where to find Kenecky and the girl. Where is Nuvironment storing the dirt?''

"God, I'm going to be sick," the botanist groaned, and put a hand over his mouth as he retched dryly. "Please let me go to the bathroom."

Garth released his grip as I rose from the footstool and stepped away. Valley staggered across the living room and through another archway into the dining room. Garth and I followed, watched as he entered a bathroom adjacent to the kitchen at the rear of the town house, slammed the door shut behind him. A few seconds later there was the sound of water running.

"Damn, Garth," I said, my heart starting to pound with excitement. "He damn well knows where the girl is. We're going to find her."

"I'd say so," Garth replied flatly as he stared at the closed door.

A minute went by, then two. The running water could clearly be heard, but there was no sound of retching. "He's had enough sick leave," I said tightly. "Let's go get him."

"Right."

We were almost to the door when we both stopped suddenly, virtually paralyzed for an instant by the sounds that came from the other side of the closed door. The voice was clearly Craig Valley's, but there was something inhuman, animal-like, in the eerie, ululating howls that were a mixture of shrieking and thick-syllabled words I knew instinctively were not a part of any language spoken on earth.

Garth hit the door with his shoulder, smashing it off its frame and inward at almost the precise moment that the howling turned into a wet, wordless, gurgling sound. Blood sprayed and spurted over our faces and clothing. I gazed past Garth in horror at the figure slumped backward on the toilet seat over the water bowl, and knew that there was going to be no saving Vicky Brown this day, because there was going to be no saving Dr. Craig Valley.

Valley had really done a job on himself. One edge of a

double-edged razor blade was embedded in the index and middle fingers of each of Valley's hands, the result of the force he had exerted to punch two holes in the carotid arteries in his neck, one on each side of his jugular. He'd certainly known what he was doing when he'd decided to leave this vale of tears, for there was no way a team of surgeons, much less my brother and me, could have found a way to stop up those spurting holes before his life leaked out of him. There was a last spasm of heartbeats, causing more blood to spray over us, the floor, walls, and ceiling, and then he was dead.

With trembling hands, I wiped at the warm, sticky blood covering my face, but only managed to smear it. And then the air in the bathroom was suddenly filled with the thick, green odor of feces as Valley's sphincter let loose and his bowels emptied; brown stains began to darken the legs of his slacks. I wanted to look away, and couldn't; I was transfixed with horror, strangely fascinated by the fact that a man could actually will himself to use his bare hands to punch holes in his neck with razor blades. He was a man who'd been in a very big hurry to die, and he'd certainly taken care of business.

Garth was also taking care of business. If I hadn't been so shaken by the horror of what Craig Valley had done to himself, I'd probably have seen the blood-coated, cordless telephone that had dropped onto the carpeted floor beside Valley's left foot. But it was Garth who had seen it first, and now he rudely kicked the head botanist's foot to one side, picked up the telephone and examined it. Then he held it out for me to examine its face.

The mode control button was switched to *talk*; the line was still open.

"Hello," Garth said evenly into the mouthpiece. "Who's this? Anybody there?"

Even from where I was standing, I could hear the dial tone suddenly come on. Garth cursed with disgust, then hurriedly punched the REDIAL button. I moved closer, listened as the handset whirred and clicked, automatically redialing the last number that had been called. The noises stopped, and a phone at the other end of the line began to ring. A woman answered on the third ring.

"Nuvironment. Good afternoon. How may I help you?"

Garth glanced at me, raised his eyebrows slightly. My heart was pounding even more rapidly, and I imagined that if I'd tried to speak my words would have caught in my throat. But not Garth.

"This is Dr. Craig Valley," my brother said evenly. "I called a few minutes ago, and my party and I were cut off. Please reconnect me."

There was a pause, which to me seemed ominous. When the woman spoke again, suspicion was clearly evident in her voice. "Dr. Valley? Craig? You sound very different."

"I have a sore throat."

"I see," the woman replied coldly, and from the tone of her voice I was afraid that she did. "Whom would you like to speak to, sir?"

"Just reconnect me to whoever I was speaking to before."

"You have to give me a name."

"Let me talk to Mr. Blaisdel."

"This isn't Dr. Valley," the woman said tersely. "Who is this? I demand to know who this is."

So much for cute private detective tricks. Garth pressed the HOOK button, got another dial tone, and called the police.

While we waited for the police to arrive, we took turns availing ourselves of Valley's kitchen sink to wash the blood off our hands and faces as best we could, drying ourselves with a roll of paper towels we found in a cabinet. I was still trembling, but Garth seemed more outraged than shaken. We didn't talk much, probably because there didn't seem much to say; there was no question in our minds that Craig Valley had opted to kill himself rather than risk supplying us with information under the duress Garth had guaranteed he would supply. As obviously mad as Valley had been, suicide still seemed a rather dire means of trying to keep one's mouth shut. It had to make us both wonder just how much else was involved besides the sexual abuse of a child.

Craig Valley hadn't punched holes in his throat because he'd been worried about a load of dirt, or because we'd labeled one of his religious idols a child molester; he had to have been afraid of us finding out something else—a secret he had given his life to protect. All we'd wanted to know was the dump site of a load of Amazon rain forest soil, and Valley's decidedly bizarre response to our inquiries made me strongly suspect that when we did get to the site we were going to find a lot more than just a big pile of bug-infested dirt.

It certainly appeared that something big and complicated was afoot, as it were, and that didn't bode well for our relatively small and simple quest.

"Shit," Garth said dispassionately as he tossed a wad of paper towels into the garbage can beneath the sink, then glanced at his watch.

"Yeah, shit," I said in agreement. More than twenty minutes had passed since Garth had called the police to report Valley's suicide, and there was still no sign of officialdom. We had other things to do, to say the least. With a little luck, and a lot of pressure, if need be, applied in the right places, there still seemed a chance that we could find Vicky Brown before nightfall; it wasn't as though we didn't know where to go next. "You can never find a cop when you need one."

"We've got better things to do than wait around here," Garth said, looking down at his blood-stained shirt, tie, and jacket. "I've got a good mind to split."

"We've got better things to do, but I think we'd best stay put if we don't want to get grounded even longer; the police will get cranky if we're not here when they do show up. What do you suppose Valley meant by that business with the 'second beast'? Just more loony talk?"

It was not surprising that Garth, always the better of the Frederickson brothers in biblical studies taught at our mother's knee, would know the answer; considering some of the things we'd been through over the past decade, I should have known, but it was Garth who came up with the words.

"It's Revelations, Mongo," he said in a weary voice as he

sighed and rested a hand on my shoulder. "Chapter six, verses three and four. 'And when he had opened the second seal, I heard the second beast say, Come and see.'

" 'And there went out another horse that was red: and power was given to him that sat thereon to take peace from the earth, and that they should kill one another: and there was given unto him a great sword.' "

4.

THE police finally arrived while we were going through papers in Valley's study, which we'd found on the second floor of the town house. There didn't seem to be much of value in his files—a lot of Jesus White Christian racial smut and creepy apocalyptic literature, including a dozen or so thin but savage tomes by William Kenecky, but no bills, letters, or anything else that might indicate where Nuvironment was storing the hundred tons of dirt Craig Valley had undoubtedly arranged to get for them.

The detective in charge of the investigation was decidedly unhappy; he was unhappy to find us searching the study, and he was unhappy simply to find us—or, more specifically, to find Garth. The detective in charge of the investigation didn't like Garth, and he had reason.

Malachy McCloskey was just under six feet. He was about Garth's age, but looked decidedly older—something he would undoubtedly blame on Garth. His thick hair was steel gray, with an occasional streak of the original black showing through. He had black eyes, acne-scarred cheeks, and features that seemed to be fixed in a kind of permanently brooding expression. For as long as I'd known him, about fifteen years, he had been a slovenly dresser, and he hadn't changed his habits for this occasion; he was wearing green socks and a green tie with a blue suit which looked as if it hadn't been pressed in the decade or so since he'd bought it off some pipe rack.

McCloskey didn't much care for me, either, since I was Garth's brother. Years before, soon after both Garth and McCloskey had earned their detective shields, Garth had turned McCloskey in to Internal Affairs for accepting gratuities from businessmen—free drinks and meals, that sort of thing. It was petty stuff, and Garth had been virtually the only person involved who'd been interested or taken it seriously. McCloskey had been given a mild reprimand and told to go and sin no more. He hadn't sinned again, as far as I knew—but he also hadn't moved up the promotional ladder as fast as Garth had. Naturally, he'd blamed Garth for "putting a blight" on his career—and he still did. Malachy McCloskey was definitely not a man I was happy to see at this time and place, while Garth and I were busily going around disturbing the scene of an investigation.

"The famous Fredericksons," McCloskey said in his gravelly voice, making no effort to hide his disgust as he entered the study, stopped, and shoved his hands into the pockets of his crumpled, coffee-stained trench coat. The dark eyes that darted back and forth between Garth's face and mine were clouded with suspicion and hostility. "I might have known. You two really made a mess of things, didn't you?"

"How so, Lieutenant?" I asked as I straightened up, smiled broadly, and gently pushed a desk drawer closed with my hip.

"For one thing, those Goddamn bloody footprints all over the floor downstairs, and the bloodstains in the kitchen sink, which I assume came off the two of you, and now the fact that you're up here rifling through the victim's possessions. What the fuck is the matter with you two? Don't you know that you're disturbing evidence at the scene of a crime? I have a mind to haul your asses out of here right now, take you to the station and book you."

"There's no crime, Lieutenant," I said. "Not unless you want to charge the stiff in the bathroom with killing himself. Garth explained over the telephone that it was a suicide."

"The police aren't in the habit of taking the word of citizens in matters involving little things like death, Frederickson. You know that, and so does that famous big brother standing next to you. There has to be an investigation and a coroner's report, and we definitely don't like coming to a scene that's been all fucked over by civilians like you. Come on."

Garth and I dutifully followed McCloskey, who was moving as if his back hurt him, downstairs, where a moderate crowd of uniformed police, forensic people, police photographers, and a couple of stray reporters were milling about. We'd heard them come in five minutes before, but had been too intent on looking for some scrap of paper that might tell us where to find Vicky Brown to go downstairs immediately; that little lapse in judgment was beginning to loom as a serious mistake.

The three of us stepped back in the hallway downstairs as two white-uniformed paramedics wearing gauze masks and rubber gloves carried Craig Valley's rubber-bagged body past us on a stretcher. McCloskey led us into the living room, over by the fireplace, then abruptly turned around. Anger had mottled his face, making the acne scars on his cheeks appear white and shiny. "You two are arrogant sons-of-bitches!" he snapped. "For Christ's sake, you had to have heard us come in, and you didn't even bother coming downstairs!"

"Who do you suppose left the door open for you, McCloskey?" Garth asked in an even tone.

"You know that doesn't mean shit, Frederickson!" the police detective shouted at my brother, causing heads in the dining room to turn. "When you were a cop, you'd have flipped if you'd walked into the situation I did!"

"You're right, McCloskey," Garth said in the same even, mild tone. "I apologize for Mongo and myself; we acted improperly. But, when I was a cop, I think the first thing I might have done after walking into this situation is to ask the aforementioned civilians just what the hell they were looking for, and why the man who was just carted out killed himself.''

McCloskey flushed, and for a moment doubt swam in his black eyes; it was quickly replaced by renewed anger. "I was getting around to that, Frederickson, so you don't have to be a smart-ass. The duty officer told me what you said to him over the phone. Now, do you expect me to believe that you were just talking to the man, and then suddenly, for no reason, he jumps up, runs into the bathroom, and sticks two razor blades into his throat?''

"I didn't say there was no reason."

"Then what was the reason?"

"I think he was afraid we were going to force information out of him.''

McCloskey was openly incredulous. "And so he killed himself rather than talk to the two of you?''

"That's right. That's how Mongo and I figure it, McCloskey."

"Did you thump him a little bit?"

Garth shook his head. "I ripped his shirt. I think he was afraid I was going to thump him if he didn't tell us what we wanted to know.''

"Was his fear justified, Frederickson?"

"I didn't hit him."

"What information were you looking for?"

"Talk to Mongo," Garth said tersely, nodding in my direction.

"I'm asking you."

"Talk to Mongo, McCloskey," Garth repeated, and turned away. "I don't feel like talking to you any longer. Your interrogation technique stinks.''

"We're looking for a load of dirt, Lieutenant," I said quickly as the blood drained from McCloskey's face and he took a step toward Garth. My brother's brusque manner could, at the very least, get us a ride to McCloskey's precinct station house, and it was time Vicky Brown couldn't afford for us to waste. "It's why we came here. Valley could have told us where to find the dirt, and when we find the dirt we'll also find a little—''

"What the hell are you talking about?" the detective snapped. "I find the two of you here all covered with blood, and you try to feed me some—!"

McCloskey was interrupted by the ringing of the telephone on the desk behind him. Startled, he jumped back, spun around, and glared at the telephone.

"That could be for me, Lieutenant," Garth said easily. "I'd appreciate it if you'd answer it."

McCloskey did. He listened for a few moments, the muscles in his jaw clenching and unclenching, then handed the receiver to my brother. Garth turned his back to us, spoke in a low voice, listened. Finally he turned back and hung up the receiver.

"What was that all about?" McCloskey asked curtly.

"Mongo and I burst into the bathroom just after Valley slit his throat," Garth said to the gray-haired police detective. "He'd just made a call on that cordless telephone you found on his chest. I used the redial button and found out that he'd just finished speaking to someone at an outfit called Nuvironment. The receptionist there wouldn't tell me who he'd been talking to, so I just had somebody checking to see if there's any way to trace a call to see what extension is used. There isn't."

McCloskey frowned. "This 'somebody' works for the phone company?"

Garth nodded.

"Did you identify yourself as a police officer, Frederickson?"

"No. I'm not a police officer."

"Then he's a contact—one of your own."

"Yes."

"Give me a name. Who is it?"

"I'm not going to give you any names, Lieutenant. If you want a personal contact at the phone company, get your own."

"I don't *need* a personal contact there, Frederickson!"

"Take it easy, Lieutenant," I said quietly. The man was working himself up into a real snit. I'd known that McCloskey had resented Garth for years, blamed him for his own poor career performance; but until that moment I had not realized how threatened McCloskey was by Garth—and, perhaps, by me. It could make Lieutenant Malachy McCloskey a potentially very troubling nettle in our sides.

McCloskey ignored me, and kept shouting at my brother. "I'm a Goddamn *cop*, Frederickson, and I have a legal *right* to request privileged information from the phone company! You don't; not anymore. Giving out that kind of information to unauthorized civilians can constitute an illegal act."

"For Christ's sake, McCloskey," Garth said with disgust. "I could have told you the call was from my mother. Don't you understand that it's not important? If you'll stop acting like a horse's ass, Mongo and I will tell you what is important."

Garth's manners might leave something to be desired, but I found his description of McCloskey right on the mark. I was getting impatient. The afternoon was rushing on, and we had to go home to change clothes before going on to our next stop. I glanced at my watch—which turned out to be a mistake.

"You two guys really think you're something!" McCloskey shouted. All activity in the other room had stopped, and everyone was staring at us. "The famous Fredericksons! I'm sick of hearing the other cops talk about the two of you all the time, and I'm sick of reading stories about you in the newspapers! I'm here to tell you that I don't believe half of the shit they print about you. Dr. Robert Frederickson and *ex*–Police Lieutenant Garth Frederickson may be fucking famous, but what you are *not* is fucking police officers. *I* am in charge of this case. This is a police matter, and I will *not* tolerate any more interference from you two—not now, and not in the future. I don't care how many powerful friends you have in Washington. Now, do I make myself clear?!''

Reading us the riot act seemed to mean that he wasn't going to hassle us any more about disturbing the scene of an investigation—which he would have had every right to do. That was good.

I glanced at Garth and was alarmed to see that he was leaning against the mantel in almost exactly the same pose he had assumed while I'd questioned Craig Valley. He seemed very relaxed, almost bored, as he stared out the window behind the desk. In my brother, such exaggerated calmness was a warning sign. That was bad.

"You've certainly made yourself clear, Lieutenant," I said brightly. "We were way out of line. My brother has already apologized for the two of us; I apologize again."

McCloskey grunted. "What the hell did you say you were looking for?"

"Dirt," I replied even more brightly.

Lieutenant Malachy McCloskey studied me, a thoroughly puzzled expression on his face. "What?"

"We're looking for the dump site of a load of one hundred tons of dirt, Lieutenant," I replied. Now that I seemed to have his undivided attention, I let my smile fade. "Valley knew where the dirt had been dumped, and that's what Garth and I were questioning him about when he killed himself."

"You're telling me that a man killed himself rather than tell you where to find a load of *dirt*?"

"Yes, Lieutenant."

McCloskey glanced at Garth, but my brother continued to stare casually out the window; when the policeman looked back at me, he seemed even more puzzled. I couldn't blame him.

"Why would he do that, Frederickson?"

"I don't know, but I have a strong feeling that the police should take steps to find out. Garth and I really don't care. It isn't the dirt itself that interests us, and Valley knew that."

"Just what does interest you?"

"Why don't you sit down, Lieutenant, and I'll tell you all about it."

He did, and I did.

5.

CREDIT Detective Lieutenant Malachy McCloskey: the gray-haired, scar-faced man might be decidedly sour, insecure, resentful, and even downright bone-headed, but his heart was still alive and in the right place. When I had finished explaining what we were up to and why we were in such a hurry, how Craig Valley had almost certainly been connected to the sample of Amazon rain forest soil found in a letter sent to Santa Claus by a sexually abused child, the man's craggy, pitted face was ashen, his black eyes misty with tears. He had children of his own—seven of them, as well as two grandchildren who were probably around the same age as Vicky Brown.

"Jesus Christ," McCloskey said in a husky voice. "Forget what I said before, about you two messing up the scene and all that; if I'd been in your place, and it had taken the cops forty minutes to get here, I'd probably have torn the whole house apart."

"There's nothing here," I said. "We went through all the paper we could find, but if he wanted to keep the dirt—or anything else—a secret, I doubt he'd have written anything down. Besides, he was just an errand boy."

McCloskey shook his head angrily. "That fucking Kenecky . . ."

Garth turned to us, shrugged. "What difference does it make whether it's Kenecky or somebody else raping the girl? Whoever it is should have his prick stretched and permanently stapled to his asshole."

"I think it does make a difference," I said, glancing back and forth between Garth and McCloskey, who still looked haunted. "If Kenecky's the abuser, it could mean that Valley's religious and racial nuttiness were more than curious personal traits he shared only with the good reverend; the apocalyptic theology and neo-Nazi shticks could be common threads in the whole operation Kenecky and Valley were a part of. For all we know, Henry Blaisdel himself could be a religious fruitcake, and these biospheres he wants to build could have, at least in his mind, religious overtones. If Kenecky is our man, it means for sure that the powers that be are willing to harbor a fugitive—and those powers are probably scuzzball neo-Nazis with a religious bent, which makes them dangerous. Now maybe we can get the F.B.I. involved. At the very least, Lieutenant, the NYPD might now be persuaded to put a little more than just their good wishes into this case."

McCloskey's black eyes, dry now and once more glinting with more than a hint of paranoia, darted over my face. "Is that supposed to be some kind of criticism, Frederickson?"

"It is not, Lieutenant; the police have been more than helpful—without them, the dirt we found wouldn't have told us anything, and that's the only clue we had to begin with. But now there's more than just a letter to Santa Claus from a sexually abused child; there's a corpse, and a possible tie-in to a federal fugitive. It should warrant a case file."

"I'll talk about it to my superiors, Frederickson," McCloskey said. Suddenly he seemed nervous.

"Are you going to talk to the people at Nuvironment?" I asked.

"About what?"

"About the dirt; we find the dirt and we find the girl. All Garth and I care about is determining the whereabouts of Vicky Brown and notifying the proper authorities if it turns out that she's being sexually abused—which she is."

"You expect me to walk into the offices of one of Henry Blaisdel's corporations and accuse the people there of complicity in the sexual abuse of a child?"

Garth grunted loudly, pushed off the marble mantelpiece, and walked to the opposite end of the room, where he leaned against the archway leading into the outer vestibule. McCloskey's bright eyes, once more hostile and resentful—and, perhaps, slightly fearful—followed him.

"All you have to do is ask some questions, Lieutenant; with what's happened here, and with the background information we've given you, you have the right. You find out where they dumped the dirt, and Garth and I will take care of the social work."

I watched McCloskey think about it; the more he thought about it, the further I could see him slipping away. I realized that he was a man not only worried about his past, but also about his present and—most important—his future. There was a small war being waged inside him, and I could see the casualty figures moving across his face.

"All you've really got is a letter from a kid," he said at last in a low voice as he lowered his gaze and stared at the carpet. "And what's in there could be the product of the girl's imagination."

"Want to read the letter, McCloskey?" Garth asked in a mild tone. I hadn't been sure he'd been listening.

"It doesn't make any difference. It's still just a letter, and there's no proof whatsoever that Nuvironment is involved in anything illegal. I think the captain would want me to have more than a suicide, a kid's letter to Santa Claus, and your word for the way things are before I go and risk stepping on Henry Blaisdel's toes. He pulls a hell of a lot of weight in this country, and particularly in this city, in case you didn't know."

I said, "Why don't you call your captain now, Lieutenant? Tell him what's happened here, and what we've told you. See if he'll okay your going to talk to the people at Nuvironment. Since Garth is the one who tracked down Valley's last telephone call, we'll tag along just to serve as material witnesses, as it were. Get them to tell you where they dumped the dirt, and we're gone."

"I don't need you to tell me how to do my job, Frederickson."

"I understand that. But no decent people would refuse to cooperate in an investigation that could involve the physical and emotional well-being of a child. But some people just don't like to talk to private detectives—and these people definitely won't talk to Garth and me if we're right about them having something to hide. Your presence in your official capacity could, let us say, help them to focus their attention on the seriousness of the matter. If we hurry, we can still get over there for a chat before they close the office for the day."

"It could get tricky, Frederickson," McCloskey said in a very low voice. "It's not something I'm going to rush into."

"For Christ's sake, Lieutenant—!"

"Now you listen to me, Frederickson!" the other man snapped as he abruptly raised his head and glared at me, pointing a thick index finger at my chest. "That big, stony-faced, self-righteous brother of yours standing across the room dumped on me pretty good a few years back. I was wrong, sure; inexperienced. Maybe I got what I deserved, maybe I didn't, but the fact of the matter is that I've had to walk a pretty tight line ever since then. I'm still walking a tight line, and I'm going to be doing it right up until midnight of December thirty-first; that's less than a week and a half away, and that's when I retire. Now you guys got real lucky, and now you've got it all; you're rich, and you're famous. Now, I'm not saying I could have done as well as you or the mighty Garth Frederickson over there, since he teamed up with you—but it didn't help that I had and have a stain on my record that Garth Frederickson put there. For sure, I'm telling you that I'm not about to jeopardize my pension, or a cushy job as head of security that I may have lined up, rushing into muddy waters that the famous Fredericksons have been stirring up. The difference is that you can afford to offend powerful people, or make mistakes; I can't. I'm going to go by the book, on this and every other matter that comes up in the next few days. If you don't like it, that's tough shit. Are you reading me, Frederickson?''

"It sounds to me like you've already retired, Lieutenant,'' I said, knowing I would probably regret the words, and not caring.

"Fuck you and your smart-assed insults, Frederickson! I'm not personally responsible for that kid; if I felt I was personally responsible in every case like the thing you're working on, I'd have gone crazy years ago. I said I'd talk to my superiors, and I will!''

I was trying to come up with an even better insult when Garth, uncharacteristically, ended up acting as mediator. "McCloskey,'' he said, speaking to the vestibule, "are Mongo and I free to go?''

"I need a statement signed by the two of you.''

"Sure,'' I said. "Uh, do we have to come with you to the station right now? There's something else Garth and I would like to do this afternoon, and we're a bit pressed for time.''

McCloskey wouldn't look at me. "I guess tomorrow morning is all right,'' he mumbled. "First thing.''

"First thing.''

It seemed we were excused. Garth and I went out onto the street, hurried to the corner to hail a cab.

"I could have used a little assistance back there, brother,'' I said. "Having a police detective along with us could make things a whole lot easier where we're going.''

Garth shook his head. "I knew you were wasting your time. McCloskey's as dead as Valley, and there's no sense in trying to get help from a corpse.''

The Blaisdel Building on Fifth Avenue was an imposing edifice indeed, a great tower of pink marble, steel, and smoked glass with an archway entrance three stories high at its apogee. The first few floors were filled with chic boutiques where you'd pay at least two hundred dollars more for any item than you would anyplace else. According to reports in various publications, the top three floors comprised Henry

Blaisdel's penthouse—"a fantastic adventure in interior design incorporating all that is best in the world," as *Architectural Digest* had put it. But the writer had confessed that her description was speculative, since she hadn't been allowed up there; nobody—excepting, I assumed, family members, servants, and top executives—was allowed up in the penthouse. Blaisdel himself hadn't been seen in public for more than a decade; what he needed was brought to him, and when his presence was required somewhere else he went by helicopter, parked by a very special permit atop his building, to his private jet to . . . wherever. By contrast, Howard Hughes had been a party animal.

We entered the cavernous lobby, looked around until we found a directory on the wall to our right. Nuvironment was listed simply as a single word with the indication that its offices occupied all of the ninth floor, just above the tree-filled atrium and shops. The shopping floors had their own elevator system, and when we went to the bank of elevators serving the rest of the building we found no buttons for the penthouse or the ninth floor. Nuvironment was obviously not a company that encouraged drop-in business. Or drop-in anything, for that matter.

"You want to look for some stairs?" Garth asked tersely.

"No," I said, glancing at my watch. No New York City cabdriver had been willing to pick up an odd couple like Garth and me with our bloodstained clothes, and we'd ended up having to jog back to our brownstone to change. It was now 4:45. I had no idea what time Nuvironment closed up shop, but I wanted to get there before it did. While it was true that tomorrow was another day, it was also true that every hour that went by was another hour of potential pain and degradation for Vicky Brown, who could be somewhere close by, perhaps only a short cab ride away. "It looks like we're going to have to make an appointment after all."

"They're not going to agree to talk to us now, Mongo—if they agree to talk to us at all. A phone call will just put them on their guard."

"What choice do we have? Stairs aren't going to get us in there; if they don't have an elevator stop, the door on the fire stairs will most certainly be locked from the inside. Obviously, they have their own private way of getting in and out." I searched in my pockets until I found a quarter, started walking toward a bank of pay phones near the entrance, stopped when I realized that I was suddenly alone. I turned, saw that my brother was walking rapidly in the opposite direction, toward an archway that led to the boutiques on the first floor. "Garth?!"

"I'll see you later, Mongo!" he called over his shoulder.

"Hey! Don't you want to hear what these people have to say, even if it's only over the phone?!"

Garth hesitated, then abruptly stopped, turned around, and walked back to me. His face was pale, and his mouth was set in a grim line. "You talk to them," he said curtly. "You're a better talker than I am. I'm telling you right now that they aren't going to help you."

"How do you know?"

Garth put a finger to the side of his nose. "This tells me. There's evil here; I can smell it."

"You've got a nose for evil? For Christ's sake, Garth, that's all I need to hear—more wacko talk. Maybe we'll luck out. Maybe they'll be as anxious as we are to investigate a matter of child abuse—especially since it's their company's good name that could conceivably be damaged."

"That's precisely why they're not going to cooperate with you, Mongo; that, and because they have other things to hide. If they do talk to you over the phone, or even if they let you go up, they're just going to jerk you around. You're wasting your time."

"Garth, will you tell me what other choice we have?!"

"You go ahead and waste your time, Mongo. I'll see you back at the house."

Feeling slightly resentful, I shook my head as I watched Garth walk away. I pushed my way through a stream of people heading for the exit, made my way to the pay phones, went into a booth designed for wheelchair users. There was no phone directory, but Information had a number for Nuvironment. I dialed it.

A woman with a pleasant voice answered—the same one I'd heard Garth speaking with over Valley's cordless telephone. "Nuvironment. Happy holidays. How may I help you?"

"You people are kind of hard to get to."

"Excuse me, sir?"

"My name is Dr. Robert Frederickson, and I'm in a big hurry to talk to somebody with authority up there. Can you tell me what elevator to take to get up to you?"

"We're not open to the public, Dr. Frederickson. I'm sorry."

"I'm not the public. I have urgent business to discuss with your boss, and it has to be right now."

"Oh?"

"How do I get up there, lady?"

"But sir," the woman said in a voice that had become decidedly less cordial, "if you have a scheduled appointment, then surely you were told—"

"I don't have an appointment. I want one."

"With whom, Dr. Frederickson?"

"Henry Blaisdel."

There was a prolonged silence, then a decidedly frosty: "Is this some kind of joke, sir? I really don't have time—"

"This is decidedly not a joke, ma'am," I said, trying to keep my tone even. I was rapidly losing confidence in my ability to get past this keeper of the gate, and I could feel anger building. "It's a matter of great importance; Mr. Blaisdel will agree, I assure you. I need to see him now. I'll only take a few minutes of his time, but it will be the best few minutes he's ever spent. Don't tell me he's not in, because he almost never goes out."

"Sir, if this is not a joke, then you're seriously misinformed."

"Misinformed about what?"

"Mr. Blaisdel never sees anyone."

"He'll see me when he finds out what business I have with him."

"And what business might that be, sir?"

"I want to see Mr. Blaisdel about a very serious public relations problem he could have," I said carefully. I hadn't wanted to get into a heavy conversation over the phone, especially not with a receptionist, but it seemed clear I had no choice if I wanted to get into Nuvironment to see some-one, anyone. "This problem involves one of Mr. Blaisdel's favorite holdings—your company, and the biospheres you're attempting to design and build. This is serious, lady, so I hope you're listening very carefully. Somebody up there—I'm sure without Mr. Blaisdel's knowledge, and certainly without his authorization—illegally imported a hundred tons of some very special soil. I also have very good reason to believe that Nuvironment's reputation is being endangered by its involve-ment with loony members of the religious far right. In short, there are a lot of things going on down here at street level that the man who lives on the top three floors should know about and take steps to stop if he doesn't want to see your company's name roughed up in the newspapers. I'm not a blackmailer, and my only interest in all this is getting certain information from you people that will help me find a young girl who's being badly sexually abused. I want to talk to Mr. Blaisdel now, because I want the girl safe tonight. Now, have you got all that, lady, or do you want me to repeat it?"

"Please wait a moment, sir," the woman said nervously.

There was a click, and a tinny-sounding version of "God Rest Ye Merry Gentlemen" started playing. Mercifully, the music didn't last longer than one chorus. There was a second soft click, and the woman's voice—now sounding even more nervous—came back on. "Dr. Frederickson?"

"I'm still here."

"Just where are you, sir?"

"Down in the lobby."

"Please wait there, Dr. Frederickson. Somebody will be coming right down to meet you. How will he recognize you?"

"Tell him I'm the short guy. He can't miss me."

"Yes, sir."

I hung up, stepped out of the phone booth and waited. Less than a minute later an eager, boyish-faced man who was probably in his early to mid-thirties emerged from a knot of homeward-bound workers, peered around, saw me, and broke into a wide grin that looked to me to have more than a trace of nervousness in it. He was all yuppie, with a finely tailored gray pin-striped suit, rep tie, highly polished black shoes, pale pink shirt. I'd have bet he was wearing suspenders. He had a bright face with a midwestern look about it; blue eyes; a full head of brown hair, which was cut short. His height was no more than five feet five or six. He hurried across the lobby to me, delicate hand extended.

"Dr. Frederickson," the man gushed in a voice that was at once pleasant and yet somehow unformed, like a boy's. However, up close I could clearly see from the lines in his face that he was closer to forty-five than thirty-five, and he had a tic in his left cheek; his was one of those faces that don't stand up well under close inspection. "It's so good to meet you! It's so *embarrassing* that our receptionist didn't recognize your name, and so amusing for you to tell her you're the short guy in the lobby. As you can see, I'm not so tall myself. My name is Peter Patton."

"Nice to meet you, Mr. Patton," I said, studying his curious face with its tic that wrinkled the flesh under his left eye every few seconds. Something about the man in the gray suit brought to mind Dorian Gray, and the blue eyes were dull, belying the bright prattle that flowed from his mouth. "I take it Mr. Blaisdel has agreed to meet with me?"

The pasted-on smile that had never reached his eyes faded. "Oh dear. I thought the receptionist explained to you that Mr. Blaisdel never makes appointments to see anyone."

"And I thought I'd made clear to the receptionist that what I have to say to him is important enough for him to make an exception."

"That's impossible. However, I understand that your business involves Nuvironment. I'm the executive director of

Nuvironment, and I'm sure I'll be able to address your concerns satisfactorily.''

"I certainly hope so, Mr. Patton," I said, and deliberately pulled back the cuff of my jacket to look at my watch. "There's only one thing I want to know, and that's—"

"Please, Dr. Frederickson," Patton said, reaching out and touching me lightly—but all too familiarly—on the shoulder, "this is no place to talk. Come up to my office where we can be more comfortable.''

I didn't care where he answered my one question as long as he answered it, and so I dutifully followed him as he ran interference against the crush of traffic coming through the lobby in the opposite direction. We went past the two banks of elevators, then down a corridor to a door at the end that looked as if it might be a utility closet. Patton removed an elegant silver key chain from his pocket, selected a key, opened the door. It led to a small vestibule with a single elevator that had no call button. My escort unlocked a small wooden cabinet on the wall to the right, pushed a button inside. The elevator door sighed open.

"Why the private elevator?" I asked as I followed him in, watched him push a gray button—the only button—to the left of the door, which sighed shut.

"We're not a commercial enterprise in any sense of the word, Dr. Frederickson. We don't sell anything. We're strictly a research and development corporation.''

"And, from what I hear, a whopping tax write-off.''

He gave me a quick, furtive look. "You seem to know —or think you know—quite a lot about Nuvironment, Dr. Frederickson. We have absolutely no need to interface with the public; the private elevator is merely a convenience for our staff, as is the fact that we have our offices in Manhattan. Outsiders who do have occasion to talk with us are met in the lobby and brought up, as you are. It gives it all so much more of a personal touch, if you know what I mean.''

I didn't have the slightest idea what he meant, and since he wasn't likely to be keeping a hundred tons of dirt on the premises, I didn't care. The door opened, and I followed him out into a gold-carpeted, walnut-lined reception area. He pushed open a door of heavy smoked glass, held it for me, then led me through the first door on the left. I found myself in a spacious corner office with a wrap-around arrangement of picture windows that looked out over Fifth Avenue toward Central Park. On one wall was a large painting that might have been the company logo—a brightly glowing, transparent sphere containing lakes, forests, and people suspended in the coldness of space.

"Let me get right to the point," I said, closing the door behind me and ignoring his gesture indicating that I should sit in one of the two thickly cushioned, leather chairs set up in front of his steel and glass desk. "I need to know where you dumped your hundred tons of Amazon rain forest soil."

Patton, who had moved behind his desk but remained standing, merely stared at me, the tic in his left cheek the only punctuation on a face that was otherwise virtually blank.

"I'm not interested in any laws that may have been broken, Patton," I continued. "My concern is strictly private, and it has to do with the physical and psychological welfare of a child who I have good reason to believe is being sexually molested. I'm sure you'd share my concern if you knew the details, but I don't want to take any more of your time than I have to. I give you my word that I'm not interested in doing anything that will jeopardize the reputation or interests of Nuvironment. All I want to do is find the kid and make sure she's going to be all right. If I can find the dirt you people brought into this country, then I'll find the kid. Tell me where to look, and I'm long gone."

"Please sit down, Dr. Frederickson," Peter Patton said quietly.

"No thanks. I'm in a hurry."

"Would you like a cup of coffee?"

"I told you what I wanted."

Peter Patton, moving very deliberately in a manner that reminded me of a marionette, slowly eased himself down into his leather swivel chair, folded his hands on the glass desk top, then looked up at me. "I don't know what to say, Dr. Frederickson," he said at last, his voice still very soft. "You're obviously very upset, and I can understand why. I'm also upset at the thought of a child being sexually abused. However, I really don't know what you're talking about."

"No? Ever heard of a man named William Kenecky?"

"Of course. He's a televangelist—a rather strident one, I'm told—who's been indicted on charges of tax evasion."

"Are you people hiding him?"

He stiffened in his chair, frowned. "Good heavens, no. What on earth would make you think such a thing?"

Things weren't going well. I'd been plain enough in explaining what I wanted to know, and why, and had gone out of my way to reassure Patton that my interest had nothing to do with any criminal investigation. Then I'd tried to turn up the pressure by pointing out that Nuvironment could be accused of harboring a fugitive from justice. Zip. One of two things was true: either Patton and Nuvironment really weren't involved at all in the importation of the rain forest soil, a possibility I gave absolutely no credence to, or Patton was going to stonewall me totally, regardless of what was being done to Vicky Brown, rather than risk jeopardizing whatever else besides dirt the company was trying to keep secret. Suddenly I felt foolish standing there in front of the man with the tic in his cheek. It was enough to give me newfound respect for Garth's nose.

"Are you denying that your company arranged for the importation of special soil from the Amazon basin?"

"Of course I'm denying it. It isn't true."

I said nothing.

"You don't believe me?"

Now I sat down—if only to indicate to Patton that I fully intended to take as much time with him as necessary. If I couldn't get him to tell me the truth, I intended to make it very clear to him that I knew he was lying—and that I'd keep digging and digging, burrowing just as deep as I had to.

"Nuvironment very much wanted a load of that soil not too long ago, right?"

Patton's delicate hands clenched and unclenched almost imperceptibly, but his gaze remained steady, and his voice even. "You've come into possession of some very sensitive information. I don't know how you got it; there are such things as company secrets that are perfectly legitimate, you know."

"Do you deny that you tried in the past to get the soil?"

"No. As a matter of fact, we tried twice. After we were first discouraged by the Customs Service, we appealed; we were given an even more negative reaction the second time, if that's possible. That was the end of the matter."

"Why was it the end of the matter? From what I understand, you need the stuff."

"The 'stuff,' as you call it, is very high in microbial count and activity, and would indeed have proved useful in our experiments. But the Customs Service disapproved our request, and that was that. This is a very important company, Dr. Frederickson, and if you'd checked you'd have discovered that we have an impeccable reputation. It just so happens that there are sterilization and injection methods—legal ones—we can employ to approximate those soil conditions, so we didn't—don't—need the actual soil."

"But I assume it would be expensive and time-consuming to produce a hundred tons of artificial rain forest soil."

Patton shrugged his frail shoulders. " 'Artificial' isn't quite the right word for it—but yes, what you say is true. However, at this stage we are not particularly concerned with time or expense."

"That's hard to believe, Mr. Patton."

"Nevertheless, it's true. The construction of even a prototype biosphere is years—maybe decades—away, and there are still many other avenues of research besides soil types to explore. We don't really need that soil—not now—as much as you seem to think we do."

If Mr. Peter Patton, with his Dorian Gray face and the tic in his left cheek, was a bald-faced liar, he was a very good one; there was nothing but sweet reasonableness and sincerity in his oddly unripe voice. I suppressed a sigh. "What other people or companies are into this biosphere business?"

"Oh, thousands of concerns do related research—every earth science is involved, after all. But nobody that I know of would actually try to build a biosphere on a scale suitable for long-term human habitation; it would take the resources of a government—or Blaisdel Industries—to do it. Since the expenditures involved are considerable, the government is quite willing to let us proceed on our own. Blaisdel Industries gets grants and tax write-offs in return, certainly, but this whole operation is much more a labor of love on Mr. Blaisdel's part than you can imagine. It's his testament to his belief in the future of the human race. The day will come, he believes, when Nuvironment biospheres will provide the means for the human species to colonize the other planets of our solar system. In the meantime, discoveries are constantly being made; certain patenting procedures which must be observed are the reason we're so 'secretive,' if that's what you think we are. Licensing those patented processes is the only payoff we have, for now."

"Maybe somebody's trying to steal a march on you, Patton; maybe some other corporation is just as interested in biospheres as you are, is farther along, and you don't even know about it."

"Then perhaps you should investigate that possibility, Dr. Frederickson," Patton replied evenly. "Frankly, I doubt it's possible."

"So do I, for a number of reasons," I said, watching his face carefully. "One of those reasons is a man by the name of Dr. Craig Valley. You know him?"

"You needn't try to trap me, Dr. Frederickson," Patton said irritably as he put a hand to his left cheek; it was the first time I had seen him take notice of his tic. "Of course I know him—and I assume he's the man who's been serving as your source of information. As you must know, Dr. Valley once worked for us as a consultant. We stopped using him at about the same time he was discharged by the New York Botanical Garden, and for the same reasons. He was showing signs of serious mental instability and proving increasingly unreliable."

"Rain forest soil was definitely imported into this country, and Craig Valley was definitely involved in smuggling it in."

"If you say so," Patton replied tersely. "I wouldn't know. If he did do such a thing, he certainly didn't do it on our behalf."

"Maybe some of your people here are doing things behind your back."

Patton snorted. "Impossible, Dr. Frederickson. I most certainly do *not* have a 'laid-back' management style, I assure you. Nothing here happens without my knowledge."

I waited a few seconds before saying quietly: "Then why don't you tell me where the soil is stored, Patton? I don't care if you've got a ton of heroin hidden under it, along with William Kenecky and a hundred other fugitives, crazy or otherwise; all I want to do is find the kid."

He waited a few seconds before answering me, and when he spoke his voice was even softer than mine. "I can't help you, Dr. Frederickson."

"What about William Kenecky, Patton?" I asked, leaning back in the leather chair as I continued to study his face.

"What about him?"

"Would you describe him as a religious zealot?"

"I suppose so," Patton said, taking his hand away from his twitching cheek long enough to glance at his watch. "What's your point?"

"What about Craig Valley? Was he a religious zealot?"

"I really don't know much about Dr. Valley's personal life."

"Well, let me assure you that he was a religious zealot—a really loony one, right out of the same fruitcake mold as William Kenecky. One of the traits shared by people like that is that they think they can do just about anything they want,

including buggering little girls, because they enjoy special
favor with God; that's their excuse for everything. I've seen
it again and again. Now, I hear you talking, and you sound
very sincere, but I can't help but wonder if you're a good liar
because you're one of that gang. What about it, Patton? Are
you a religious zealot who thinks God wants you to protect a
child molester?''

"That's a most offensive question, Frederickson!" the
executive director of Nuvironment snapped as he rose from
his chair, drew himself up to his full five feet five inches,
and tugged at the bottom of his tie. "Now, I think I've given
you more than a generous amount of my time, and I'd thank
you to—!''

"A little more than an hour ago Craig Valley, your man at
the Botanical Garden, killed himself, Patton. He did it by
punching holes in his carotid arteries using double-edged
razor blades which he held in his bare hands. He made a
phone call before he died; as a matter of fact, he didn't even
bother to hang up before he offed himself. The last person he
talked to works here at Nuvironment. Isn't that a son-of-a-bitch?''

That sat Peter Patton back down. He looked like a man
who had been punched in the stomach; his blue eyes were
wide with shock as he stared at me in disbelief; his mouth
hung open, and his breathing was rapid and shallow. Oddly
enough, his tic had stopped. I casually crossed my legs and
stared back at him, raising my eyebrows slightly.

He finally managed to say, "Dr. Valley is . . . dead?''

I lowered my eyebrows to a squint, just to let him know I
remained more than a bit skeptical about anything and everything he had to say, regardless of the histrionics that went
with the words. "You didn't know?''

He tugged at his tie again, then loosened it and undid the top
button of his shirt, took a deep breath. "How would I know?''

"The police didn't call you?''

Patton shook his head, and it occurred to me that he could
be telling the truth about that, at least. Lieutenant Malachy
Seamus McCloskey was evidently still talking to his superiors,

and maybe a few other people, making sure that his about-to-retire ass was well armored before he started mucking about and asking questions in a company, and a favored one at that, owned by Henry Blaisdel.

"Was it you he called, Patton?" I continued. "Were you the person he was talking to when he slit his throat?"

"How could you know?" Patton asked the wall behind me. His face had gone very pale. He abruptly shifted his gaze to my face. "I mean, how could you know who he called if he committed suicide while he was making the call?"

"The wonders of modern technology, Patton," I said evenly. "He called here."

Peter Patton wiped a thin film of perspiration from his forehead with a linen handkerchief. He carefully refolded the handkerchief and put it back in his jacket pocket, put his hands back on the glass desk top, palms down, and sighed heavily. "As a matter of fact, I was the one he called," he said softly, licking his lips. "My lord, you say he killed himself afterward?"

"Not afterward, Patton; during."

Something moved in the depths of Patton's eyes, and he narrowed them slightly. "If you were there while he was making the call, why couldn't you have stopped him from killing himself?"

Not being quite ready to go on the defensive with the skilled liar sitting across from me, I ignored his question. "What the fuck did you say to him that caused him to slit his throat?"

"This is terrible," Patton said hoarsely, apparently deciding that turnabout was fair play as he proceeded to ignore my question. "If this gets into the newspapers . . . Mr. Blaisdel detests any kind of publicity about himself or his companies, even when it's good publicity."

"Your concern for Craig Valley is touching, Patton. But don't worry about me leaking anything to the media. I really don't give a damn why Valley called you, or what you talked about. Like I keep saying, the only thing I care about is finding the child I mentioned. To do that, I need to know where you're storing that dirt.''

His tic had started up again, this time with a vengeance, and Patton pressed the tips of the index and middle fingers of his left hand tightly against it. "*Please* believe me, Dr. Frederickson. I can't help you. I don't know anything about the soil you're searching for. As far as the call from Dr. Valley is concerned, I can't even tell you what we talked about, because we didn't really *talk* about anything. He was incoherent; babbling, really. The few things I could make sense of sounded very abusive, to tell you the truth, and I took it that he was blaming me—or Nuvironment—for all of his personal difficulties. I think he blamed us for getting him fired from the Botanical Garden, but it wasn't true. I swear to you that I simply put him on hold almost immediately after he started to become abusive.''

"On hold? Why didn't you hang up on him?''

Patton again shrugged, and smiled almost shyly. "I suppose I should have. But, after all, he was obviously very distressed. I guess maybe I was hoping he would calm down and that I'd be able to talk some sense to him. When I came back on the line, he wasn't there; I assumed *he'd* hung up. Now, to find out that he killed himself . . . it's just very shocking, and I'm afraid that now I'm going to feel at least partly responsible for his death. Who knows? Maybe I could have saved him.''

"I want to talk to your boss, Patton.''

The other man blinked, frowned, shook his head slightly. "What?''

"You said you can't help me—or won't.''

The frown deepened until it was pretty close to a scowl. "You're a very persistent man, Dr. Frederickson.''

"That's only one of my many faults. One of my few virtues is that I can be very closemouthed, when it suits me, and I keep my word. I told you that I won't involve Nuvironment in any scandal, and I won't—if you tell me what I want to know. Now, another one of my faults is that I have this real nasty streak in me that comes out when I get disappointed. In this case, I just might take it into my head to talk to the newspapers about . . . whatever. I *know* Blaisdel wouldn't want me to do that, so I figure maybe I'd better talk to him about the dirt, William Kenecky, and the little girl. You just put me in touch with him on the phone; I'll do the talking.''

Patton snatched his hands off the top of the desk and stiffened in his chair. ''You may carry out your threat, Dr. Frederickson, and it's possible that you could ruin my career—but it won't get you what you demand. It won't get you an appointment with Mr. Blaisdel, because he never sees anyone, and it won't get you the information you seek, since Nuvironment had nothing to do with any importation of soil. We've done nothing wrong, absolutely nothing, and if you try to make it appear that we have . . . well, that will be on your conscience.'' He paused, touched the side of his nose. ''Also, of course, there are libel laws.''

Peter Patton himself was nothing if not persistent—so persistent, and adamant in his denials, that I was almost tempted to believe him. But if I did believe him—if Nuvironment had nothing to do with the importation of the rain forest soil, and if Craig Valley really had called Patton just to vent his spleen hysterically before slitting his throat—it meant that Garth and I would have to start all over again, from scratch, without the vaguest notion where scratch might be. That being the case, naturally, I decided not to believe a word he was saying—although it wasn't clear where that was going to get me, either.

''This business about the child bothers me a great deal, Frederickson,'' Patton continued.

''Yeah; I can see that.''

''There could be one other explanation—and that bothers me a great deal, too.''

''What would that explanation be?''

''The explanation would be that we have competition that I'm not aware of; such a competitor wouldn't be interested in long-range goals, but only in reaping the benefits of certain research findings. It now occurs to me that we may have a spy here, skimming off the cream of our research."

"Oh," I said, unable to think of anything else to say. Suddenly I felt very depressed.

"If that were the case," Patton said as he leaned forward slightly in his chair, "we would certainly want that person exposed." He paused for a few moments, continued carefully, "I certainly wish you were working for us, Dr. Frederickson."

"Jesus Christ, Patton, are you offering me a job?"

"Yes. And why not? I happen to know that you and your brother now deal almost exclusively with corporate clients. I understand that your fees are high, and Nuvironment would be more than willing to pay for the two of you to investigate the possibility of industrial espionage in our company. You could begin after New Year's."

It was an interesting proposition, inasmuch as it seemed to imply that Peter Patton was willing to give us the run of the place to search records and investigate personnel as we saw fit; that wouldn't seem to make much sense for the head of a company that was trying to hide something in addition to a hundred tons of dirt. The problem, of course, was that it was Patton who had come up with the idea; if he thought it was a good one, then it was difficult to see what Garth and I would gain. And we weren't about to put off our search until after New Year's.

"We already have a client who's taking up all our time," I said distantly, still pondering his offer and wondering why he had made it. "Vicky Brown; the child. Remember her?"

"Yes," the pale-eyed man with the tic replied evenly. "But you believe that I'm denying to you information that could lead you to her; in effect, you're accusing me and my company of abetting the sexual abuse of this child. I deeply resent that, Dr. Frederickson. If allowing you to investigate our operations will assuage your suspicions, I'm willing to pay you to do it."

"Then you really don't believe there's a competitor trying to steal your secrets?"

"It's always good to have a thorough security check once in a while."

"But you don't believe you have a spy."

"No."

"Then how would you explain the soil?"

"I think you've made a mistake; the people who analyzed the soil for you made a mistake. Or, some other concern—perhaps an agricultural lab at some university—brought in a small sample of the soil for their own purposes. I happen to like children very much, Frederickson, and I would do nothing to cause one to be harmed. I'm as interested in the welfare of this Vicky Brown as you are."

"And you're willing to give Garth and me complete access to all your operations here?"

"Not only here, but at any of our research facilities around the world."

"How many of those are there?"

"Sixteen. You won't find any rain forest soil in any of them, I assure you. As I said, you can begin January second."

"Why not right now?"

Patton again glanced at his watch. "I'll be happy to give you a tour of our facilities right now, if you'd like, but it won't do you much good. So much of our work is highly technical that you'd really need the appropriate personnel here to explain to you what they're doing and give you access to their computer files."

"Why can't you do that?"

"I'm a manager, Frederickson, not a scientist. Besides, I'm not sure you'd believe anything I told you, anyway. Just about everyone has gone home now, and the offices will be closed through New Year's. In fact, I'm scheduled to leave tomorrow morning for a European ski vacation. If you like, I'll postpone it."

"I don't need your personnel to search your computer files. I'll bring in my own experts."

Patton shook his head. "I'm afraid I couldn't authorize that; and, if I could, I doubt your people would be successful in interpreting all the data that's stored here. Please, Dr. Frederickson; I'm trying to be cooperative, and responsible."

And he was certainly putting on a good show. On the other hand, I could search computer files for a year and still miss what I was looking for. Rummaging through the offices of Nuvironment—now or after New Year's—wasn't the answer to the problem of finding Vicky Brown. Somebody had to *tell* me what I needed to know. In effect, Patton was offering me nothing except a show.

"I'd still like to talk to Blaisdel."

Patton rested his hands in his lap, sighed deeply. "I will submit a memo to that effect, Dr. Frederickson; that's all I can do. The memo will be ignored."

"Why don't you just pick up the telephone and call him?"

"Because—"

As if in response to my suggestion, the phone on his desk rang, startling both of us. Patton frowned and stared at the phone as it continued to ring—five, six times. He obviously hadn't been expecting any phone calls.

On the seventh ring Patton grunted with annoyance, reached out and punched a button on a speaker-intercom console connected to the phone. "What is it?" he snapped. "I thought I left instructions that there were to be no—"

"I'm sorry to interrupt you, Mr. Patton," a strong, authoritative male voice said. It was a distinctive voice, vaguely familiar; I was certain I knew the voice, but couldn't recall where I had heard it. "If you're on the intercom, please pick up the telephone receiver."

Patton punched another button, snatched the telephone receiver out of its cradle, and held it to his ear. "What's the problem?" he said curtly. He listened for a few moments, and his pale face darkened. "Just bring him in here," he said at last, and slammed down the phone.

I had a pretty good idea who "him" was even before the office door opened and Garth, blood streaming from a gash on one cheek and the other cheek rapidly swelling, and with both arms twisted up behind his back, was roughly ushered into the room by two burly men whose suit jackets weren't sufficiently well tailored to hide the bulge of guns in shoulder holsters. It looked, not surprisingly, as if Garth had given as well as he'd got; the shirts of both men were ripped and spattered with blood, their hair was tousled, and the left eye of the man on Garth's right was almost swollen shut.

Now I realized where I had heard the voice on the intercom before—on national television, broadcasting various baseball "games of the week" for a year or two. The name of the man twisting Garth's right arm was Hector Velazian, and he had once been a twenty-five-game winner in the majors before drugs and booze had melted the muscle in his mind and arm. He'd been rehabilitated, but had never gotten back his form. He'd retired, landed a job as a broadcaster, then lost that when his old demons had caught up with him. That had been at least five years before. The last I'd heard of him, he'd been identified by some stringer for UPI after languishing for a week in a Mexican drunk tank. He'd looked positively ghastly in the news photo that had appeared at the time, but now—except for the black eye Garth had given him—he appeared fit and trim. And mean, with his dark, Latin features twisted in frustration and anger.

The man attending to Garth's left arm was Billy Dale Rokan, another retired major league baseball player who'd fallen afoul of various illegal substances, along with a well-publicized statutory rape charge. It appeared that Peter Patton was a baseball buff; but instead of collecting cards, he collected former players. However, the men's jobs certainly seemed to agree with them; Billy Dale Rokan, like Hector Velazian, looked fit enough to trot out on the field again.

"Hello, brother," Garth said easily, with just the faintest trace of a smile. "How's your meeting going?"

"I thought I told you to wait in the car."

"We didn't bring the car."

"I thought you were going to wait there anyway."

"I figured we'd better check with you before we called the police, Mr. Patton," Hector Velazian intoned in his deep, resonant, announcer's voice. "We checked his identification, and it turns out he's a private investigator with this outfit called Frederickson and Frederickson. I've heard of him; he's a heavy." The Latin paused, nodded in my direction. "Him, too. That's his brother."

The lighter of the Fredericksons said, "Why don't you guys let go of my brother before I start throwing around office furniture?"

"Mr. Patton?" Billy Dale Rokan said.

"Let him go," Patton said tersely.

"But Mr. Patton—!"

"I told you to let him go!"

The two ex-ballplayers released Garth's arms, but then moved in to flank him tightly, their shoulders between him and the slight man sitting behind the desk. Garth rubbed his shoulders, then shoved his hands into his pockets, looked up at the ceiling, and yawned.

"We caught him down in the third-level basement, Mr. Patton," Rokan said as he wiped blood from the corner of his mouth. "He tripped off a couple of alarms. When we found him, he was trying to pick the lock on the freight elevator. He had no business being down there."

"Indeed," Patton replied mildly as he looked at my brother. "Just what is it you were doing down there, Mr. Frederickson?"

"I was trying to find a way to get up to Blaisdel's penthouse," Garth replied matter-of-factly as he looked at me. "What the fuck do you think I was doing down there?"

"Why would you want to do that?"

"I just thought Henry might like some company. I hear he's a virtual shut-in."

Patton pressed his fingers against his tic and rocked back and forth in his chair for a few moments. Finally he stopped rocking and nodded curtly to Velazian and Rokan. "Leave us."

"But—"

"It's all right, Hector. Both of you can leave. And close the door."

The two guards looked at each other, shot hostile glances at Garth and me, then backed out of the office, with Rokan closing the door behind them.

Garth, who looked—to me—dangerously calm and unperturbed by his tussle with the guards, didn't even glance at Patton. He asked me, "Did he tell you where we can find the girl?"

"Uh, not exactly."

"I told you nobody here would cooperate, Mongo. There's something very funny going on here, and it has to do with a lot more than a lousy load of dirt. I told you I could smell the evil here. You're trying to cut a deal with some very freaky people, and you're wasting your time."

Peter Patton cleared his throat loudly. "Please sit down, Mr. Frederickson," he said evenly. "You seem overwrought. I'm sorry my people had to be so rough with you, but Nuvironment provides security for the entire building, and you were in an area that's closed to the public."

Now Garth slowly turned to face the man behind the desk. "I'm not overwrought, pal," he said very quietly. "I just get more than a trifle impatient with anybody who'd protect a maniac who gets his rocks off by tearing up the vagina and rectum—and mind—of a child. You know what I mean?"

Patton flushed and leaned forward in his chair. "That is an absolutely outrageous accusation, Frederickson. As I was saying to your brother, I'll sue you for everything you've got if you dare to repeat it to anyone."

"Mr. Patton denies that he or his company had anything to do with bringing in the dirt, Garth," I said in a flat voice, watching Patton's tic-ravaged face. "Indeed, he's raised the possibility of a competitor stealing Nuvironment's research findings, and he's offered us a retainer to look into the matter. He claims to be as concerned about Vicky Brown's welfare as we are. He's even offered to open up the Nuvironment offices for our inspection. You should have been here during our discussion; he really seems quite sincere."

"So?" my brother said without much apparent interest. He was staring hard at Patton. "Did you accept the retainer?"

"I was about to tell him that I couldn't possibly commit to such an arrangement before consulting with my partner."

"You know, this man's a liar. He's jerking you around."

Patton started to rise out of his chair; he apparently had second thoughts, because he immediately sat back down. "You have no right to talk to me like that, Frederickson," he said tightly, in a dry voice that cracked. "I deeply resent it. I have a good mind to press charges for trespassing."

"Mongo, listen to me," Garth said without taking his eyes off Patton's face. "If this joker really wants to hire us, it's only to put us off the track. This son-of-a-bitch really is ready to sacrifice the kid in order to protect Kenecky and cover up whatever it is they're really trying to do. I don't want to rush you through this important meeting, of course, but I thought you might like to join me for steaks and whiskey sours."

"Yeah, you're right," I said with a sigh. "I am kind of hungry, and we're running into so much resistance trying to get certain people to give this kid a break that we have to take pains to keep our strength up." I got to my feet, smiled thinly at the ashen-faced executive sitting behind the glass and steel desk. "Well, Mr. Patton, what can I say? My brother informs me that you're a liar—which means that you prefer protecting a child molester to giving us just one simple piece of information. Frankly, I don't understand it. I just hope Henry Blaisdel and you people in Nuvironment don't have second thoughts about all of this when we do find your lousy pile of dirt—which we are most definitely going to do. You might even think about preparing a letter of resignation, because, as of now, all bets are off on Garth and me keeping whatever it is we find to ourselves."

As I turned and started toward my brother and the door, Peter Patton, now red-faced, leaped up from his chair and came stalking around his desk. "Wait a minute!" he shouted in a squeaky voice. "Just who the hell do you two think you are?! One of you is a trespasser, and both of you are slanderers! I can bring charges! The Frederickson brothers aren't going to be so high and mighty if they get their private investigator licenses revoked, will they?! As a matter of fact, I think I definitely will—!"

The executive director of Nuvironment abruptly stopped speaking when his air supply was cut off—the result of Garth's grabbing him by the tie and collar and lifting him up on his toes. Patton's eyes went wide, and his mouth opened and closed as he struggled to breathe.

"You've got a lot more to worry about than causing trouble for the Fredericksons in various city agencies, Mr. Patton," Garth said in a perfectly mild, conversational tone of voice that somehow reminded me of the sound of a sharp knife cutting through silk. "We don't need licenses to search for the child. When we find her, and we most certainly will, I'm going to make a judgment about her condition. With your cooperation, Mongo and I could probably have found her this evening; now it's going to take longer. If I decide that this unnecessary delay has resulted in additional damage to her mind and body, more than she's already suffered, this Frederickson brother is going to come back here and kill you. Now, there's a very serious threat from one of us that you can add to your charges of slander and trespassing. Have I made myself clear, Mr. Patton?"

Garth casually cocked his head to one side and raised his eyebrows slightly, as if waiting for a response from Patton, whose face was now turning a dark purple.

I said, "Uh, Garth, I think it might be a good idea for you to set Mr. Patton back down on his feet. He seems to be having a bit of difficulty breathing, and it could be difficult for us to go on about our business if you're arrested on a murder charge."

"You're a mealy-mouthed fuck," Garth said to Peter Patton in the same mild tone as he released his grip and the other man staggered backward, gasping for breath, and finally collapsed over the top of his desk.

"Come on, Garth," I said tersely as I quickly opened the door and tugged at my brother's sleeve. "I think it's time we went back to corporate headquarters for a strategy conference."

Garth stood staring at the gasping Patton for a few moments, then abruptly turned and stalked past me out the door. I left the office, slamming the door shut behind me, and hurried after Garth as he headed toward the private elevator.

6.

IF Garth was at all concerned about what had happened on the ninth floor of the Blaisdel Building, he certainly didn't show it as we walked back along Fifth Avenue through the wall-to-wall sound of Christmas music created by competing groups of Salvation Army bands, steel bands, all-purpose bands, and enterprising soloists tootling or sawing away on everything from tubas to double basses to kazoos. Rainbows of light splashed over the sidewalks, spilled by shop windows crammed full of Christmas displays of every description. Fuller-bodied music seeped out of the churches—the *Messiah*, the Brandenburg Concertos, choir-powered Christmas carols . . .

In a way, I wished it wasn't Christmas; it just made our job, our dilemma, more depressing.

On the other hand, I reminded myself, if not for the fact that it was Christmas, we would never have learned of a little girl who was lost somewhere, hurt and in need. And taking care of such business was really what Christmas was supposed to be all about.

True, Garth seemed distant and distracted—but I knew it was because he was thinking about Vicky Brown, not pondering whatever consequences might arise from his having roughed up and threatened Peter Patton. I was distracted by thoughts of Vicky Brown as well, but it was becoming increasingly obvious that I was being distracted by a lot more things than Garth was; I'd decided that the problem had to be attacked immediately, and the air cleared.

"I need to talk to you," I said as we entered his third-floor apartment in the brownstone and I tossed my parka over a coatrack in a corner of the wood-paneled foyer.

"I know," Garth said evenly as he took off his overcoat, hung it over my parka, then preceded me into the living room. "You want a drink?"

"No."

Garth's apartment, except for the furnishings, was virtually identical to mine, and now he went to the wall of glass at the south side of the room, gazed out into the brightly lighted night. "You weren't happy with the way I handled Patton," he said, his voice slightly muffled by the glass. "You didn't say anything, but I could see."

"There are a few things I'm not happy with, Garth," I said curtly. "Like, say, your little excursion into the bowels of the Blaisdel Building. What the *hell* did you think you were doing, for Christ's sake?!"

"Well, I wasn't trying to get into the freight elevator—that part of their story was bullshit, intended to put me into an even worse light if the decision was made to press charges; it's arguable as to whether going into the basement of a building warrants a trespassing charge. I could have been looking for a men's room."

"Is it just my imagination, or have you failed to answer my question?"

"I wanted to try to find out if they had a security alarm system in the building—and, if so, how good it is. They do, and it's state-of-the-art. The interesting thing is that the shops all have their own individual security alarm systems. The best one isn't for Nuvironment or any of the other office complexes up there."

"The penthouse?"

"Yeah."

"Are you sure the state-of-the-art system just covers Blaisdel's triplex?"

"I'm sure. And they have security guards to oversee the security system; that's how I got caught."

"Well, that's not all that surprising, is it? Henry Blaisdel isn't exactly John Doe."

"I never said it was surprising. You asked me what I was doing down there, and I told you."

"I still don't understand what you thought you were going to accomplish."

"I wasn't trying to accomplish anything but what I did—check out Blaisdel's and the building's security system. Those people in there have Vicky Brown—or they know where she is. Have you forgotten that?"

"No, Garth, I haven't forgotten Vicky Brown. But there is the possibility, however remote, that Patton is telling the truth."

"That isn't a possibility, Mongo."

"He admits talking to Valley, and he didn't have to do that. Craig Valley was mad as a hatter, so any direction he pointed us in has to be suspect. He arranged to bring the dirt into this country, sure, but he could have been acting for somebody else; that would make sense if it's true that he blamed Nuvironment for his troubles, which is Patton's story. Patton flat out denies knowing anything about the dirt, Vicky Brown, or William Kenecky."

"He's lying."

"How the hell can you be so damn sure? You were skulking around in the basement while I was talking to the man. And I don't want to hear about your damn nose."

Now Garth turned away from the window and stared at me for some time. Shadows moved in his brown eyes, and he seemed to be searching for words. "I can't explain it any other way, Mongo," he said at last as he came over to me and laid a hand on my shoulder. "I think it may have something to do with the nitrophenylpentadienal poisoning. I really can't describe to you what I was feeling and sensing while I was zonked out on that stuff, except to say that certain things about certain people became instantly clear to me. That still happens to me; I just know certain things. I knew that anyone you talked to in Nuvironment was going to lie to you even before you went up there. I sensed it.''

"You know what that's called? Prejudice."

"You call it what you want, Mongo," he said quietly, taking his hand off my shoulder and moving away. "But I knew you weren't going to get any cooperation, so I figured my time would be better spent seeing if there was a way for us to get in there without anybody finding out about it. If Patton takes us through, he'll make sure we don't find what we want; if he offered to hire us, it was only so he could keep track of us—or to see if you were open to a bribe."

"That had occurred to me, Garth."

"Your visit served to warn him. Now, any records they have pertaining to the dirt and its dump site are going to disappear. We should have waited until tonight and tried to break in."

"Before we even tried to talk, and just because you thought you smelled evil when we walked into the lobby?" I said, making no attempt to mask my increasing impatience and rising anger. "You've got to be kidding me. Let me tell you something, brother. I'm getting just a bit tired of this new mystical, soft-spoken barbarian number of yours. I know I don't have to remind you that you're not a cop any longer— and if you were, I'm sure you wouldn't have acted the way you did up there; you wouldn't have engaged in a potentially illegal act of entry, and you wouldn't have manhandled and directly threatened Patton. Now you've put us both into a potentially vulnerable position. I don't know how hard Patton wants to push things, but if he does want to make trouble I suggest that your former employer, namely the New York Police Department, will lift our licenses faster than you can say Lieutenant Malachy McCloskey. I just don't see how losing the means to make our livelihood is going to advance our present cause.''

Garth flushed slightly. His eyes flashed, and he abruptly pushed back a thin strand of his wheat-colored hair before sweeping his arms around him in a gesture: the contents of his apartment, and mine, and the building itself. "Mongo," he said tightly, "there was a time not so long ago when all of this shit that we have now wouldn't have mattered so much to you—not when compared to what's happening to Vicky Brown. Now you're worried about us losing our licenses because we've offended a piece of shit like Patton. Do you really care so much about protecting all of this?''

In reply, I mumbled something under my breath that I did not intend for him to hear.

"What?'' Garth said irritably, taking a step back in my direction.

I motioned for him to come even closer and bend down toward me, which he did. "I said, you sure are getting to be a self-righteous, insensitive, narrow-minded pain in my ass," I whispered in his ear, and then brought my right fist up into his nose. I thought I felt and heard the cartilage snap; blood spurted over the front of my slacks and shoes and over the carpet.

Garth, his nose streaming blood, straightened up and stepped back. His brown eyes were wide with shock, pain, and bewilderment; then, finally, came understanding. He took a handkerchief out of his pocket and pressed it to his nose.

"I think you broke it," he said evenly. He seemed to be merely stating a fact, not registering a complaint.

"Yeah," I said, still seething with anger. "But you bled all over my pants and shoes, so I figure that makes us even."

"I'm sorry, Mongo."

I sucked in a deep breath, waved at my brother in disgust, slowly exhaled. "It's all right."

"I have been acting a bit self-righteous, insensitive, and narrow-minded lately, haven't I?"

"Yeah."

"And overly zealous?"

"Yeah. That too."

Garth grinned at me. "What about stupid?"

Despite my best intentions, I couldn't keep from laughing. "Okay, okay, enough; stop. You've engaged in sufficient self-recrimination to enable me to forget the outrageous things you said to me. Just watch yourself in the future, brother."

Garth's smile vanished, and the laughter winked out of his eyes. "You're also absolutely right about our not having to lose our licenses in order to find the girl; but I looked at that twitching son-of-a-bitch behind that desk, thought about the fact that he could probably tell us where to find the girl, but wouldn't, and I . . . just lost it. These days . . . ever since getting drugged with the nitrophenylpentadienal, I just go a little crazy where hurting kids are involved."

"I know, Garth," I said quietly. "But you've always felt deeply for anyone who was hurting; it's one of the reasons why I've always loved you so much. I think what the poison did—and what you have so much trouble explaining—is to take away some of your controls while giving you other, different ones. I think you've become as close a thing to a true empath as anyone alive on the planet today. You don't just feel sympathy for people; you virtually experience their mental and physical pain. I love you for that, too—but I also pity you. I guess, in a way, you really *can* 'smell evil,' as you put it."

Garth grunted, shrugged his broad shoulders, then walked out of the living room to the bathroom. He was gone for about fifteen minutes. When he returned, he had three strips of adhesive tape over the bridge of his nose, and he had stuffed cotton into his nostrils to stanch the bleeding. The nose looked straight enough, but the flesh under both eyes was already beginning to swell and darken; he was going to wake up in the morning with two significant shiners, and I hoped he owned a good pair of dark glasses. I almost felt bad—until I remembered the words that had triggered my little outburst of violence. Also, I observed that my punch in his nose seemed to have had a positively therapeutic effect on the empath who was my brother.

"I'll call Patton tomorrow and apologize, Mongo," he said quietly as he sat down on the sofa in the living room and put his feet up on his coffee table. "You're right; it was stupid for me to grab and threaten him like that, and I've put us in a vulnerable position."

"Let's not go overboard with the sackcloth and ashes, brother. What's done is done, and we should forget about it until and unless he tries to throw some grief our way. Besides, he told me the office was being closed down and he was flying off to Europe. If he's hiding things, and I *do* agree with you that he is, I doubt he'll want to make waves and call more attention to himself and Nuvironment."

"The son-of-a-bitch knows," Garth said softly, the muscles in his throat and jaw beginning to twitch. "He knows where the girl is."

"Okay, he knows. But we don't have any room left to move in that direction. And I agree that any record they may have had of the shipment is gone by now."

"Which means that we're going to have to start looking elsewhere."

I nodded. "For openers, we'll check out all the maritime shipping companies—especially any that we find out are owned by Blaisdel Industries. Also, we can try to find out what other companies do business with Nuvironment—plastics, steel, glass, whatever. If they've reached the stage where they're actually trying to build a biosphere, they need a lot more than just dirt. If we can identify some of their suppliers and talk to them, we may be able to pick up a clue."

"Right," Garth said, getting to his feet. "That means a lot of browsing through the business journals. Let's go; the library's open until nine."

"Tomorrow, Garth," I replied. "It's beginning to look like we're going to have to pace ourselves. It'll only take one of us to do the shipping companies. I'll do that, since we don't want your black eyes to scare anybody away. You'll work the library."

Garth shoved his hands into his pockets, frowned. "I hate to lose any time, Mongo."

"I know, Garth. So do I. But we're not going to find the girl tonight. And no matter what information there is to be found in the library, the fact remains that we won't be able to talk to anybody until tomorrow; offices are closed now."

"Okay, you're probably right," Garth said quietly. He pulled the cotton from his nostrils, wriggled his nose, then looked at me inquiringly.

"It's not bleeding anymore."

"I don't think you broke it after all, Mongo."

"I didn't? Shit. I hit you as hard as I could."

"Well, you had a bad angle. Don't feel bad about not breaking it."

"I must be getting old."

Garth smiled, came over to me, and gently laid an arm over my shoulders. "We're both getting old, brother."

"You want to go out and get something to eat?"

Garth shook his head. "I'm just going to have a sandwich and a beer while I look through the Manhattan yellow pages for companies selling things that might be useful in building a biosphere. It's probably a waste of time, but I need to feel like I'm doing something."

I nodded, walked across the living room, stopped and turned back at the entrance to the vestibule. I decided that I wanted to share something else that was bothering me. "How high would you rate my paranoia index?" I asked.

"Extremely high—which is perfectly normal for a New Yorker. Why?"

"All right, let's look at what we've got. First, a nutty plant man who killed himself rather than risk telling us something he didn't want us to know. Then we have Patton playing games—but he offers to give us the run of his offices and labs after the first of the year, which is a little less than a week and a half away. Why?''

"He told you Nuvironment was closing down until then."

"Yeah, but why make the offer at all? He's got more than enough time to destroy files, sure. But what about his people? Valley knew something, and he killed himself rather than reveal it. Why should Patton be so willing to give us access to his people—after the first of the year? I'm thinking—''

"You're thinking that it may not matter what we discover after the first of the year because by then it won't matter to them? That whatever it is they're so anxious to cover up won't make any difference then? That by then it will be too late for us, or anybody else, to stop them?"

"Yeah," I said, blinking in surprise. "Something like that."

"The thought occurred to me too, Mongo. You're not the only one with a high paranoia index."

I smiled thinly. "But then, you've got a nose for evil, don't you? I must have some of the same genes in my nose."

"I really wish that fruitcake Valley hadn't killed himself," Garth said seriously. "After he told us where to find Vicky Brown, I'd have liked to ask him to be a bit more specific about when the world was going to end, and just what he thought was going to happen when it did."

7.

MALACHY McCloskey seemed oddly subdued and distracted when Garth and I went in the next morning to make our formal statements concerning the suicide of Dr. Craig Valley; I had the feeling that the few days he had left before retirement were weighing heavily on him, and that we made him decidedly nervous. Despite the fact that the police detective apparently believed our story, the process was still maddeningly time-consuming, and it was past eleven by the time we got out of the precinct station. Garth headed for the 42nd Street library, while I hailed a cab.

Pier 42, on the Lower East Side, was the last maritime shipping facility left in New York City, and it was used primarily for the importation of bananas. But bananas came from the tropics, and I considered it a good possibility that one of the container ships might have been persuaded to bring in some soil along with its bananas.

I visited five offices and warehouses, talked with secretaries, warehouse foremen, and longshoremen. Not a few people thought I was joking when I asked if they knew anything about a load of a hundred tons of dirt. Then I told them why I wanted the information and quickly got their cooperation. What I didn't get was any useful information.

It was four o'clock by the time I finished working the area around Pier 42, and I realized with a growing sense of frustration that by the time I went back for my car and then made it through the rush hour crush of traffic in the Holland Tunnel, all of the shipping offices in Jersey City and Hoboken, across the river, would be closed.

I hailed a cab, went to the library to help Garth.

My brother was not encouraging; just in Manhattan, there were close to a hundred companies that supplied glass or plastic.

The next morning, the day before Christmas, I was up bright and early, driving Beloved—a modified Volkswagen Rabbit— down the East Side and through the Holland Tunnel to New Jersey, where most of the shipping companies had fled over the years to lower taxes and modernized container-shipping facilities.

I started in Jersey City, visiting companies in alphabetical order. At my first stop I found that a Christmas party, complete with jug wine, cookies, and a huge grab bag, was already in progress, although it was only nine thirty in the morning. I decided that did not bode well.

It didn't. Everywhere I went, Christmas parties were in progress, sometimes covertly, and more than one person I talked to had glassy eyes and liquor breath. Christmas music was everywhere, on the streets and in the offices; people were smiling, eager to cooperate.

Nobody knew anything about any shipment of Amazon rain forest soil.

By noon, I had covered less than half the companies on my list, and I still had Hoboken to visit. I tried to keep my frustration and anger tamped down, because I knew these emotions would only drain me of energy, but it was difficult; the good cheer that was evident everywhere only underlined the fact that somewhere—perhaps only a short distance away—there was a little girl who was not going to get any puppy for Christmas, only rending physical and psychological pain. To make matters worse, Christmas this year fell on a Friday, which meant that it would be three full days before Garth and I would be able to resume our search through corporate America.

After yet another fruitless visit, I put on my parka and trudged out of the shipping company office into a raw, gray afternoon that perfectly matched my mood. There was a cold drizzle that I was certain would soon change to snow, making my trip back into Manhattan even more slow and miserable. I was suddenly very tired, and depressed; my instincts told me that the rest of the day was going to be equally unproductive. I thought I might be coming down with a cold. I wanted to get back into Manhattan well before the heavy traffic started, but I knew I couldn't; I had to keep slogging along until I ran out of offices or they closed, because there was always the possibility that the very next one I went into might be the one that had shipped the dirt. If I quit early, I thought, Garth would have the right to punch me in the nose.

And I had another reason for wanting to stay on the job right up until the time I had to leave to meet Garth for dinner; I thought I just might have picked up a tail, and I wanted to be sure; if someone was following me, I wanted to make certain I didn't lose him.

The man I thought might be following me wore a tan parka with a fur-lined hood hiding his features, brown corduroy slacks which were tucked into the tops of old-fashioned rubber galoshes. The parka was bulky, but I gauged him to be of medium build, about five feet nine or ten. He had a kind of spring in his step and upright posture that somehow reminded me of how certain athletes move. Three times I had caught a glimpse of him as I had emerged from different shipping offices. There was always the possibility that he was a salesman of sorts making similar rounds, but he carried no briefcase or notebook. If he was a tail, and I was almost certain he was, he was the lousiest one I'd ever come across.

Just to test the waters, I casually walked three quarters of the way around the block, then abruptly headed down toward the river. I stood for a few minutes in a snow-covered meadow in a deserted park, watching legions of gulls hitching a free ride on the ice floes in the Hudson. Out in the harbor, the Statue of Liberty was just barely visible in the misty gray air. I walked out of the park, turned left, then right, then stopped to pretend that I was looking in a store window while I studied the reflections in the glass.

Lo and behold, my man with the springy step dressed in a tan parka floated through the sheen of the glass; he was on the opposite side of the street.

It was the best thing that had happened to me all day, and I loved it. Why anyone would want to waste his time following me while I wasted my time was beyond me, but I wasn't going to question providence.

As I turned away from the store window and walked at a decidedly moderate pace back toward Beloved, I noticed something else that was making a return appearance—a long, black limousine parked on my side of the street about a block and a half away. The limousine was out of place in the neighborhood, and I decided that my tail was being chauffeured about in style.

It was definitely amateur hour, I thought. Peter Patton, undoubtedly under orders from Henry Blaisdel, wanted to keep an eye on me. Apparently not willing to bring in professional help from the outside, Patton was using a company car and, no doubt, company personnel to do it. It was, of course, absurd to use a stretch limo to tail somebody, but Patton obviously didn't realize that. Or he didn't care; the stretch limo and obvious tail could be an attempt at intimidation, or even a show of contempt.

Outstanding.

If my man had wheels, it seemed to mean that he was under orders to keep following me wherever I went, as long as it looked like I was taking care of business. If I was getting too old to break Garth's nose, it probably meant I was getting too old for heroics—especially when there was so much to lose if I made a mistake. I certainly didn't want to come out on the losing side of a confrontation, and my tail's chauffeured limousine meant that I should have time for consultation with my burly backup troops. I made a mental note of the license plate of the limousine, then continued walking at a leisurely pace to where I'd parked Beloved.

Reasoning that maneuvering a stretch limo through rush hour traffic was no easy task, I took care to keep Beloved in the right-hand lane as I went back through the Holland Tunnel into Manhattan and headed uptown. The black limousine dutifully followed, keeping no more than three or four car lengths behind. I was beginning to feel insulted; I couldn't decide whether the driver thought I was blind, very stupid—or if he just didn't care if I knew he was behind me. I suspected it was the latter.

I'd left Jersey City not a moment too soon, because it was five minutes to seven by the time I'd negotiated my way back up to West Fifty-sixth Street. Normally, I'd have driven Beloved right into the brownstone's underground parking garage, since Rick's Steak House, where I was to meet Garth for our Christmas Eve dinner, was only a block away. However, I was afraid that the driver of the limousine, whose intelligence

I was seriously beginning to question, might think that I was bedding down for the night and drive away with the man in the tan parka; after leading them as far as I had, I couldn't risk that. It is well-nigh impossible to find a legal parking place on the streets in midtown Manhattan at any time; and it was hopeless on Christmas Eve. Consequently, I did something I had sworn I would never do, since it is the equivalent of handing over your wallet to the police department and the tow truck operators; I parked in a tow-away zone, right beneath a sign that read: NO PARKING OR STANDING AT ANY TIME.

"I'll make it up to you if you get towed away, Beloved," I mumbled as I got out and locked the door. "A tune-up, at the least, and I'll personally touch up any scratches."

The limousine stopped at the end of the block. I made a show of checking to see how close my tires were to the curb, used my peripheral vision to watch as the man in the tan parka got out of the limousine. He quickly stepped back into the shadows—but not before I had gotten a good look at him. It must have been warm in the car, because he'd unzipped his parka and flipped back the hood. He was wearing a brown corduroy jacket the same color as his pants, a light blue shirt with no tie. He was fair complexioned, with modishly cut light brown hair. I patted Beloved on the trunk, then stepped into the light where I was sure he could see me. Then I headed into the rich, deliciously gloomy wooden interior of Rick's.

I was met just inside the door with a bear hug and kisses from Kim, a beautiful young lady with the blackest hair I'd ever seen. Garth had taught the woman, a former prostitute and functional illiterate, how to read, and then gotten her a job at Rick's. She was now what Garth and I thought of as the World's Best Waitress. And I suspected that she deeply loved Garth.

"Merry Christmas, Mongo, my love," Kim said in her husky voice.

"Merry Christmas, Kim, my love," I mumbled as I tried

to extract my head from her ample bosom. "Is Garth here yet?"

Kim's smile wavered slightly, and shadows moved in her jet black eyes. "He's in the back, at your usual table. He seems so . . . morose. What's the matter with him, Mongo?"

"Troubles, babe," I said as I finally managed to escape from her powerful grip. I reached up and patted her cheek as I moved past her toward the rear. "Bring me my usual, will you?"

"You look morose, too!" Kim called after me as I pushed my way through a wall-to-wall throng of celebrants. "It's Christmas Eve! I'll be back in a little while to cheer you both up!"

Garth, wearing dark glasses to cover the black eyes I had given him, was sitting at our regular table, a banquette in a comfortably dim corner on the far side of a filigreed wooden partition that separated the dining area from the bar. He looked up from his diet soda, nodded as I sat down across from him.

"How'd you make out at the library today?" I asked, leaning across the table so that I could be heard above the din of Christmas music blaring from a jukebox in the bar.

My brother shrugged his broad shoulders. "Lots of information—too much information, really. Blaisdel owns lots of companies. It would take a month just to sort it all out."

"Any companies besides Nuvironment that might be involved in the design and construction of biospheres?"

"Lots—or none. The man owns companies that make just about everything you can think of, all around the world. Some of his companies did a lot of defense work in the late fifties and early sixties, but he doesn't seem to have had too many government contracts in the last few years. It would take too long to check everything out systematically, so I'm following hunches, making some calls."

"What hunches?"

Again, he shrugged. "What difference does it make? They're just hunches. How did you make out?"

"Nothing at Pier Forty-two, and nothing in about half the companies in Jersey City. But I still have half of Jersey City, and all of Hoboken, to work on."

"Great," Garth said in a flat voice as he sipped at his soda. "I don't think you're going to get anywhere there, Mongo; however they brought in the dirt, they've covered their tracks. On the other hand—"

"On the other hand, I've got some good news," I interrupted, reaching across the table and squeezing Garth's heavily muscled forearm. "They may think they've covered their tracks, but they're still nervous about the comings and goings of the Frederickson brothers. You may not believe this, but Patton—or whoever—put a tail on me, complete with chauffeured limousine, and he is *bad*. I mean, like el stinko. I can't think of a better Christmas present right now, under the circumstances, and he's waiting for us right now out at the bar, all gift wrapped in a brown corduroy suit and a tan parka. He's medium height and build, with his hair cut in a style that went out with the Beatles. You can't miss him."

Garth stared at me for a few moments, a strange expression on his face. He took another sip of his soda, then set the glass down on the table and smiled wryly. "You've got it mostly right—except that he's wearing a blue parka."

"What the hell are you talking about? He's *my* tail, and I'm telling you he's wearing a tan parka."

Garth grunted, rose from the table. "Excuse me for a little while, brother. I've got to go to the head."

"I can see that my report got you all excited."

"Sure has."

Garth was gone less than thirty seconds.

"That didn't take long," I said as he settled himself back down on the leather-covered bench across from me. "You must have a small bladder."

"I just wanted to take a look in the bar. I'd tell you to go take a look, but it might arouse suspicion. Think carefully now, Mongo. If you did go in there now to look over the clientele, especially people wearing parkas, what do you suppose you would see?''

"No shit? Twins?"

Garth nodded. "Matching outfits, to boot—except for the parkas. My guy is the one in blue. That was what I was about to tell you when you interrupted me. While I was in the library, I could feel this guy watching me—and he kept checking out the books I'd called up from the stacks after I'd finished and put them in the cart. I took a little walk before coming here, just to see how serious he was. He stayed right with me; in fact, he'd probably have stepped on my heels if I'd stopped. A real clown. He had a car trailing him, too.''

"Jesus Christ. I hope this isn't somebody's idea of a practical joke."

"It's no joke, Mongo," Garth said seriously. "They're from Nuvironment. Patton sent them to keep tabs on us."

"Your nose again?"

"If you like."

"It doesn't make any difference. I agree with you. Who else would put tails on us?"

"Did you get a look at your man's driver?"

"No. The limo had smoked windows, and they were up all the time. You?"

Garth nodded. "Just a glimpse—but it was a memorable one. A big, ugly guy; shaved head, flat nose. He's got the thickest neck you're ever likely to see this side of a livestock show." Garth paused, closed his eyes, and rubbed his temples. Finally he opened his eyes, looked at me, and shook his head. "I'm sure I've seen him someplace before, and I feel like I should know him; but I just can't place him."

"Is he out in the bar?"

"I didn't see him—and I definitely would have if he was in there. Both drivers must still be in their cars."

"And both parked on Fifty-sixth."

"Maybe not. It would make more sense for one of them to park on Fifty-seventh, in case we went out the back."

"Whatever. Brother, I would say that a lovely Christmas

present has been dropped into our laps just in the nick of time.''

''Right.''

''But we have to cut out the drivers.''

''Right,'' Garth said, and smiled thinly. ''I knew I wanted to have a chat with my companion, but, naturally, I wanted to check with you first. I'd hate to do anything that would cause you to criticize me again.''

''Go to hell, Garth,'' I said, rising and signaling for Kim. ''You made sure your twinny followed you right in here, just like I did; if he hadn't, you'd have been all over him and his King Kong chauffeur—and you'd have been right, if slightly unwise, to do so. So don't give me any of your shit about criticism from me. That business with Patton was different, and you know it.''

I gave Kim a big tip, told her we'd be back as soon as possible, then walked slowly through the bar with Garth, past the corduroy-suited twins, and out the door.

Outside, Garth nudged me, and I nudged him back; there was no sign of any limousines. Apparently, it had been assumed that we were through for the day when we'd gone into Rick's, and the twins had been left behind, on their own, just to make certain we were safely tucked into bed.

''Where to?'' Garth asked.

''I've always considered my roof garden a wonderful place to entertain, no matter what the season.''

''Good idea. The alley and fire escape?''

''Let's do it.''

We walked to the intersection, but instead of crossing it to the next block and the front entrance to our brownstone, we turned right, quickening our pace slightly as we angled across the street. I cast a quick, furtive glance over my shoulder to make sure the tan and blue parkas were following us; they were, moving up the sidewalk in tandem, about twenty yards behind us. We slowed down to make sure the twins wouldn't miss our big move, then, halfway up the block, we ducked into the narrow alleyway that separated our brownstone from the one on the block behind us. Instantly, Garth pressed back against one wall, and I stepped back against the other.

The twin in the blue parka was the first to poke his head cautiously around the corner of the alley. Garth grabbed the fur-lined hood of his parka, rudely yanked him into the alley, and slammed him up against the brick wall. When the second twin appeared a split second later I treated him to a drop kick to the solar plexus, doubling him over. I grabbed the back of his parka, pulled him into the alley to join his brother.

My twin, the one in the tan parka, wasn't going to be able to breathe, much less speak, for a bit longer, so I turned my attention to the other one, who was staring wide-eyed into Garth's stony face.

"Yes, he does bite," I said to the man, who then directed his attention down to me. He wriggled a bit, but Garth held him tightly up against the wall. "Before he does, I have one question; answer it, and we'll all be on our way to see what Santa brings. Where did Nuvironment dump its hundred tons of rain forest soil?"

There was some gasping and wheezing from the twin at my feet. Slowly, both hands grasped to his stomach, he managed to get up. He took a few tentative deep breaths, looked at his brother, and nodded.

"Praise the Lord," Garth's twin said.

"Praise the Lord," my twin wheezed.

"Amen," Garth said, and clipped his twin hard on the jaw. He crouched down to catch the slumping body of the unconscious man over his shoulder, then effortlessly straightened up, reached over his head, and pulled down the fire escape. "Any criticism, Mongo?" he continued, looking at me.

"Well, maybe you're just a trifle impatient, brother," I replied, studying the thoroughly shocked face of the twin in the tan parka. "But then, so am I. No criticism."

"You got your gun?"

"No."

"Are you too old to break one of the guy's kneecaps if he tries to run away?"

"At the moment, he doesn't look like he wants to find out."

"Good," Garth said, and, with the twin in the blue parka still draped over his shoulder, began climbing up the fire escape. "If he doesn't want to come up on his own, I'll be back down in a couple of minutes to get him."

"So?" I said to my ashen-faced twin as his eyes followed the progress of his brother on my brother's shoulder as Garth climbed up into the night. It had begun to snow heavily, and they disappeared from sight as Garth passed the first floor. "The price of declining this party invitation is to answer my question. If you do, Garth will bring your brother back down. Where's the dirt? Don't bother trying to lie, because we'll be taking the two of you with us to make sure the dirt's where you say it is."

My twin didn't bother trying to lie; he didn't bother saying anything at all. His pinched features and dark brown eyes clearly reflecting alarm and concern for his brother, he suddenly stepped to the fire escape and began climbing up into the snowy darkness. I clambered up after him—again noting his springy step, and the easy manner in which he moved.

We arrived at the top, climbed over the brick parapet to find my brother standing over his twin, whom Garth had sat down right on top of the burlap covering one of my prize-winning rosebushes. When my twin rushed over, Garth grabbed him by the lapel of his parka, sat him down on top of a second rosebush. The twin in the blue parka had regained consciousness, although he still looked more than a bit groggy. He looked around him, saw his brother sitting beside him, reached out and took his hand. If he was about to praise the Lord again, he apparently thought better of it when he glanced up into Garth's face. Both men slumped forward on their rosebush perches, bowed their heads.

"That idiot Patton sent you two idiots to tail us," Garth said to the men, his voice barely audible above the rising wind that whipped his wheat-colored hair about his head. "Mongo and I should feel insulted, but we don't have time to go into that. We're looking for a little girl, and you're going to tell us where to find her. Your employers dumped a shipload of some special dirt somewhere around here. Where is it?"

The twins exchanged surprised looks, and that bothered me; they shouldn't have looked surprised. It could mean that something Garth had said—perhaps something about our assumptions—was wrong, and that would be bad news indeed.

"What's the matter?" I asked my twin, the one in the tan parka. "Talk to us, for Christ's sake. Is it so hard for all of you people to believe that our only interest is the welfare of the child? Don't you care at *all* about her? What the hell's the matter with you people?"

"We won't tell you anything," my twin said. "Praise the Lord."

"Praise the Lord," his brother said.

"Amen," Garth said, and both men immediately flinched and put their hands over their faces.

But Garth didn't hit anybody. Instead, he grabbed the front of his twin's blue parka and yanked him up off the rosebush. He unceremoniously marched the man to the parapet, then, still maintaining a firm grip on the front of the man's parka, roughly sat him down on the brick.

My twin started to rise, and I kicked him in the left thigh—not hard enough to do any real damage, but with sufficient force to sit him back down again. "You have to forgive my brother's impatience," I said to the man as he furiously massaged his thigh. "I know he's making a terrible first impression, but he's not really as mean-tempered as he seems. It's just that he gets very crazy about child molesters, and people who protect them. Right now, you and your brother fit into the second category."

"Lies!" the man shouted at me. "Lies! We know who you are! You two are the spawn of Satan! You won't trick us! You won't defeat Christ's legions in the final hour! The second seal has been opened, and you and your brother chose to ride with the red beast!''

"What does he have to say, Mongo?!" Garth shouted over the wind.

"He says we're the spawn of Satan!"

"Tell the prick he's got that right! This guy doesn't want to say anything at all! He must think he can fly! Ask your guy if he thinks his brother can fly!"

"Tell us where the dirt is, pal," I said to the man sitting in front of me. "That's all we want to know; we check it out, and then you and your brother can be on your way. Patton will never know that you told us, I promise you."

"I don't know what you're talking about, spawn of Satan!" The fear and shock in the man's brown eyes had now turned to hate which was so clearly reflected in his twisted features that it startled me.

"Oh? Why were you following us?"

"You can't trick me! I won't tell you anything!"

"Then don't try to tell me you don't know what we're talking about, because you do. At least you know about the dirt. Maybe you don't know about the child, so I'll give you the story. Listen to me carefully: a lunatic by the name of William Kenecky is repeatedly raping and sodomizing a child by the name of Vicky Brown. You babble a lot of the same religious bullshit as Kenecky, but I don't think that either you or your brother molests kids. And you have absolutely no reason to protect Kenecky. We'll find Kenecky and the girl if you'll tell us where the dirt is being stored. You'll take us there, and then you'll see that what I'm saying is true." I paused, sighed heavily. Suddenly I was filled with a great weariness, as if the man's blind zealotry and stupidity formed a great weight that was pulling at my heart, dragging me down. "It's Christmas Eve, man," I continued quietly. "Imagine how you'd feel if she was your kid. Can't you give her a break?"

"Mongo?!" Garth shouted. "What's happening over there?! Do I launch this guy or not?!"

"Keep him on hold!" I shouted back over my shoulder as I kept my eyes on my twin's face. I didn't like what I saw there; the gleaming, crazed look in his eyes could mean that he was beyond threats to either himself or his brother, and thus beyond reason. It frightened me. I said, "Don't you think Jesus would want you to help this child?"

The man shook his head. "It doesn't make any difference if you kill Floyd or me. Soon we'll both be in Paradise."

"Good for you—but that doesn't answer my question. Don't you think Jesus would want you to cooperate with us in stopping a child molester from abusing a little girl's mind and body?"

"You're lying about Reverend Kenecky! He would never—!" He abruptly stopped speaking, but it was too late; the child molester had already been let out of the bag.

"Mongo?! Has he told you where we can find the dirt?! My arm's getting tired!"

I glanced over my shoulder at Garth, and didn't at all care for what I saw. My brother had pushed the twin in the blue parka back over the edge of the parapet, and the only thing that was keeping the man from falling four stories was Garth's grip on the front of his parka. The man's legs pumped up and down, and his fingers clawed at the brick wall he was bent back over. Garth lowered him a little more. I didn't think Garth would drop him—but I had to admit to myself that, under the circumstances, I wasn't absolutely sure. Vicky Brown's plight had him more worked up than I'd ever seen him, and he'd already made it very plain to me that he cared nothing for the rights—and, presumably, the lives—of victimizers or their allies. He had truly lost patience with the evil in the world in the most profound sense; to Garth, evil people were no longer people. And even if he didn't drop dear Floyd intentionally, there was always the chance that his gloveless hands might become stiff and numb in the cold, and lose their grip.

Cold hands just wouldn't make a very good defense at our

murder trial—and our being brought up on charges of murder wouldn't do anything to help Vicky Brown.

"Uh, Garth, hold off for a while, will you?! My friend here and I are just getting into a serious chat! Why don't you bring your guy over and join us?!"

For a moment I didn't think he was going to do it. Our eyes met, held. Then he shrugged before abruptly pulling brother Floyd back up over the parapet. He dragged him back across the roof and again sat him down on my rosebush, next to his twin.

"These guys seem to have popped out of the same fruit-cake as Valley, Mongo," Garth said easily. "I think I may have to start breaking things in them."

"You hear the way my brother talks?" I said, looking back and forth between the two men, whose faces had suddenly become oddly vacant. "He's the bad guy—but you're in luck, because I'm the good guy. I say, let us reason together." I paused, moved in front of the man in the blue parka. "Floyd, your brother tells me he doesn't believe Reverend William Kenecky would sodomize a young girl. Well, what if he would? Just *suppose* he would—and is. Just suppose that Garth and I can prove to you that Kenecky is a child raper. Would you help us then?"

The twins looked at each other—with Floyd displaying what might have been a slight frown of disapproval at his brother's talkativeness. But neither spoke.

"What the hell is it that you Nuvironment people are trying to hide that's worth all this aggravation?" I continued, struggling to remain calm and keep my tone even. "Why did Patton have you follow us? What on earth is he afraid we may find out?"

Again, there was no response. The twin in the tan parka had bowed his head again, and appeared to be praying.

"Show them the letter, Garth."

"You show it to them if you want," Garth replied tersely, taking the well-worn envelope containing Vicky Brown's letter out of his pocket and handing it to me.

I removed the letter from the envelope, shielded it from the gusting wind and snow with my body, held it out in front of them. "Is this a lie? Read it."

Neither twin would look at the letter. "We won't be tricked," the man in the blue parka said.

I refolded the letter, put it back in the envelope, and handed it back to Garth as I continued to study the faces of the brothers. Suddenly I felt pity for them. Appeals to reason and Garth's threats were getting us nowhere; I wondered what might happen if I appealed to their madness. Christmas Eve was no time to be beating on people, no matter the reason.

"I can see that the two of you are very devout," I said seriously. I was rewarded with a flicker of interest in their eyes. "Garth and I respect that, but it's difficult for us to understand just what it is you believe. I know it's the millennium and all that, and every thousand years all sorts of people take it into their heads that the world is going to end; it's part of the human condition. But what's interesting about you two is that you seem to be convinced that it's going to happen tomorrow or the next day. What do you know that we don't? If the world is really going to end that soon, maybe Garth and I should start thinking about getting our affairs in order."

"You mock," the twin in tan said. "You don't believe it."

"I'm just curious as to the specifics of what you believe. Is what you believe supposed to be a secret?"

He shook his head. "It's clear for all who have truly taken Jesus into their hearts."

"What's clear? That the world is going to end?"

"Yes!" the second twin snapped. "Jesus is coming!"

"When?"

"Soon. Very soon."

"How do you know that?"

"Let him who has eyes see. Let him who has ears hear."

"How is the world going to end?"

"In fire," the twin in tan said. "As it is prophesied."

"What's going to happen then? What's on the celestial agenda after the world ends in fire?"

"Those who truly have Jesus Christ in their hearts will be spared, including those who have died before. Those of us who are clean will be swept up to the sky to be with Jesus while demons ravage those of you who have been left behind and who have survived the fire. There will be hell on earth for you. After seven years, Jesus will finally descend to vanquish the demons and establish His kingdom here on earth. We will join Him, and we will live forever. People like you will be dead. And damned."

"So you really believe this nonsense Kenecky has been feeding you?"

Both men had been shivering. Now they stopped, and their eyes flashed. "It's all in prophecy!" the twin in tan shouted. "It's clearly written for all to see! The fact that you have not seen and do not believe is what damns you. Reverend Kenecky has Christ in his heart; when Reverend Kenecky speaks, it is the same as Christ speaking."

"Even you can't believe that Christ wants him to rape little girls—and that's what he's doing. I think you know now that it's true, even if you won't read Vicky Brown's letter. I think you know Vicky Brown—and you certainly know Kenecky. Garth and I wouldn't be up here in the cold chatting with you unless we were absolutely certain that what we say is happening is happening. And you say that a man who screws kids has Christ in his heart? Give us a break."

The twins exchanged uncertain glances, and it seemed to me that each was waiting for the other to say something. I felt a rush of excitement. Mine had certainly been the voice of sweet reason, and I could see by the expressions on their faces that what I said had troubled them; I dared to hope that my words would serve as an antidote to the poison in their heads—at least long enough for one of them to give us the single piece of information we needed to go on. I glanced at Garth, gave a slight nod. Obviously, he didn't share my optimism; he simply shook his head slowly.

"So come on," I continued evenly. "I'm telling you the truth about Kenecky. Where are Kenecky and the little girl? That's all we want to know."

The twin in the blue parka said tightly, "It doesn't matter what's happening now. Next week, it will end. Everything that we have known will end."

I blinked slowly in astonishment. The voice of reason croaked, "It doesn't matter?"

"Floyd's right," the twin in tan blurted. "And even if Reverend Kenecky is doing something to Vicky, it must be God's will. Perhaps the reverend's attention to her is God's gift to the child. You simply don't understand. God may be working for Vicky's salvation through the reverend. What he does with her would be like a sacrament."

The owner of the voice of sweet reason suddenly saw spots swimming in front of his eyes, the result of spiking blood pressure. Suddenly I felt as if I were burning, and then all reason was swept away as rage mixed with loathing and horror and exploded. I screamed something unintelligible and jumped on the man in the tan parka, knocking him backward onto a bed of snow-smothered pachysandra. I ripped off my gloves, but couldn't manage to get my hands around his throat because of his parka. Blind with rage, nauseous with a sick sense of something I couldn't quite identify, I rained blow after blow on his face, and didn't stop even when blood started flowing freely from his nose and mouth. I couldn't stop; while one part of my mind clearly recognized that the man I was sitting on was flesh and blood, another part of me felt as if I were punching a phantom, something unspeakably evil that had plagued the heart and soul of humankind from the time we had learned to walk upright. We had split the atom and soared in space, but all the knowledge we had gained had not been sufficient to slay this evil; the evil embodied in the man I was beating was immune to knowledge, for it spurned reason. I hated this evil and knew that it was too deeply ingrained in the man ever to be expunged. Even as my fists shredded the flesh of the man's face, I somehow felt that I was attacking superstition and stupidity, the things that had broken men's and women's bones in the Inquisition, the things that had caused the deaths of countless men, women, and children in countless wars.

I was a tad worked up.

"You shit-for-brains, rotten, fucking son-of-a-bitch!" I screamed as I grabbed the man's hair and shook his head back and forth. "You tell me where Kenecky and the girl are, or I'll kill you! I'll kill you!"

And then Garth's powerful fingers grabbed the back of my parka, pulled me off the man even as I continued to punch and kick at the air. He lifted me up and away, then set me down on my feet—but he kept a firm grip on my coat as I again lunged for the man. The bloody mouth of the twin in tan hung open, and he seemed to be in a state of shock.

"He can't tell you anything while you're punching out his lights, Mongo," my brother said dryly, sounding slightly bemused. "Once you'd abandoned your perfectly rational and perfectly useless approach to these jokers, you should have let me take care of business. You just get too emotional."

"Let me go, Garth!"

"Calm down."

"I am calm!"

"Get calmer."

I stopped struggling, then started with surprise when the man I had been beating on, his face smeared with blood, abruptly sat up and started to shout—at least at first I thought he was shouting, but then realized that he had gone into a kind of trance and, like Craig Valley, was "speaking in tongues." His eyes were wide and out of focus, his head thrown back as he howled at the sky.

Then the second twin, apparently caught up in his brother's ecstasy, started. The man in the blue parka grasped his brother's hand as he screamed, swayed, shouted, and stamped his feet. A chill that had nothing to do with the freezing cold went through me.

Then, still holding hands and screaming, moving in unison

as if through some secret means of communication, the two men abruptly leaped to their feet and rushed between Garth and me.

"Hey, what the hell?!" I shouted, grabbing for the man in the tan parka as he hit me in the chest with his elbow and rushed past.

Garth lunged and grabbed for the other twin, and ended up holding an empty blue parka.

Stunned and horrified, Garth and I turned as one, cried out as the twins, still holding hands and shrieking their language which no one could understand, sprinted the short distance across the rooftop garden, jumped up on the parapet, and without hesitation hurled themselves out into the snow-swept darkness that echoed with the bells and music of Christmas Eve.

8.

"YOU two are in a lot of trouble," Detective Lieutenant Malachy McCloskey said as he finally—ten minutes after we had been ushered into his office—looked up from the paperwork on his desk. The man with the acne-scarred face looked as if his chronic sciatica was acting up; he sat at a twisted angle, as if favoring his left buttock. He was unshaven, and his gray hair was rumpled. He'd obviously been rousted out of bed two or three hours before, and he was still missing his bed. Two or three hours was the length of time we'd had to wait after first coming into the precinct station; it confirmed to us that McCloskey had been given the standing assignment of dealing with all things now wrought by the Fredericksons. Levers had been pushed, strings pulled, and Malachy McCloskey, better than most people, would know how easily a man could get ground up in that kind of political machinery.

If Garth felt any discomfort at now being more or less at the mercy of a man who probably hated him, he didn't show it—just as he hadn't displayed any embarrassment or discomfort as we'd sat on the wooden benches outside and he'd had to endure the furtive, curious glances of his former colleagues. Only three men on a shift of twenty-eight had come over to say hello and ask after his—our—health; it was as if they sensed, correctly, that the man with the full beard was very different from the Detective Lieutenant Garth Frederickson they had known and worked with.

"I'm sorry you had to get out of bed on Christmas Eve, McCloskey," Garth said evenly.

McCloskey shook his head impatiently, ran his right hand over his grizzled cheeks, then scratched his head. "Christmas Eve, my ass," he said in his raspy voice. "It's Christmas Day. My daughter's here from Iowa with my two granddaughters. I really would have liked to see their faces when they open their presents."

"Maybe you can still make it," I said brightly, flashing a broad smile.

McCloskey looked at me for a long time, and he didn't smile at all. "I seriously doubt that, Frederickson," he said at last.

"Come on, Lieutenant; give us a break."

"Give *you* a break?"

"What do you want from us? You've got our statement—and a very long one, I might add. We're the ones who called the police, and we came over here right away."

"Big deal. You knew you'd probably have been arrested and handcuffed if you hadn't."

"I don't know that at all. You've read our statement; you've probably read it more than once. Garth and I haven't done anything wrong."

McCloskey's black eyes flashed. "Jesus Christ, man, you've—"

"We've been fully cooperative, is what we've been—which is more than I might say of the police. We've been cooling our heels here for better than three hours now."

"You've got to be kidding me. You think you and your big brother get points for calling in and then coming over here? Considering the fact that two men were splattered all over the sidewalk in front of a certain building on Fifty-sixth Street, a building wholly owned by the famous Fredericksons, it's not too hard to figure out where they fell from, is it? You really think you have any choice but to cooperate?"

"We've explained what happened."

"And you really expect us to believe that they *jumped* from your roof?"

"Yeah. We expect you to believe that."

"*Both* of them?"

'You've got it. They were linked together, holding hands, when they jumped. Garth and I tried to stop them, but they were too quick for us."

"And you claim they were *happy* about jumping off the top of a four-story building?"

"That's not what our statement says at all. We don't claim to be psychiatrists, but to us it appeared that they'd worked themselves into a kind of trance with glossolalia—'speaking in tongues.' They were experiencing religious ecstacy, and it led to their taking their own lives."

"Religious ecstacy?"

"A trance, self-hypnosis, religious ecstacy—call it what you want. I told you they were speaking in tongues."

"How the hell do you know they were speaking in tongues—whatever that means?"

"Glossolalia is characteristic of some so-called Charismatic or Pentecostal Christians," Garth interjected in a flat tone. "They believe that speaking in tongues is a gift from God, and they view it as evidence that they're filled with the spirit of God."

"Do they normally kill themselves while they're speaking in tongues?" McCloskey said tersely.

Garth shook his head. "This group is beyond the pale, Lieutenant. Once you've heard someone speaking in tongues, you don't forget what it sounds like. Mongo and I have heard it before in connection with this business. Craig Valley was making babbling sounds like that just before he killed himself, and we said so in our previous statement. Remember?''

McCloskey dismissed Garth's words with a weary, slightly contemptuous, wave of his hand. His cold, black eyes fixed on my face. "You know what I think?" he said after a long pause, to me. "I think your big brother here killed those men."

"You think wrong," Garth said evenly. "You should look at a man when you're accusing him of murder, Lieutenant."

"I'll damn well look at you, Frederickson!" McCloskey snapped, wheeling in his chair to face Garth, then wincing and putting a hand to his back. His body was now arched into a position that resembled a question mark, but his obvious pain served only to fuel his anger. "You were roughing them up! You're an arrogant son-of-a-bitch who thinks he can get away with anything! They wouldn't tell you what you wanted to hear, so you threw them off the fucking roof! You lost it, Frederickson, and you killed two men!"

"No," Garth said simply. "That's not what happened."

"Bullshit! You roughed up Patton, and you threatened to kill him! You're damn lucky he doesn't want—"

"But I didn't kill him, McCloskey; and I didn't kill those two brothers."

"But you were damn well roughing them up, weren't you?! I know Goddamn well you were, but I don't see any mention of it in your statement!"

"Look, Lieutenant," I said quickly, "I can understand why it might be hard for you to believe that two men could suffer religious hysteria and kill themselves—if it hadn't happened once already, with that crazy orchid keeper. I don't think even you believe that we jabbed razors into Craig Valley's throat. Well, we didn't kill Valley, and we didn't kill the two you found on the sidewalk. They killed themselves, just like Valley; just like Valley, they possessed information they considered vital, and which they didn't want us to have."

"Where to find a fucking pile of *dirt?!*"

"Yes, Lieutenant. Except that it's not the dirt they're worried about; it's what else we'll find when we find the dirt. Garth and I have already suggested that that's something the police might want to give serious thought to looking into, but that's your business."

"And you say they killed themselves rather than risk having the two of you force the information out of them?"

"Yes."

"Then you admit you were roughing them up?"

"Garth and I don't admit to anything except for what you've got in that statement in front of you."

"What were they doing up on your roof, Frederickson?"

"They followed us home."

McCloskey laughed without humor, rolled his eyes. "And they followed you all the way up onto your roof?"

"Well . . . actually, we did sort of have to invite them to come up there. After all the time and effort they'd put into following us up to that point, it seemed the only decent thing to do."

"Don't be a smart-ass with me, Frederickson," McCloskey said in a low, decidedly ominous voice. "You're the one who's asking me to take this statement seriously. I don't think the two of you realize how very, very close you are to the inside of a jail cell."

"All right, Lieutenant. We were rather insistent that they join us on the roof."

"Oh, I know you were—the same as I know that you took them up there so that you could rough them up and frighten them."

"No, Lieutenant. We took them up there to talk."

"On your roof, in the middle of winter?!"

I glanced at Garth, looking for help. My brother seemed merely bored. "Well, uh . . . it was more private than the street, and certainly no colder."

McCloskey picked up a piece of paper off the cluttered top of his desk and slowly crumpled it in his right hand. "I've got the famous Fredericksons," he said softly, an odd catch in his voice. It was as if he was only now fully realizing how much serious damage he could do to us, and was trying to decide what he wanted to do about it. "I wonder what a jury would make of the nonsense you're telling me? Two men fall to their deaths from your roof after you forced them to go up there with you. What did you want to do? Just talk. Why did they die? Religious ecstasy. Jesus Christ, I really think the famous Fredericksons may have gone too far this time."

I was really thinking just about the same thing when Garth shifted in his chair and, in a maddeningly casual tone, asked, "Who were they, McCloskey?"

"Huh?" McCloskey blinked in surprise, but quickly recovered. "Look, I ask the questions here. Don't you remember the routine?"

Garth tilted his head toward me. "Mongo, do you happen to have the number of Haggerty, Haggerty, Schwartz and Haggerty?"

Ah. The bugles of the cavalry. "I certainly do, brother."

"I think it may be time to call our lawyers. What do you think?"

"I'm not sure. Let me ask the good lieutenant here."

The good lieutenant's face was flushed a deep red. "You sons-of-bitches," he said in a voice that was quavering with rage. "You're goddamn right it may be time for you to call your lawyers, and I don't give a shit if they come from one of the most high-powered firms in New York and Washington. You tell those pin-striped shits that I'm thinking of booking the two of you on charges of first-degree homicide, and if they want to plea-bargain maybe the DA will let you off on an aggravated manslaughter charge, with relatively light prison sentences of five years. While you're in prison, maybe both of you can learn a new trade."

"Mongo?" Garth said evenly. "I don't think he grasps the situation. Call our lawyers."

"No, no, Garth. Just a second." I looked at McCloskey, smiled, and hoped that I grasped the situation Garth was referring to. "Lieutenant, Garth has trouble communicating when he's upset. I, on the other hand, tend to be almost infinitely patient, even under the most trying circumstances. So I'm going to try to interpret what he just said for you."

I didn't think McCloskey's face could get any redder—but it did. "Are you calling me stupid, Frederickson?! I heard what he said! And you heard what I said!"

"Yes, but we don't seem to be *communicating*. If you think you're going to be safely retired at this time next week, with the Fredericksons out of your hair because you've booked us, you're wrong. This case is a haunt; three men are dead, and somewhere a little girl is being sexually abused by a fugitive from justice. The NYPD threw this—us—in your lap, but if you think you can walk away from all of this with a clear conscience simply because you've laid heavy charges on us, you're a lot stupider than I think you are. The kid will haunt *you*, McCloskey. So if you want to retire in peace, I suggest that you start showing us a little cooperation and *listen*."

That got his attention. He blinked slowly, swallowed hard.

"*We've* been cooperative, Lieutenant," I continued quickly, wanting to follow up before he'd had too much time to think about it. "But Garth asks you for one teeny-weeny bit of information, and you go nova on us. We've found out quite a few things up to this point, and we've freely shared our information with you. Who knows what else we may turn up? Frankly, Lieutenant, I don't think you're going to book us. You know why you're not going to book us? Because Nuvironment definitely does not need the negative publicity we'll be sure to generate for them. This is what Garth really meant when he asked me if I had the number of our lawyers."

"You just hold on, Frederickson. I don't work for Nuvironment."

"You're doing great, Mongo," Garth said dryly. "It never fails to amaze me how you're able to interpret my words for me."

"I know you're not working for Nuvironment, Lieutenant," I said, casting an evil glance at my brother. I felt like a tap dancer in combat boots on a bare stage in a concert performance where someone kept speeding up the music. "And I certainly never meant to imply that you would cave in to pressures from people above you. But let's face it: the fact that you're here celebrating Christmas with us instead of with your daughter and grandchildren means that you've been assigned a watchdog role—and you can bet your about-to-retire ass that the decision to put you in the position you're in was made at a high level. They want you to *handle* us, Lieutenant, not arrest us. Nuvironment definitely will not want publicity about the religious freaks the company appears to be linked with. And, frankly, when all is said and done, I just don't think a jury, after we tell them what's happened, is going to believe that the famous Fredericksons, with all they now have to lose, would throw it all away by throwing two guys to their deaths off their own roof. Come on, McCloskey."

"But they might believe that the deaths arose out of aggravated assault," the detective said through clenched teeth. "They might convict for manslaughter."

"Maybe, maybe not. Still, I seriously doubt that either the NYPD or the DA's office would want to be cast in a bad light. If you'll recall, this started out as a *pro bono* investigation of a child sexual abuse case by two noted, if you'll permit me to say so, private investigators. As far as Garth and I are concerned, that's still all it is. At the beginning, we went to the appropriate authorities, and they pledged to cooperate with us. *We're* going to keep at it, Lieutenant—even if it's through our lawyers, from behind bars. In my opinion, you and the department aren't going to improve your images if it looks like you're harassing us because of pressure from a private corporation that has right-wing—and possibly neo-Nazi—religious loonies on its staff, tolerates child sexual abuse, and is almost certainly harboring a fugitive. We didn't kill those men, Lieutenant, and I think you know it. What Garth was trying to say is that it's still possible for us to work together. No lawyers to stir up excitement—no charges."

McCloskey took some time to think about it. He clenched

and unclenched his fists, finally leaned back in his chair and swiveled around to face Garth. "That's what I thought you were saying, Frederickson," he said quietly.

Garth looked at me, smiled thinly. "That Mongo has such a silver tongue, doesn't he, McCloskey? But then, I thought what I was saying was obvious."

"So who were those guys, Lieutenant?" I asked. "What's their story? We know they worked for Nuvironment, but there must be more. I'm sure we can read all about them tomorrow in the newspapers, but we're probably going to be so busy dodging reporters that we won't have much time to read. What can you tell us about them?"

McCloskey slumped in his chair, sighed, and rubbed his knuckles into his eyes. "Christ, Frederickson, I'm tired," he said, apparently speaking to Garth. "I wish I could get out of here like you did. I've got a real bad feeling about this thing. I don't think I can afford a mistake, and nobody is willing to tell me what the ground rules are."

"One more week," Garth said not unkindly. "I hear what you're saying. Under the circumstances, every day for the next seven days is probably going to feel like a week—or maybe a year. Mongo and I can't really advise you, but it seems to me that you'll be in the clear as long as you do your job."

"Yeah? I'm not sure my job shouldn't be to arrest the two of you and charge you with murder."

"Then do it," Garth replied evenly. "Either arrest us, or believe that we're innocent and that your job as a cop is to help us stop a madman from sexually abusing a little girl. It's your retirement you're looking for—but it's your choice as to how best to do your job until next week at this time." Garth paused, then actually laughed. "Hey, McCloskey, if you want, Mongo and I will serve as your character witnesses if you get brought up on any departmental charges in the next seven days."

McCloskey almost smiled. "Spare me," he said, and sighed again. He stared at the ceiling for some time, then continued:

"The stiffs' names were Floyd and Baxter Small; that's what their identification said. There was nothing on them to indicate that they worked for Nuvironment."

"But they did," I said. "Nobody else would have had an interest in following us."

"You say."

"Call Patton or somebody else at Nuvironment and see what they have to say. I don't believe Patton went to Europe."

McCloskey looked away. "It seems Patton doesn't have a phone—listed or unlisted. And nobody's going to be up there in the office on Christmas Day."

"Call Henry Blaisdel and see what he has to say. As a matter of fact, I'd like to talk to him if you can get him on the phone."

"It isn't the first time the Smalls have made it into the papers," McCloskey said, ignoring what I thought had been a most helpful suggestion.

Garth grunted. "I don't recall either of the names, McCloskey. Where would Mongo and I have read about them before?"

"It would have been a small item, maybe a year or two ago. It seems the Small brothers were pro golfers—but not anywhere near top rank. They played on a secondary circuit that toured a lot of the third world countries. They were playing in some tournament in Botswana, of all places, when they both came down with the crazies. It seems they were taking part in some kind of Christian athletes' prayer meeting in the hotel where they were staying when they had a vision of Jesus. They tore up their passports and all their money, stripped off their clothes, and went running through the lobby screaming at the top of their lungs. They ran right through a plate-glass window, and they were lucky they didn't cut their heads off. There were difficulties in getting them new papers so they could come back here. It made the papers. Immigration has copies of their new passports on file, if you're interested."

"Jesus," I said. "And you said you didn't believe us when we told you they went into a religious trance?"

"They didn't kill themselves in Botswana," McCloskey mumbled, avoiding my gaze.

"Obviously—but only because the prayer meeting was held on the first floor. Patton, or maybe Henry Blaisdel, seems to have a thing for athletes. He's got two ex-ballplayers on his staff; they serve as muscle."

"That doesn't prove anything."

"It's a link."

"To what?"

It was Garth who answered. "One of Blaisdel's favorite charities is something called Born Again Christian Athletes for Christ, McCloskey. That strikes me as rather redundant, but that's what they call themselves. You can look it up. I came across it in the library. In the article, the word 'fanatical' was used more than once. Apparently, they're not to be confused with any of the other organizations of Christian athletes."

"You didn't tell me that," I said to my brother.

"It didn't seem important at the time; I was looking up Blaisdel's companies, not his charities."

"Thank you for the information, Lieutenant," I said, turning back to McCloskey.

"Yeah."

"The problem is that it doesn't do any of us any good, since the Smalls are dead. Nuvironment, the people working there, is the key to this thing. I'm certain Patton is still lurking around here someplace; but if you can't find him to talk to, then you're going to have to talk to Henry Blaisdel."

"*Don't* try to tell me how to do my job, Frederickson."

"Those two worked for Nuvironment—they were being chauffeured around in limousines, for Christ's sake. Peter Patton is covering up something big, and he'll obviously risk a lot to make sure nobody finds out what it is. It's a lot more than a shipment of dirt, or a case of child sexual abuse. Men die for him—or they die to hide his secret. You've got a lot of seriously crazy religious zealots on the loose here, Lieutenant, and I'd think you'd want to find out just what it is they're up to."

McCloskey was beginning to look seriously distressed. "Being religious—or supporting a Christian athletes' group—is no crime, Frederickson."

"Aiding and abetting a fugitive from justice is—and every time Craig Valley or either of the Smalls opened his mouth he sounded like a clone of William Kenecky. Sometimes religion of that brand can kill. Remember the Inquisition? Every single Nazi or neo-Nazi group in the world, in this country, has used that kind of religious interpretation as a foundation stone for the rest of their murderous nonsense. Maybe it's time you asked the F.B.I. to come in."

"On the basis of your fantasies?"

"Three men are dead by their own hand, Lieutenant. That's no fantasy. And all three were in a religious trance when they died. That's no fantasy."

McCloskey shook his head. "I hate the fucking F.B.I., just the same as your brother hated the fucking F.B.I. when he was a cop. We don't need those arrogant, glory-hogging fucks in here."

"Then what are you going to do about it, Lieutenant?"

"I don't know," McCloskey said after a long pause. "I'll tell the captain what you said, see what he wants me to do."

"Garth and I are getting back on it right after you let us out of here. You know that."

"Shit," the man with the pockmarked face said. "You guys are to trouble what a magnet is to steel filings."

"We're looking for a little girl, not trouble. We're the ones who are being hassled."

"Mongo and I understand that you're caught between a rock and a hard place, McCloskey," Garth said evenly. "If we do come across something unsavory—criminal—in connection with Nuvironment, would you rather we not tell you?"

McCloskey's black eyes flashed. He sat up abruptly, winced with pain—and then deliberately straightened his back. "Don't you condescend to or patronize me, you son-of-a-bitch! I'm still a cop, and until next week I'm still on active duty! Don't you forget it! You find out anything, you'd *damn* well better let me know about it!''

"Okay," Garth said in the same even tone. "I didn't mean to offend you."

"Well, you did offend me! And let me tell you—!''

McCloskey was interrupted by the sudden ringing of the phone on his desk. He grunted with disgust, snatched up the receiver. "Yeah, what is it?" He listened, and the blood slowly drained from his face, making him look even more exhausted and haggard. "What the fuck?! No, leave everything as it is. I'll be right there." He hung up the phone, rose and snatched his overcoat off a rack in the corner, headed out the door. "You two come with me!" he shouted over his shoulder.

Garth and I looked at each other, then rose and followed after McCloskey. "I wonder what that was all about?" I said as we walked through the squad room, ignoring the heads that turned in our direction.

"I assume we'll find out soon enough," Garth replied in a low voice. "Incidentally, all that talk about athletes jogged my memory; I remember where I've seen that big, ugly chauffeur before."

I abruptly stopped, looked at my brother. "Where?"

"On a football field. It was Tanker Thompson."

"Tanker Thompson? Are you kidding me? I thought he was in prison."

Garth slowly shook his head. "He's out now, working for Nuvironment."

Thomas "Tanker" Thompson, born-again Christian or not, was not a man I wanted at my back, whether in a car or on foot. When he'd played defensive tackle for one of the now-defunct U.S.F.L. football teams, he'd weighed upwards of three hundred pounds, and had been quick as a cat. His problem had been that he was a virulent racist; considering the number of pro football players who are black, he'd apparently never had a problem getting himself worked up for game day. One day he'd gotten himself a little too emotionally worked up. After a missed tackle and an exchangé of words with a black running back from another team, Thompson had chopped the man in the larynx with the side of his hand. Despite an emergency tracheotomy performed on the field, the other man had died two days later. Tanker Thompson had been convicted of aggravated assault, and had become the first athlete in the United States to go to prison on a sports-related charge. A while back, in a "where they are now" column in some magazine, I'd read that he'd undergone a "spiritual conversion" while in prison, and was devoting all his time to religious studies. Obviously, he had been let out on parole, and was now on the payroll of Nuvironment.

It figured.

Still pondering the unpleasant implications of having a murderous behemoth of an ex–football player assigned to watch over us, I followed Garth out of the station house into a cold, gray Christmas dawn that seemed ominously still and foreboding. I smelled snow; lots of it.

Malachy McCloskey, still pale-faced and looking very agitated, was standing at the curb, nervously tapping his palm on the roof of a squad car that had its motor running. "Let's go, you two!" he shouted when he saw us, then hurried around to the other side of the car and got in behind the wheel.

"Where are we going, Lieutenant?" I asked as Garth and I got in the back.

McCloskey slammed his foot down on the accelerator, and Garth and I were pressed back in our seats as the car sped away from the curb. He switched on the flashing red light atop the car, but not the siren. "Central Park," the gray-haired man said tersely as he cut between two cabs.

"And I'll bet we're not going to a sunrise service."

"Hardly," McCloskey replied, and grunted. "I think someone's left you two a Christmas present, and it wasn't Santa Claus."

9.

It wasn't a present, but a message.

The good Reverend William Kenecky certainly was no longer going to be abusing Vicky Brown—or anyone else, for that matter. Somebody had crucified the self-styled "scourge of the Lord," nailed him upside down and naked, with his skinny arms and legs grotesquely splayed, to the trunk of a massive, gnarled oak tree about twenty-five yards off a narrow, twisting path in the heavily wooded section of Central Park known as the Ramble, a notorious trysting place for homosexuals. He was missing his genitals, which had been cut off—or out; he looked like he'd been cored like an apple, and I hoped he'd been dead when it had been done to him. He was a sight, and if I hadn't so detested this skinny, spiritually bent creature that had walked like a man, I'd have vomited. I was glad I hadn't eaten in a while. I glanced at Garth to see how he was reacting to this less than cheery Christmas morning sight; my brother didn't look sick, only thoughtful.

We were standing just behind the police lines—strips of yellow tape that were flapping in a stiff, cold breeze from the northwest. On the other side of the tape, uniformed police officers, detectives, police photographers, and technicians from the coroner's office were going about their grisly business. Measurements were made as strobe lights flashed; the scene somehow reminded me of one of Kenecky's shows on television. Twenty yards behind us, crowded together on the narrow trail, a phalanx of reporters and television camera crews were being held at bay by a second phalanx of police officers.

Reverend William Kenecky's last picture show, I thought. Shit.

McCloskey, his grizzled, scarred face once again wearing its riot-act expression, separated himself from a knot of uniformed officers and detectives and stalked over to where Garth and I were standing behind the fluttering yellow tape.

"It's no wonder the two of you are famous," the detective said in a thick voice. "Lots of people die around you. I'd always heard that about the Fredericksons, but now I'm seeing it for myself."

I was getting just a tad weary of Malachy McCloskey's increasingly uninspired quips about my brother and me; I started formulating what I thought would be an appropriate response, one that would undoubtedly include unflattering references to the man's ancestors, as well as the suggestion that he perform an unlikely act of sexual self-abuse. Fortunately, Garth spoke before I did.

"I haven't noticed any of the good guys dying around us lately, McCloskey," Garth said calmly. "And we never met the gentleman hanging on the tree over there. We used to watch him on television; for a piece of shit, he was a great comedian."

"You're a cold son-of-a-bitch, Frederickson."

Garth raised his eyebrows slightly. "Am I? If that means that I don't feel a lot of sympathy for that skinny, kid-fucking scumbag over there, I guess you're right. It must be a personality defect. At least somebody put him out of his misery; but the child he abused may have to live with the nightmare memories of what he did to her for the rest of her life. Because of Kenecky, Vicky Brown may never be able to lead a normal life."

"Maybe you've got a point," McCloskey said, looking down at his feet.

I asked, "Did you find the genitals, Lieutenant?"

McCloskey shook his head. "There's no blood from the spike wounds in his palms or feet, and precious little from the hole where his prick and balls used to be. You can't see it from here, but he's got a bullet hole just behind his left ear. It looks like he was executed someplace else, then mutilated after he was dead; the corpse was brought here and put up for public display—all for the benefit of you two, of course. Somebody's trying to assure you that the girl's not going to be harmed anymore.''

"It looks that way, doesn't it?" Garth said in a flat voice.

McCloskey used the toe of his right shoe to draw a small circle in the snow and leaves on the frozen ground. "It looks like you guys were right about the girl, Kenecky . . . and maybe a few other things. I apologize to you if I seemed a little . . . insensitive. You know I've got kids of my own. And grandkids. I guess seeing this creep hanging up there brings a lot of things home to me. It makes me think of my own. You know what I'm saying?"

"Yeah," I said. "Speaking of those other things we may be right about, want to bet that the lab people find traces of Amazon rain forest soil under his fingernails?"

"You've made me a believer."

Garth asked, "Any idea of how long he's been dead, McCloskey?"

"The coroner's people tell me that's going to be hard to pin down until they get him on a cutting table. The low temperature complicates everything. The initial estimate is that he died somewhere between six and fourteen hours ago. There are burns on the flesh that could have been caused as a result of the corpse being packed in dry ice." He paused and laughed grimly, without any trace of humor. "I guess whoever did this wanted him to look fresh for you."

I grimaced in frustration. "If he's been dead up to fourteen hours, and the corpse was packed in dry ice, he could have been brought here from anywhere in the country."

McCloskey shrugged. "Or he could have been killed only a few blocks away, and then kept on ice until now, Christmas morning, as a special gesture. Unless forensics finds something very special on or in him, it's going to be almost impossible to tell where he was killed."

"We come back to the postmark on the letter," Garth said to me. "He had to have been killed somewhere around here, which means that the girl has to be close by. That's why they went to so much trouble to mask the time of death."

I thought about it, then slowly, reluctantly, shook my head. "I don't think we can assume that anymore. We know now that Kenecky was tied in with a multinational corporation, with operations all over the world. True, the letter was certainly mailed somewhere in the New York region; but now we have to consider the possibility that it was brought here from someplace else. It could have been written anywhere."

"Shit," Garth said with disgust. "And all we thought we were looking for was a needle in a haystack. In fourteen hours, he could have been brought here from just about anywhere in the world. That's thousands of haystacks."

"You two sound as if you're still worried about finding the girl," McCloskey said carefully. "If you don't mind my asking, what's the point? I thought you agreed that Kenecky was killed and hung up here to assure you that the girl was going to be all right. And you did say that was all you cared about. They got your message, and they sent back one of their own."

"And their message is a mutilated corpse," Garth replied evenly. "Before, all we knew was that Vicky Brown was being sexually abused by a lunatic; now we find out that the girl is living with—or under the control of—a whole barrel-ful of lunatics who think that death doesn't mean a goddamn thing because they're all going to be resurrected and go floating up to the sky in a few days. And one of those lunatics is most definitely murderous." He paused, looked at me. "I don't think that sounds like a very healthy environment for a child. Do you, Mongo?"

"Absolutely not. And I'm sure the lieutenant agrees."

"This is police business now," McCloskey said curtly.

"Finding Kenecky's murderer is police business," I said. "Finding the girl in order to make certain she's all right is our business. I wouldn't be surprised if we met at the end at the same dirt pile."

"You're probably right about that," McCloskey said distantly. He was looking somewhere over my right shoulder; his face was grim, as if he didn't like what he saw there.

"The girl is our client."

"Your *client*?"

"Right," I said, and smiled thinly. "We're acting *in loco parentis* for Santa Claus."

Garth asked, "Will you let us know if you find out anything more specific about when and where Kenecky was killed?"

McCloskey frowned. "I don't know if I can do that, Frederickson."

"I know you can't do it officially, McCloskey. How about unofficially? In return, we'll make sure you hear right away about any relevant information we may dig up."

"You're legally bound to do that anyway."

"You're not listening carefully to Garth, Lieutenant," I said. "He told you we'd get the information to *you*, personally. You wouldn't want anyone else—especially the F.B.I. —horning in on your case, would you?"

McCloskey looked at me, smiled grimly. "You should negotiate for us with the Russians, Frederickson."

"Is that a compliment, a yes, or a no?"

"It's a maybe. Give me a couple of days."

"How long will it be before the autopsy is performed?"

"A couple of days."

"That sounds fair, Lieutenant. Thank you."

Garth said, "Do you need us anymore, McCloskey?"

"No."

"Then we'll be on our way."

"Hey," McCloskey said as we started to walk away.

We stopped, turned back. "What is it, Lieutenant?" I asked.

The surly-looking man with the acne-scarred face jerked his thumb back in the direction of the crucified corpse on the tree behind him. "I've never seen anything like that, and I don't want to again. I'm thinking that the famous Fredericksons should watch their asses."

I nodded. "You too, Lieutenant. Like Garth says, these guys are crazy; if you get in their way, the fact that you're a cop won't mean shit to them. Now they've shown that they'll kill others, as well as themselves, to keep their secret. If you do get a lead on the location of that dirt pile, I'd take a lot of firepower with me."

"Yeah? What are you two going to use for firepower?"

"Ah," I said, smiling. "Garth and I have our stealth and cunning."

"Merry Christmas, McCloskey," Garth said.

Malachy McCloskey nodded to both of us. "Merry Christmas to you."

We went home. Incredibly, Beloved had not been towed; she was still at the curb where I had parked her, beneath the NO PARKING OR STANDING AT ANY TIME sign. I put her in our underground garage, then went to bed. However, despite the fact that I'd been up all night, I found I was too wired to sleep. It was the same with Garth; he called me on the phone and asked, without any trace of irony, if I was sleeping. We got cleaned up, then went out and ate a desultory Christmas brunch at Rick's.

"Can you think of anything we can do today, brother?" Garth asked as we finished our steak and eggs.

"No—except to have another bloody Mary or two. We need to get some rest."

"Agreed," Garth said, and signaled the bartender, raising two fingers.

"I may as well go back to Jersey City tomorrow and try to check out some more shipping companies. I may not find out anything, but it seems like a forced move; we don't really have any choice but to keep plodding on."

"They're not going to be open on a Saturday which is the day after Christmas."

"I'll check out the situation anyway. If there are ships coming in, somebody's going to have to unload them."

Garth nodded. "There are a number of suppliers I want to

check out. I'll start my calls, see if anybody is open. If not, it will just have to wait until Monday."

"Christ, they'd need hundreds of tons of glass, plastic, steel, whatever, to build a biosphere big enough for people to live in. You'd think somebody would remember orders like that, even if they didn't remember that it was for Nuvironment."

"They'd remember—unless they've been told not to remember."

"Or unless all of the supplies have been ordered and delivered through companies owned by Blaisdel."

"Right. But you're correct about them needing an awful lot of shit, including a few million gallons of sea water. And they'd need a lot of expertise. They've gone outside before, to the Botanical Garden; there may be other outside experts they've used. I think I'm going to check back with Sam Zelaskowich and see if he knows of anyone else, in any other institution, who's done consulting work for Nuvironment."

"Good idea. But you're going to have to be very careful—for Zelaskowich's sake."

"I know, Mongo. I will be." He paused, nodded to the bartender as he brought us over our drinks, then continued: "All we need is one lousy lead, the name of one person who won't end up dead on us. There are records somewhere, and there are people who have the information we want."

"Where are you going to start?"

"I'm not sure," Garth answered after what seemed an unusually long pause.

Something about the tone of my brother's voice made me wonder if he was being evasive; but since I could think of no reason why he would be evasive, I let it go. We finished our drinks, Garth grabbed the check, and we headed for the cashier. Outside, the sky was leaden with thick, dark clouds. It was, I thought, going to be a very long Christmas Day.

The good news was that I slept; the bad news was that I woke up at two thirty in the morning. I made a large pot of coffee, exercised, then sat for a half hour in my sauna and tried to relax. It was useless; the more I sweated, the more nervous I became. Something was nagging at me—something besides the obvious difficulties and frustrations of the situation we were dealing with. I kept struggling to find the source of my unease as I showered, dressed in a terry-cloth jumpsuit, and went into the kitchen to make myself something to eat.

I'd just popped two slices of rye bread into the toaster when it came to me.

Three men associated with Nuvironment had killed themselves rather than divulge information they didn't want Garth and me to have; all three had implied that they, at least, expected something to happen very soon, namely the end of the world. Peter Patton, on the other hand, certainly hadn't seemed to share their sense of urgency; indeed, he'd offered to give Garth and me the run of his place. Next week. After the first of the year.

Under any circumstances it would be most unlikely that anyone would be at the Nuvironment offices in the middle of the night to answer the phone. In addition, it was a holiday weekend, and Patton had said that the offices were being closed down until after New Year's. Still, acting on an impulse that sprang out of my unshakable sense of foreboding, I picked up the telephone and dialed the number for Nuvironment.

There was no ringing; instead, a recorded voice came on, courtesy of the New York Telephone Company, to tell me that the number I was trying to reach had been disconnected.

It left me with a very cold, knotted feeling in the pit of my stomach. I buttered my toast, ate it with my fourth cup of coffee. But I put the eggs I'd been about to cook back into the refrigerator; I wasn't hungry anymore.

At eight thirty I rolled Beloved out of the garage and noted with decidedly mixed feelings the black limousine parked just down the block. As I headed downtown, the limousine tailed along, about six car lengths behind me. Nuvironment might have closed up shop permanently, but Peter Patton was obviously taking no chances on having any loose cannons messing up his act—whatever that act might be; the tails were still on duty. It was almost comforting to be followed, implying as it did that it still might be possible for us to learn something, and I made no effort to lose the Cadillac.

I returned to Jersey City, found a few of the shipping offices open and operating with skeleton crews. Nobody knew anything about a shipment of a hundred tons of Amazon rain forest soil.

The one thing I did discover was that my tail was none other than Tanker Thompson himself, apparently alone, and looking even meaner and uglier in person than he had on television. He was truly massive, with his six-and-a-half-foot height and three-hundred-pound body, and a neck that was almost as thick as his head. Perhaps because it would be difficult for such a big man to move with much stealth, he didn't bother. When I stopped my car, he stopped his only a few yards behind; when I got out and walked, he got out and walked, keeping no more than a block or so between us. There was an arrogance in this open, casual approach that tended to infuriate me, and once I almost stopped and turned around, intending to confront him. But I knew that he would simply keep coming at me until I found myself staring up into his bruise-colored face with its flattened nose and small, black eyes. There was no question but that Tanker Thompson frightened me, and I knew that it would be a waste of time to try to talk to him. I just wasn't ready for a confrontation with the murderous ex–football player, and I quickened my pace.

I finished visiting all the offices that were open in Jersey City, then headed for Hoboken. I was thoroughly dispirited, certain now that I was wasting my time, but just as certain that I would have no peace of mind if I didn't play out the string.

It was five thirty by the time I got back into Manhattan. With Tanker Thompson still on my tail, I came out of the Holland Tunnel, headed for uptown and home. I resisted the impulse to wave at the black limousine as I pulled into my garage.

Garth wasn't in his apartment—a fact that disturbed me somewhat, since I couldn't figure out who or what he would be visiting at six in the evening on the Saturday after Christmas. I left him a note asking him to come up as soon as he got in, then wearily climbed the circular staircase in his den that led up to my own apartment.

I poured myself a stiff Scotch, downed it quickly. I started to pour myself another, then thought better of it. I busied myself making linguini with homemade clam sauce, ate it with a half bottle of Chianti while I watched the Cable News Network—always with half an ear turned to hear the door opening or the phone ringing. I finished the linguini and wine, fell asleep in my chair in front of the television set.

10.

I awoke with a start, knocking the food tray on my lap to the floor. CNN was showing something that looked like a farm report, with a two-hundred-pound woman kneeling and chucking a six-hundred-pound pig under the chin as she spoke about how the new, sophisticated farmer always has a computer linkup to check the latest prices of futures in pork bellies. I glanced at my watch; it was four thirty in the morning. My first reaction was annoyance with Garth for not waking me up when he'd come in.

My second reaction was fear that he hadn't come in.

I bolted out of my chair, kicking the tray and wine bottle out of the way, and hurried down the circular staircase to his apartment, went into the bedroom. His bed was made, unslept in.

This time Santa Claus was more than just late; he was missing.

The first thing I did was make myself instant coffee, using

hot water from the tap in the kitchen, just to give myself time
to calm down. I sipped at the tepid liquid, grimaced. Then I
made a systematic search of his apartment for a note he might
have left me. There was none. Next, I sat down at the
telephone in his den and pulled out his list of the numbers of
all the hospital emergency rooms in the city; there was no
Garth Frederickson in any of them. I searched through his
desk until I found his private phone directory, found the
number I wanted, and dialed it.

Malachy McCloskey answered on the sixth ring. "Yeah,"
he mumbled sleepily. "What is it?"

"Lieutenant, this is Robert Frederickson."

It took a few moments for the words to register. "Frederickson?
How did you get this number? Do you know what the hell
time it is?"

"They've got Garth," I said tersely.

There was another lengthy pause, then: "Huh? Who's got
Garth?"

"Nuvironment, Patton, that bunch of lunatic ex-athletes—
whoever it is that doesn't want us snooping around, and
whoever it was who scooped out William Kenecky. Now,
I'm calling you because we said we'd keep you informed,
and I'm calling you because I know you've been unofficially
assigned by the department to keep an eye on us, but most of
all I'm calling because I need you. I know there's a forty-
eight-hour wait before you can file a missing persons report,
but by then I'm afraid I may find Garth nailed upside down
to a tree in Central Park. Can you help me out, put something
on the wire now?"

"When was the last time you saw your brother, Frederickson?"
McCloskey asked, fully awake now.

"Christmas Day. I left early the next morning, because we
were pursuing different avenues."

"What were the avenues?"

"I went over to Jersey to check out shipping companies, to
see if one of them had been used to bring in the rain forest
soil. Garth was going to stay home and make phone calls to

various suppliers who may have done business with Nuviromment. He was gone when I got home last night. I fell asleep waiting for him, and I just woke up a little while ago. He isn't here." I paused, took a deep breath, slowly exhaled. "I'm just a little bit upset, Lieutenant. It's kind of hard to get that image of Kenecky out of my mind."

"Take it easy, Frederickson. I hear you. Are you sure he's not sleeping over at his girl friend's house, or something like that?"

"His girl friend is vacationing in Barbados—and he wouldn't be sleeping over there anyway, not while we're working on this matter."

"What kind of suppliers was he checking out?"

"Plastics, glass, steel, what have you. I don't know where he planned to begin, and it wouldn't matter if I did; if he did come across something important, and got snatched as a result of it, whoever he talked to isn't likely to admit it. We're talking very nutty and dangerous people here, Lieutenant. I need your help."

"I'll put out an APB on him, Frederickson."

"That's not good enough, Lieutenant, because it's too much. Whatever screws these guys have left in their heads are pretty loose; they'll kill Garth if the police start making loud noises all over town." If they hadn't killed him already, I thought . . . but I couldn't bring myself to put that idea into words. I debated whether or not to tell McCloskey about Tanker Thompson, decided not to. Even if the police picked up Thompson, the man wasn't going to tell them anything— and it could goad Garth's captors into killing him. Thompson was just a foot soldier; it was the general who had to be found and put away. "You've got to move fast, but you have to go after the right people. If you're going to put out an APB, put it out on Peter Patton; I doubt very much that he's in Europe. Also, it's time for the big brass there—maybe along with the mayor—to have a chat with Henry Blaisdel. Somebody has to tell him that his people have gone too far, and that he'd better pull them back before it's too late."

"That's crazy, Frederickson. I'm not even sure how I can justify an APB. Now you want me to go after Patton, or risk offending one of the most powerful men in the world, just because your brother is missing?"

I took another deep breath, screwed my eyes shut. "You said we'd made you a believer."

"Believing something isn't the same as having evidence, Frederickson," McCloskey said in a strained voice. "You're asking me to make some very big moves without anything solid to back them up."

"You saw what they did to Kenecky. Do you want Garth to end up looking like that? I'm begging you, Lieutenant. I need help on this. I can't find Patton, or get to speak to Blaisdel, on my own, and they're the keys to finding out where Garth is right now. I know you can't make the big moves on your own hook, but at least you can go to your captain, lay out the situation, and then see what he'll authorize. I realize I'm asking for a lot, the same as I realize we're chasing shadows here, but I don't know what else to do."

There was a long pause during which I could hear McCloskey breathing, then: "You and your brother have been right about a lot of things, Frederickson. Your brother may still show up, but in the meantime let me see what I can do."

"I appreciate that very much, Lieutenant. How long will it be before you can give me some kind of answer as to what you can and can't do?"

"I don't know. How can I get in touch with you, Frederickson?"

"I'm going to be on the move, Lieutenant. You can leave a message with my answering service, or I'll be in touch with you. If you're going to be out, you can leave a number where I can reach you—if you care to."

"Where are you moving to, Frederickson?"

"At the moment, I'm not sure. I just know I can't stand to do nothing. I'll appreciate anything you can do, Lieutenant. Good-bye."

I hung up the phone and immediately went to the computer

terminal in Garth's den. I punched up the code we had agreed to use for this case, but nothing came up on the screen except the word Nuvironment, and the names of Peter Patton and Henry Blaisdel; it was about as much as I had in my electronic file. I'd hoped there might be some indication of how he'd planned to proceed, what companies he had planned to contact first. Nothing. However, I understood the paucity of information; when you're in a hurry to stop the sexual abuse of a little girl, you get impatient punching information into a computer.

I shut off the computer, opened his desk drawer, and, in a way, found what I was looking for—but it was useless to me. The drawer was crammed full of photocopies of lists of various manufacturers and distributors, but there were no handwritten notations beside any of them.

And yet, as if by waving a magic wand, Garth had somehow picked, out of hundreds of possibilities, the right company or individual to lean on. He had hit pay dirt—or a land mine, depending on how you looked at it.

I closed the drawer, then clasped my hands against my thighs to stop them from trembling. As far as I could tell, Garth had left absolutely no indication of what he had planned to do, or where he had gone. It was unlike Garth—and contrary to both company and personal policy. Ever since we'd started working together, we'd always left bread crumbs for the other to follow, even while working on the most benign cases. Garth had violated procedure, left no tracks, and I wondered why. I hoped his lapse wasn't going to cost him his life.

Despite the fact that it was still very early, I called Samuel Zelaskowich, on the outside chance that Garth had picked up another lead from the botanist. To my surprise, he sounded wide awake; he explained that he did some of his best work in the early morning hours, and in fact had just returned from a five-mile walk. No, I wasn't disturbing him; no, Garth hadn't contacted him; no, he was sorry to say that he knew of no other consultants who had worked for Nuvironment. I thanked him and wished him a good day.

Feeling like there was an electric current running through me, I forced myself to go into Garth's kitchen and make a pot of coffee, just to give myself something to do while I struggled to calm myself down. Then I sat at the kitchen table, sipped coffee, and tried to think. It didn't take me long to reach a decision as to what I was going to do next, and it gave me a chill that the hot coffee couldn't touch.

Still concentrating on calming and centering myself for what lay ahead of me in the day, I made myself eggs, bacon, and toast, ate slowly. By the time I had finished eating and cleaning up the dishes, the sun was coming up, glowing reddish-orange, lending some warmth to what looked from Garth's kitchen window to be a very cold day. I went to the bank of windows in the living room and looked down on Fifty-sixth Street; the black limousine was there, parked across the street. I certainly hoped it was Tanker Thompson's day off, and that whoever was manning this shift was no more than a third of the ex–football player's size. I also fervently hoped there was only one.

I rummaged through Garth's kitchen drawers until I found the item I wanted, put it in my pocket. Then I went upstairs to my own apartment. I hadn't carried a gun for more than a year, since there hadn't been any need. Now there was. I took out both my Beretta and my Seecamp; they had been carefully cleaned and oiled before I'd put them away, but I went through the same procedure all over again. I loaded both guns, strapped the Seecamp to my ankle, and put the Beretta in my shoulder holster. Then I put on my coat and went down to the basement garage.

I drove Beloved up and out of the garage at a leisurely pace, punched at the garage door control hanging on the visor as I turned left. I drove three blocks, just to make sure my tail was awake and taking care of business. He was. Still driving at a leisurely pace, I headed toward the West Side Highway. There was virtually no traffic on the streets on this early Sunday morning, so the limousine was always clearly in sight in my rearview mirror—and he wasn't far behind.

This total lack of guile made me suspect that the driver of the other car was none other than Tanker Thompson. Just what I needed for my nerves.

I went up the ramp onto the West Side Highway, heading north. The limousine came up right behind me, no more than two or three car lengths behind. I knew exactly where I wanted to go, and what I wanted to do when I got there, but the timing was going to be very tricky. The on-again, off-again Westway project, designed to replace the crumbling West Side Highway and Henry Hudson Drive with a six-lane expressway, had left in its wake a checkerboard of cleared areas and aborted projects in various stages of construction beneath the present highway, closer to the river. Four months before, in the course of acting as liaison in some very delicate negotiations between federal prosecutors and a certain Mafia don who was willing to inform on the family that had put out a contract on his life, I had met said Mafia don in an isolated, half-finished parking garage—really no more than a concrete slab with a corrugated steel roof—on a landfill jutting out into the river in the upper Eighties. That was where I was going.

Three-quarters of a mile from the exit, I stomped on Beloved's accelerator, and the well-tuned 360 Mercedes-Benz engine under the Rabbit's hood—a little indulgence I'd allowed myself in honor of my newfound wealth—roared to life. Beloved's tires spun, gripped, and the black limousine began to recede rapidly in the distance. Perhaps too rapidly. I let up on the accelerator, watched in the rearview mirror as the Cadillac gained ground, then sped up again. I slowed slightly before the exit, turned off on it, went around a corner, and immediately braked hard. When I saw the nose of the limousine appear in the rearview mirror, I yanked the wheel to the right, sped around a wooden barrier, knocked over a NO EXIT sign, and bounced down a badly rutted road leading to the river and landfill. At the bottom was a concrete ramp with a hairpin turn leading onto the concrete platform that was to have been the first floor of the parking garage. I braked hard, skidded around the turn; Beloved skidded twenty feet sideways and came to rest across the entrance.

Perfect—I hoped.

Bidding good-bye to Beloved, assuring her that she was being sacrificed in a good cause, I jumped out and sprinted toward a concrete support column fifteen yards away, to the left of the entrance. I reached the column just as the air was filled with the tortured scream of brakes being applied full force—and too late. The driver of the limousine, not knowing where he was going, had—as I'd hoped—come speeding out of the blind turn, and by the time he saw Beloved it was too late to stop. The brakes continued to scream as the Cadillac, its rear tires billowing black smoke, slid across the concrete and rammed hard into Beloved, driving her like a billiard ball ten yards down the length of the platform and up against a support column, where she burst into flame.

I drew my Beretta from the shoulder holster and sprinted to the limousine. All of the car's windows had exploded on impact in bursts of white powder, and I could see Tanker Thompson, blood streaming from a gash on his forehead, slumped over the wheel. But Tanker Thompson was certain to have a hard head, and he was already beginning to mumble and stir by the time I reached the driver's side. I shoved the Beretta into a pocket in my parka and took out the tube of Krazy Glue I had taken from Garth's kitchen. Quickly, I squirted some of the liquid on Thompson's left ear, reached around the back of his head and squirted more on the right ear. I reached in, threaded his left arm through the steering wheel, slapped the palm of his hand against his ear. I did the same to his right arm and palm.

Now we were ready to talk turkey.

Tanker Thompson wasn't going to be making any big moves now—not unless he wanted to end up holding his ears in his hands. Feeling rather smug with my cleverness, I casually ambled around to the other side of the car, where the passenger's door was sprung off its hinges. I slid into the front seat over a glistening carpet of powdered glass, once again took out my Beretta, and tapped Tanker Thompson once, smartly, on the top of his shaved head. Acrid black smoke from the burning wreckage of Beloved swept through the shattered front windshield, making my eyes sting. I wasn't sure how long it would be before police and fire trucks arrived, so I was in a bit of a hurry.

"You awake, Thompson?"

The giant with the mashed nose and bruise-colored face grunted, tried to sit up, grunted even louder when he discovered that his palms were securely glued to his ears. He raised his right elbow slightly, shifted in his seat, and studied me with small, black eyes that seemed oddly lifeless, like lumps of coal in the smear of blood that covered his face. I didn't like those eyes; they belonged in an animal, not a human. He mumbled something, of which I understood only the words "fucking dwarf."

"Tut-tut. That's no way for a God-fearing man to talk."

"What have you done to me?" he asked, his deep voice rumbling in his chest with the ominous sound of distant thunder.

"Nothing that I can't undo. Just sit still and answer my questions. If I like what I hear, I'll see if I can't scare up some nail polish remover to dissolve that glue on your ears. Where are you keeping my brother?"

"What's the matter with you two?" Tanker Thompson said with what sounded like genuine confusion and indignation. 'Why are you so unreasonable?"

"Huh?" The question itself, and his injured tone of voice, took me completely by surprise. "Why are *we* so unreasonable?"

"Yes," the huge man said in the same indignant tone. "You wanted to make sure that Vicky wasn't going to be hurt anymore. She's not. I saw to that. Then why are you continuing to try to thwart God's will?"

I shook my head slightly. "You're admitting you killed William Kenecky?"

"Yes. He was the spawn of Satan masquerading as a man

of God. Men of God don't abuse children like that. I love children, and so does God. God told me to kill him, and I did. Patton didn't handle that right. He should have cooperated with you when you first went to him—at least he should have told you that he would make things all right for Vicky. Because of him, the two of you could have caused trouble. He was a fool. God told me to kill him, too."

"Jesus. You killed *Patton*?"

"Please don't take the Lord's name in vain. Yes, I killed Patton. There is no room in God's elite for fools. Why did you and your brother keep coming and trying to make trouble after you knew Kenecky was dead? I thought you'd be pleased."

The wind had abruptly shifted and was carrying the smoke from Beloved's wreckage in the opposite direction, out the other end of the half-finished garage, dissipating it over the ice-choked Hudson River. The flames of the wreck were dying down, and there was still no sound of sirens. It occurred to me that no one had even noticed the crash, or paid attention to the smoke; this was, after all, New York City. I released the hammer on the Beretta, lowered the gun to my lap. "You've certainly been a busy beaver, Tanker," I said in amazement.

"I am Christ's avatar on earth in the Final Days; I am His sword, and He has empowered me to make these decisions." He paused, studied my face. When he spoke again, there was an almost childlike quality to his voice. "You know who I am, dwarf?"

"Of course, Tanker," I replied evenly, speaking to that childlike quality, as well as his obvious madness. Tanker Thompson was not exactly what I had expected; I had anticipated having to deal with a mindless brute, and instead found myself talking to a man who sounded like he was waiting for me to ask him for his autograph. "I'm a big football fan, in a manner of speaking, and I remember when you played. It's just too bad about that nasty little racist streak in you."

Tanker Thompson sighed. "It's true that I had evil in my

heart. I killed a man because of the color of his skin, and I hated Jews.''

"You don't feel that way any longer?"

"No."

"Then what are you doing with the company you're keeping?"

"It is God's will, part of God's plan for His avatar. God spoke to me in prison. I was forgiven for my sins, and it was explained to me how Jews are God's Chosen, and how they would play an important role in the Final Days. Kenecky and Patton had already prepared the way, but they did not have Jesus in their hearts. They had no further function in what is to come, and they were only complicating things; I was told to kill them.''

"Right," I said, not understanding a word he was saying, and not caring. There was only one thing I cared about at the moment. I swallowed hard, found that my mouth was very dry. "Tanker, did God tell you to . . . kill Garth?"

"No. He is to be destroyed with all the others when the end comes.''

I hadn't realized I'd been holding my breath until my chest and lungs began to ache. I slowly exhaled, passed a trembling hand over my eyes. "But you do have him?"

"Yes. But why did the two of you keep coming on? God wanted Kenecky killed so that you would know that Vicky is protected. I would never let anyone hurt a child, dwarf. That's not what God wants.''

"Tanker, Garth and I kept coming because we still weren't sure that the child was unharmed. We didn't know that a decent man like you was watching out for her. Now we do, so there's no need for us to continue with our investigation; all we ever cared about was the girl. If you'll tell me where my brother is, I'll go get him and we'll be out of your hair.''

Again, the giant lifted his elbow, stared at me from under its crook. I didn't like the look in his small eyes. "You lie, dwarf," he said at last. "That's a sin. You must think I'm a fool. I'm Christ's avatar on earth; He lets me see into men's hearts, and He tells me you're lying.''

"I'm grateful to you for not killing Garth, Tanker, but I don't understand why you want to keep holding him. We're not your enemies."

"You're God's enemies."

"No, Tanker. It's certainly true that we don't share your religious beliefs, but that doesn't make us God's enemies. We don't care what you believe. And it turns out that we shared the same concern. It was because of us that you found out that Kenecky was abusing the girl, and then you . . . put a stop to it. That's all we wanted. On that piece of business, we were on the same side. That must mean we were on God's side, since you're God's avatar."

"You don't understand."

"Then explain it to me. Why can't you let us be? For that matter, why does Christ need an avatar on earth in the first place? It seems to me that He's been taking care of His own business quite nicely for upwards of two thousand years."

"This is different; these are the Final Days. Satan's demons are already arriving, in human form. Kenecky and Patton were demons."

"Then why were you working for them?"

"I've already explained that to you. God had put evil in my heart so that the demons would come to me, think I was one of them. Even they were part of God's plan, since they had the power to bring on the Final Days. But then God cleansed my heart so that I could see that they were demons, and that He had no further use for them."

"Do you think Garth and I are demons?"

"No. But you're not among God's elite, either. Neither of you will be Raptured next week."

"Next week? You believe the world is going to end next week?"

"The world will begin to end; the battle of Armageddon will begin. These are the Final Days. I and the others will be Raptured up to the heavens to wait with Jesus for seven years. Those who are left behind, those who survive the first minutes, will be tormented by the armies of Satan. When the seven years have passed, Jesus and those He has Raptured will descend to rule the earth in His kingdom.''

''Uh, when next week is all this business supposed to start happening, Tanker?''

''The beginning of the new year.''

''You mean Friday?''

''Yes.''

''Got it. But after that, those of us who haven't been Raptured will be taking our lumps with Satan and his demons, right?''

''You mock, dwarf. But you'll see. All of you unbelievers will see.''

''I don't mean to mock, Tanker; I'm just trying to make an argument. If Garth and I are going to be going through so much suffering, don't you, as Christ's avatar, think it only fitting that we should suffer together? And if the Final Days are here anyway, what does it matter if Garth and I are together? Where's the sense of hanging on to him if Satan and his demons are coming around in another five days to make us all miserable? What's the point?''

''Neither you nor your brother will suffer at the hands of the demons, dwarf,'' Tanker Thompson said in a low voice that had a particularly chilling effect on me. ''Not everyone will be around to suffer the years of Tribulation.''

''Uh, why is that, Tanker?''

''Because you'll be dead.''

''Garth and I will be dead?''

''Yes. The two of you, and millions of others, will die at the beginning of the Tribulation.''

''How do you know we're going to die?''

''Because it is prophesied.''

''All the more reason for brothers to be together, no? What do you care if we're together for the last five days of our lives?''

There was no reply, and I found myself growing even colder.

"I don't understand what's happening, Tanker," I continued. "What's the story? Are you punishing Garth by holding him?"

"No."

"Then why not free him so that he and I can be together for the last five days before Satan arrives?"

Again, there was no reply. And then I realized why I felt cold as I recalled some things a few of the zanier zealots, including William Kenecky, had spoken and written about on a number of occasions; the same things had even been alluded to by a few of the zanier politicians looking to curry favor with the religious right.

Nuclear war with Russia, their line of insane reasoning went, could well be the Armageddon referred to in the Bible. Consequently, not only would it be moral to start such a war, but the people launching it would be carrying out an act of Divine Providence. These chiliasts believed that it was God's will that millions should die in order to bring on Armageddon and the eventual Kingdom of God on earth. These people didn't fear nuclear holocaust; indeed, they couldn't wait for the bombs to start falling.

I could well be talking to such a man. Tanker Thompson, Craig Valley, Floyd and Baxter Small, William Kenecky, Peter Patton, and Henry Blaisdel—lovers of death, all of them, men who viewed their own and everyone else's extermination with what could only be described as a kind of sexual frenzy.

"Tanker," I said softly, "you people are doing more than just hanging around waiting for the Rapture and Tribulation to begin Thursday at midnight, aren't you? You've got something cooked up to start the ball rolling, right? That's why you're so certain Garth and I are going to die."

Tanker Thompson smiled, nodded. "It's God's will."

"It's the ultimate in necrophilia, is what it is," I said tersely, feeling my heart start to pound. "What's going to happen? How many other people are going to escape the Tribulation because they'll be dead, Tanker?"

"Many. It will be a blessing. What's necrophilia, dwarf?"

"You killed Peter Patton. Who's in charge now? Henry Blaisdel?"

Tanker Thompson laughed softly. "God is in charge. It can't be stopped now. Praise the Lord. Jesus is coming."

"If it can't be stopped, why hang on to Garth? If it's God's will that the Tribulation should come, then no human should be able to stop it."

"No human must be allowed to try. That's why I'm here."

"Then it can be stopped?"

"Not by you."

"Where's Garth, Tanker? Is he where Vicky Brown is?"

"No."

"Where is Vicky Brown?"

"She's safe, dwarf. I told you that."

"She's in a biosphere somewhere around here, isn't she? Nuvironment has actually built one of those things, right?"

There was a long pause. I didn't think Thompson was going to answer me, so his answer came as a surprise. "Not around here," he said at last.

"The letter she wrote to Santa Claus was mailed in New York."

"Patton told me about the letter. That was what started it all. It's how you and your brother found out about Vicky and Kenecky . . . and other things."

"Yes."

Tanker Thompson made a low, guttural sound in his throat that could have been a curse. "The devil even uses children," he said. "I was a fool. I should have read it before I mailed it."

"*You* mailed the letter?"

The man absently nodded his shaved head, winced slightly when the motion pulled at his ears. "I didn't see how it could hurt. Vicky asked me to, and I wanted to make her happy. I was wrong; I should have been more vigilant. Satan was trying to trick both of us."

"So you brought the letter with you to New York City from someplace else?"

"It was in my pocket; I'd forgotten about it."

"Where, Tanker? Where did you bring it from?"

Thompson was silent, and I sensed that our conversation had come to an end. "Tanker," I continued quietly, "I don't like pain. I've experienced enough so that I know I certainly don't enjoy getting it, and I don't like giving it. You're not at all what I expected you to be; in some ways, I feel sorry for you, and I respect you for knowing that what Kenecky was doing to Vicky Brown was wrong. But I'm going to have to hurt you if you don't tell me where you're keeping Garth." I replaced the Beretta in my shoulder holster, leaned forward, and pushed in the cigarette lighter. I wasn't certain it would still be working, but a few seconds later it popped. I pulled the lighter out of the dashboard, looked at the glowing end.

The prospect of what I was preparing to do sickened me—but I was damn well going to do it. I didn't have any other choice.

"We've got as long as it takes, Tanker," I said, and swallowed hard. "Three men have killed themselves rather than tell tales out of school. Well, we know you're not going to kill yourself, because I'm not going to let you. But unless you want me to start burning off your skin piece by piece, you're going to tell me where Garth is. Then you're going to tell me what tribulations you loonies have cooked up for the rest of us, so we can put a stop to it."

"I'm certainly not going to kill myself, dwarf," Tanker Thompson said matter-of-factly. "I'm going to kill you."

And with that pronouncement, he yanked his right hand away from the side of his head. Blood spurted from the ragged flesh that had been his right ear. Stunned and horrified, I felt paralyzed as the huge hand, bloody flaps of tissue adhering to the palm, reached out and locked around my left wrist, began to twist. Instinctively, I stabbed at the back of his hand with the cigarette lighter. There was a sharp hissing sound, then the smell of singed flesh and hair. Thompson cried out, reflexively released his grip—at the same time as he pulled his other hand free, and ripped off his left ear with it. Screaming in rage and pain—but also with what sounded eerily like triumph and ecstasy—he reached for me with both his bloody hands.

Moaning with terror and revulsion, I scrambled back across the seat, fell out the door onto cold concrete that was slick with oil and antifreeze from the smashed radiator. A hulking Tanker Thompson, blood welling and rolling out of the wounds on the sides of his head, suddenly appeared above me on the seat, reached down for me with hands that still had the flaps of his ears attached to their palms. I screamed and rolled away from the horror of the grasping hands, jumped to my feet, and clawed for my Beretta. I got the gun out, backed away a few steps and aimed it at Tanker Thompson's massive chest as he climbed out of the car and started toward me.

"That's far enough, Tanker," I said in a voice that squeaked, holding the gun out in front of me with two trembling hands. "You stop right where you are, or I'm going to blow your head off."

"God will keep me alive long enough for me to kill you, dwarf," Thompson replied in an almost casual tone. "After that, it doesn't matter. In a few days, I'll be in Paradise."

Even as I aimed the gun at his chest, it occurred to me that the other man didn't even need God on his side in this face-off; I couldn't afford to kill him, since he was my only link to Garth. I lowered the gun slightly, took careful aim, and squeezed off a shot. The bullet hit Thompson in the left thigh, two or three inches above his knee. He cried out, grabbed his leg.

"The next one goes into the kneecap, Tanker," I said. "Now, you just sit down right there and we'll talk this over."

I should have shot him in the kneecap to begin with; the bullet in his leg only made him stop long enough to reconsider his strategy. He limped back to the car, grabbed hold of one of the Cadillac's hanging doors, and tore it the rest of the way off its hinges. Then he reached down and picked up the crowbar that had come flying out of Beloved's sprung trunk.

Holding the door in front of him as a shield, trailing blood from the wound in his thigh, Tanker Thompson started shuffling toward me.

It seemed like a good time to rethink my own strategy. I had myself a dilemma; I could, I thought, rather easily dart around the gimpy Thompson and get away—but I needed to get information out of the other man, not get away from him. On the other hand, the man with the torn-off ears was not a good candidate for cooperation. It was obvious that Tanker Thompson had a tremendously high tolerance for pain; and he didn't care if he died, as long as he could take me with him.

Not a good situation.

While I was doing all this heavy thinking, Thompson had continued to come forward, and I'd continued to back up—until now he'd cut off a good three-quarters of the concrete platform, and I was heading back onto a lip over the icy Hudson.

I went down on one knee, fired two bullets at his ankles and feet, which were exposed below the door. The bullets ricocheted off the concrete, missing him. He crouched down, began shuffling forward even faster, obviously oblivious to the pain from his torn ears and the wound in his leg. I figured I had two, maybe three, seconds to make my exit, if that was what I was going to do. Watching his beady black eyes that were peering at me over the top of the door, I feinted to the left, then cut to my right. There was a corridor perhaps ten yards wide I might use to try to sprint past the car-door-armored Tanker Thompson, but a flying crowbar just might catch, kill, or cripple me if I tried that.

Besides, I found that I didn't really want to make an exit after all, and my feelings involved more than the need to find my brother. Anger welled in me, rage at the mindless force of evil slouching toward me, evil that could kill not only Garth, but a good many other people—the evil of superstition, chauvinism, megalomania, and willful ignorance that had haunted humankind ever since we'd dropped out of the trees; all of that evil was embodied in the giant shuffling toward me, forcing me back toward the river. I stopped, braced my legs, and emptied the Beretta into the center of the car door. I knew the bullets wouldn't pass through the layers of steel, but the force of the gunfire stopped him, and even backed him up a little. And it made him duck down behind the door. When he again peered over the top of the door, what he saw was me flying feet first toward him through the air.

It seemed I wasn't getting so old after all—or, at least, the rage, frustration, and desperation in me was sufficient to roll back the years momentarily. I hadn't flown so high, or had so much control over my body, since my headliner days with the Statler Brothers Circus, and my timing was perfect. Tanker Thompson poked his head up from behind his shield just in time to catch my heel in his jaw. His head snapped back, and we both landed on the concrete at about the same time. I landed on my left shoulder, rolled over in a somersault to absorb the force of my landing, came up on my feet, and immediately spun around.

The giant, a reformed racist and Jew-baiter who now considered himself a kind of hit man for Christ, was down—but definitely not out. The kick I had delivered to his head would have broken the necks of most men, but it hadn't even knocked Tanker Thompson unconscious, only dazed him slightly. But it was enough—I hoped.

The tire iron had fallen perhaps fifteen feet to his right. With rage still fueling my muscles, I darted to the tire iron, picked it up with my hands on both ends, then ran to Thompson, who was just getting up on his knees. I jumped on his back, pressed the length of the tire iron up against his throat and pulled. I didn't want to strangle him, only knock him unconscious without the risk of breaking open his skull. I had no real idea of what I was going to do with him then, but I knew that I could not—would not—be finished with Tanker Thompson until I had found out where Garth was being held prisoner, or one of us was dead.

Thompson's answer to my grand strategy was simply to

get to his feet, carrying me right up in the air with him. I pulled even harder on the steel bar, but the muscles in his neck were like steel cords. He brought his left hand up, wriggled his fingers between his throat and the bar, began to push the tire iron away.

I decided it was time to get off Tanker Thompson's back and go for the Seecamp strapped to my ankle. But it was too late for that. His right hand had come across his body to where the heel of my left foot was digging into his side; thick, powerful fingers wrapped around my ankle. I had no choice but to go along for the ride as Tanker Thompson marched toward the edge of the platform. I dropped the tire iron, started yelling and pounding on the top of his head, but that had about as much effect as someone trying to stop a locomotive by dragging his heel in the gravel. Thompson never slowed his purposeful pace, and I stopped yelling just in time to suck in a deep breath as we plunged off the end of the platform, went crashing through the ice, and slipped into a black, gelid, wet night that hit my body with such a shock that I half expected to die right then of a heart attack. My heart didn't seize up on me, but I knew that I couldn't last long in that icy, underwater darkness; in perhaps twenty seconds or less, the cold would paralyze me and drain away all my energy, I would go into shock, and I would drown.

And Tanker Thompson still had hold of my ankle.

My first reaction was blind panic, a desperate need to try to struggle back toward the surface—but I knew I would certainly die if I tried that. Tanker Thompson was obviously perfectly willing, indeed eager, to die to further his purpose, namely to kill me, and he could easily hang onto a panic-stricken dwarf for the few more seconds it would take me to drown.

I had lost almost all feeling in my body, yet I managed to reach down and, using both my frozen hands as a kind of clamp, pull the small pistol from the holster on my right ankle. As we settled into the muck in the shallow water, I pushed the barrel of the Seecamp between his hand and my left ankle, pushed. The fingers came off. I twisted around, planted both my feet on his barrel chest—and then felt his fingers wrap themselves around my right calf. But Tanker Thompson had had some of the zip taken out of him; he'd absorbed my kick to his head, and he too was freezing, drowning. I pushed with all my strength—and the fingers slipped off. I shot to the surface, bumping my head on floating chunks of ice, and the pent-up breath escaped from my lungs in an explosive, gasping moan.

Seconds were all I had before I lost the ability to move, and then I would sink back down below the surface to join Tanker Thompson in icy death. I clawed at the bobbing chunks of ice, flailing with my arms and legs, and finally made it back to one of the pilings supporting the concrete platform. I gripped the wood, at the same time as I felt my feet touch gravel. I pushed and pulled, made it up over the lip of the platform, and flopped on the concrete. With my clothes and body steaming in the air, I crawled on my hands and knees across the platform to where the wreckage of Beloved still lay smoldering against the concrete support pillar. There was little smoke now, and still no sound of sirens; the wreck and explosion, muffled by an envelope of concrete and steel, had gone unnoticed. However, there were still some flames flickering in the wreckage. There was no feeling at all in my fingers, and there was no way I could manage to handle zippers and buttons, but I was able to use jagged pieces of metal literally to tear the clothes from my body to the waist. Then, slapping and rubbing my hands together, I leaned over the flames, so close that the hairs on my forearms and chest began to sizzle. More steam rose from my skin, and I backed away just before the flesh began to burn—but sensation had begun to return. I stripped off the rest of my clothes, then huddled, naked and shivering, next to Beloved's life-saving flames.

After ten minutes or so of slowly basting myself on all sides, I finally started to feel relatively warm, and I knew that the danger of hypothermia from a precipitous drop in core temperature had passed; but I was still in danger from delayed shock. And Garth would be in even greater danger if and when his captors discovered that I had prematurely dispatched Tanker Thompson off to Paradise. That could be soon, which meant that I had to get moving, no matter how unappealing the thought. I picked up the remnants of my clothes, found that they were still soaked. The fire was almost out, which meant that I had a problem or two. Even if I didn't freeze to death, the sight of a naked dwarf hippety-hopping down the West Side Highway just might attract a tad too much attention, and questions from the police.

I slipped on my shoes, squished my way across the platform to the Cadillac with the smashed front end. I was looking for something—anything—with which to cover myself, for I was already starting to shudder with cold again, and I no longer had a fire to warm myself up with. I peered in, and my eyes went wide when I saw, crumpled on the floor in the back where it had landed when it had slid off the backseat, a quilted jacket bearing the logo of Thompson's former football team. I snatched up the jacket, slipped it on. It was only about a dozen sizes too big for me, which, for my purposes, made it just right. I wrapped myself in its folds, was just starting to zip up my down and wool cocoon, when I felt ice cold hands wrap themselves around my neck. I screamed.

I grabbed a thumb that felt like a nub of frozen steel, twisted it back. The grip loosened. Still screaming in a kind of terrified series of hiccups, I wheeled around, gazed in horror at the dripping, steaming figure of Tanker Thompson. The exposed flesh of his face and hands was blue-white, the color of ice, and his clothes were covered with ooze from the bottom of the Hudson. I could not understand how he could possibly be alive, but he most indubitably was; he couldn't stay alive much longer, certainly, but as long as he was alive it was quite obvious what was on his mind.

I'd had quite enough of Tanker Thompson, who reminded me of nothing so much as some great mythical giant, a cruel

Antaeus who gained strength from contact with the elements, and who could not be killed. As he again reached for me, I ducked under his arms, then ran as fast as I could in my oversize coat and water-filled shoes off the concrete platform, scrambled up the rutted dirt access road to the West Side Highway.

I'd once again lost all feeling in my feet, and it felt as if I were hobbling on stumps as, holding up the bottom of the jacket so as not to trip over it, I managed to extricate one arm from the folds and used it to try to flag down a car.

Fat chance. This was New York City, and I wouldn't have been picked up even if I were dressed and looked like Mother Theresa.

What I got was a cop—which, considering the fact that I was close to freezing to death, was probably just as well. I knew him; his name was Frank Palorino.

"Mongo?" he said uncertainly as, shuddering inside Tanker Thompson's massive jacket, I managed to open the door of his squad car and slide into the front seat. "What the hell's going on?"

"Thanks for stopping, Frank," I said through chattering teeth. "I, uh . . . I had a little accident."

Suddenly the cop with the close-cropped black hair with matching permanent stubble on his chin and cheeks began to chuckle; the chuckle quickly grew into a full-fledged belly laugh. "A little accident? What the hell? Did you fall in the river?"

"As a matter of fact, I did," I said stiffly as I reached out and turned the heater in the squad car up to full blast. "Listen, would you mind—?"

"Where the *hell* did you get that jacket?" Palorino managed to say between bursts of giggling. "I didn't know you'd played professional football."

Frank Palorino was beginning to try my patience; I could still feel the icy cold of the river—and fear of death—in me straight to my bowels. "A passing fisherman," I stammered. "Look, Frank, give me a break, will you? Get me home."

"Sure," he said, still chuckling as he accelerated and moved into the left lane.

A few minutes and a couple of miles later, as he was pulling up in front of the brownstone, it seemed to occur to my jolly chauffeur that perhaps something not so amusing was afoot, as it were, and that perhaps he should make further, more sober, inquiries into just what a soaked dwarf swaddled in a decidedly oversize athletic jacket had been doing stumbling alongside the West Side Highway on an otherwise peaceful Sunday morning in the middle of winter.

"Mongo," Palorino said seriously as he pulled the car up to the curb, "tell me just what happened to you. How did you happen to fall into the river?"

"Thanks for the ride, Frank," I said as I got out of the car.

"Mongo, hold on. I'm serious. What's going on? What were you doing down by the river?"

"Listen, Frank," I said, shaking violently now inside the jacket as I turned back to the policeman. "Call Lieutenant McCloskey. Tell him I'll be in touch with him just as soon as I get myself a little more warmed up, and a little more together. Tell him everything I said to him in our earlier conversation goes double now. In the meantime, you can go down to the waterfront off Eighty-sixth Street. You'll find a couple of wrecked cars, and you'll probably find a frozen stiff somewhere close by. The stiff's name is Thomas Thompson. Tell Lieutenant McCloskey that it was Thompson who killed William Kenecky."

Palorino's stubbled jaw dropped open. "What? What the hell are you talking about?"

"Frank, I'm really too cold to repeat it all."

"The lieutenant's going to want to talk to you right now, Mongo."

"Frank, it's not as though you don't know where to find me," I said, then slammed the door shut and headed for the entrance to the brownstone.

I half expected Palorino to start banging at my door, but he didn't. I got in the elevator in the vestibule, kicked off my soggy shoes, and headed for the bathroom when I got up to my apartment. I turned on the hot water in the tub, shuffled back to the bar in my living room, and poured myself half a tumbler of Scotch. I shrugged off the jacket, headed back into the bathroom. The water in the tub felt like it was just this side of boiling as I eased myself down into it, which was just about the temperature I was looking for. I sat in the steaming water, gulping Scotch, until I felt a new kind of numbness, a warm sensation of comfort, slowly oozing through me.

And with the returning warmth inside and outside my body returned the realization that there was no time even to rest, much less get drunk. Garth was still the prisoner of men who thought nothing of killing themselves, and thus would undoubtedly kill him in the wink of an eye if the mood so struck them; I had to find him before the mood struck. It was not yet noon; now that I was out of danger, I certainly could not waste time sloshing around in a tub and getting wasted. I set the remainder of my drink down on the floor, got out of the tub, and toweled myself off as I reflected on the thought that there was only one place left to go. As far as I was concerned, the police should have gone there in the first place—but they hadn't, and probably wouldn't.

Lieutenant Malachy McCloskey and the rest of the NYPD could do what they wanted, but I was going to find a way to drop in on Mr. Big himself.

Constantly feeling like I was moving in a dream, I carefully cleaned, oiled, and reloaded my Seecamp, which I'd somehow managed to hang onto. I was just putting the gun in the pocket of my parka when the phone rang. I hesitated, then picked up the receiver.

"Yeah?"

"Frederickson?! What the fuck's going on?! What were you doing down by the river, and where's the stiff you were talking about?!"

Suddenly I started getting a fresh chill. "You didn't find him, Lieutenant?"

"Find who?! Frederickson—!"

"Tanker Thompson—the ex–football player. He killed William Kenecky, and he tried to kill me. Have you spoken to Henry Blaisdel?"

"Frederickson, you stay right where you are! I'm sending a squad car to pick you up. You're coming over here to the precinct station, and then you and I are going to have a long talk."

"You bet, Lieutenant," I said, and hung up.

I started for the door, suddenly felt my head begin to spin, and promptly fell on my face. I didn't pass out, but for long moments I felt as if I were clinging to the edge of a void, about to fall in. I clung to consciousness, taking deep breaths. Finally my head cleared. I managed to get to my feet, although I swayed. Mr. Big was obviously going to have to wait until I'd had some proper rest and my body had had time to recover from the pretty good shock it had been given during the course of my battle with Tanker Thompson and subsequent dousing in the icy Hudson.

But I couldn't do my resting in the apartment, because, if I did, I was more than a little likely to end up resting in a jail cell. Moving slowly but deliberately, I packed a gym bag with a couple of changes of underwear, toilet articles, some tools of the trade, and a clean shirt. Then I took the elevator down, locked up, and started hoofing it toward the Sheraton Hotel, a few blocks away. I was just turning a corner when I heard the screech of brakes behind me. I looked around, saw two squad cars, lights flashing, pull up to the curb in front of the brownstone. I kept walking.

11.

I slept right around the clock, and then some, and finally woke myself up with an enormous sneeze, followed by two or three lesser sneezelets. I wrapped myself in an oversize bath towel for a robe, called room service, and ordered a pot of coffee, French toast, home fried potatoes, bacon, a bottle of aspirin, and a bottle of vitamin C. I needed to keep up my strength—or get it back. While I was waiting for the food to arrive, I shuffled off to the bathroom to brush my teeth and shave. I didn't feel all that hot, and I was convinced that I could sleep for another week if I really put my mind to it. On the other hand, considering what I'd been through, I decided I wasn't feeling all that bad; I knew I was slightly feverish, but that beat being dead.

My order arrived about the time I finished getting dressed. I took two aspirins and a thousand milligrams of vitamin C, followed that with the food and coffee. By the time I'd finished eating and drained the pot of coffee, I was ready to roll.

It was time to go visiting.

I dressed in jeans, a sweat shirt, and sneakers, strapped the Seecamp in its holster to my ankle, then double-checked the other items in my gym bag to make sure I hadn't forgotten anything in my rush to get out of the apartment and escape the long arm and time-consuming inquisitiveness of the law. Everything was there. I zipped up the bag, called down to the desk to tell them to send the bill to my office, then left.

The Blaisdel Building was only a few blocks away, but I

had the hotel doorman hustle me up a cab anyway; I assumed Malachy McCloskey was more than a bit irritated with me, and I didn't want to risk being spotted on the street and picked up by the police. I told the cabbie to stop a half block away, and I looked around before getting out; there were no police around. When a large knot of pedestrians came by, I hurriedly paid the driver, settled in with the crowd of walkers, then darted into the entrance to the Blaisdel Building.

Although I had strongly disapproved at the time, I was now grateful that Garth had checked out the building's security system; now I knew what I was up against as I searched for a way to get up to Henry Blaisdel's penthouse triplex. I was going to have to be wary of all sorts of sophisticated alarm devices. Still, there had to be a way to get up there, short of scaling the building, and if I had to shoot a few Born Again Christian Athletes for Christ on my way up, I was more than ready.

But first I wanted to check out the Nuvironment offices—or what used to be the Nuvironment offices—on the off chance that Peter Patton, before he had been so unceremoniously ousted from office and life by Tanker Thompson, might have left something behind that could lead me to Garth, or Vicky Brown, or both.

I hurried through the lobby and down the narrow, far corridor to the locked door at the end where Patton had taken me on my initial visit. I looked back down the corridor to make sure nobody was watching me, then took a set of lock picks out of my gym bag, huddled over the lock, and went to work. It wasn't an expensive lock, and I got lucky on my third try; the door clicked open, and I went through. The private elevator in the vestibule was down, its door open. I stepped in, drew out my Seecamp, then pressed the single button that would take me to the Nuvironment offices on the ninth floor.

The first thing that hit me when the elevator door sighed open was a blast of hot air. It must have been ninety degrees in the gold-carpeted reception area, and I couldn't understand why anyone would have turned up the thermostat before they left.

The second thing that hit me, as I passed through the heavy door of smoked glass, was the smell of rotting flesh. I gagged, took a handkerchief out of my pocket, and put it over my nose and mouth. Then I started down the central corridor, giving Peter Patton's spacious office a cursory glance. Nobody was home.

There was a lot of square footage in the Nuvironment offices, including what looked like research labs of various sorts and open workplaces. Somebody—Tanker Thompson, I presumed, acting on instructions from God—had really trashed the place; every computer on the floor had been reduced to a tangle of steel and plastic, smashed circuitry, dangling wires, and all of the drawers in the desks had been pulled out and emptied. As far as I could tell, there wasn't a scrap of anything, anywhere, that would afford the slightest clue as to why Nuvironment had closed up shop, what they thought—or knew—was going to happen on New Year's Eve, or where they might be holding Garth.

There was one very large room where I suspected some answers might have been. In the center of the room was a huge display stand, a kind of great wooden box on legs, surrounded by shards of plastic. There were marks on the empty walls where maps or charts might have been hanging. The entire floor was covered with ooze, a mixture of water and sand littered with what appeared to be electrical components and large swatches of rotted vegetation. Judging from the size of the room and the depth of the mire on the floor, I judged that the container that had been on the display stand had held upwards of a thousand gallons of water. I was certain that what had been demolished had been a model of a biosphere.

Off to my right, half submerged in the ooze and caught on a piece of broken plastic, there was what appeared to be a piece of posterboard. I sloshed over and picked it up. In black letters against a pale blue background was written the word EDEN.

I found Peter Patton's corpse, the head twisted around and bent back at an impossible angle, in an adjacent room, which looked like it had once been used for the storage of maintenance supplies. After breaking Patton's neck, Tanker Thompson had flung the body onto a pile of empty packing crates; one limp arm was draped over the main thermostat, which accounted for the heat. I winced against the smell, turned, and hurried out of the room. I went to the extreme end of the corridor, turned right, and abruptly stopped. In front of me was the door to another elevator.

I slowly approached the elevator, stopped in front of it. I reached out with a slightly trembling hand for the call button, then drew back, uncertain of what to do.

There was no doubt in my mind that the elevator led up to Henry Blaisdel's penthouse, but simply getting in and riding up didn't seem like such a good idea. State-of-the-art security, Garth had said, which meant that my operating the elevator could well set off alarms, and I would find a large unwelcoming committee at the top. Then again, they might not expect intruders to come up by way of Nuvironment, since the Nuvironment offices themselves were so difficult to get to. Whatever. The more I thought about it, the more convinced I became that taking the elevator was probably as good an alternative as any, and better than most. I was going to try to break in on Henry Blaisdel by walking in his front door.

I punched the call button. Less than a half minute later the door opened, and I stepped into the spacious, mahogany and velvet-lined interior. I punched the button at the side of the door. The elevator whirred, began moving up silently, but at what I could tell was high speed.

When the elevator stopped, I crouched down at the back, Seecamp held out in front of me with both hands. The door opened, and I found myself staring out into space that was, if not exactly empty, at least devoid of people. I straightened up and, still holding my pistol at the ready, stepped out onto thick, red carpeting that covered the entire floor, and that reminded me of nothing so much as a sea of blood. Rising from this red sea were a series of Doric columns and rectangular Lucite panels on which were hung various paintings executed in what I thought of as Nazi-propaganda style: handsome men, women, and children—all white—marched arm in arm through the paintings, always heading toward a glowing figure, whom I assumed to be Jesus, waiting for them in the distance. In his right hand the glowing Jesus-figure carried a gleaming, upraised sword, and in the left a stylized swastika, a perversion of the cross. Cowering in the corners of all the paintings were writhing, ugly caricatures of blacks, Jews, and Asiatics. There were dozens of these obscene paintings, turning the floor into a kind of art museum that was a real horror show.

The *pièce de résistance*, propped up on a red velvet throne inside a ceiling-high vacuum chamber, was at the far end of the floor.

It was impossible to tell how long Henry Blaisdel had been dead, because there were no dates written on or inside the glass case that was his mausoleum, but somebody had done a pretty good job of stuffing the old boy, because his corpse looked better than some living people I know. He was dressed in a three-piece black suit with black wing-tip shoes, leaning forward slightly on his throne and staring thoughtfully off into the distance. Beside him stood a statue of Jesus with one plaster arm draped protectively over Blaisdel's frail shoulders.

I loved it. It certainly explained why Henry Blaisdel hadn't been sighted in the past few years, and I could only marvel at the number and complexity of the legal stratagems that must have been required to keep the old man's death a secret, and his fortune under the control of . . . whoever was controlling it. Certainly, Henry Blaisdel himself must have made all the arrangements before his death. He'd been a man with a purpose; judging by what the men to whom he'd obviously bequeathed his money and power had been and were up to, it was a very dangerous purpose.

To the right of the mausoleum was a circular marble

staircase. The small shards of plastic embedded in the caked mud on my sneakers clicked and scraped when I stepped on the stone; I kicked off my sneakers, tied the laces together, and draped them around my neck. Then, trying to make myself even smaller than I was, I moved slowly up the staircase, keeping to the right. There was still no sign of anybody, no sound in the massive triplex but my own hoarse breathing. I reached the top of the staircase, peered around the marble balustrade—again saw nobody in my immediate field of vision. It occurred to me that I was wasting my time, that the penthouse was as empty as the Nuvironment offices fifty-nine stories below, as lifeless as the dead old man downstairs. But I had no other place to go, no other hope . . .

Still holding the Seecamp out in front of me, I straightened up, stepped out onto the carpet at the top of the stairs. There was a corridor, lined on both sides with bedrooms—all individually and expensively decorated, but with no sign that anybody had been using them lately. There was a heavy oak door at the end of the corridor. I went through it, stopped abruptly, and sucked in a deep breath as my heart began to beat faster.

The biosphere model was on a huge table identical to the one I had seen on the ninth floor. It was at least twenty feet long and ten feet wide, with the clear plastic dome over it virtually touching the twelve-foot-high ceiling. Bolted to the side of the table was a wooden plaque with gold lettering: EDEN. I pulled over a straight-backed chair, climbed up on it in order to get a better look at this model of Henry Blaisdel's idea of Paradise.

Beneath its massive plastic sky, Eden was shaped like the letter F. The base of the F was to my right, and perhaps a third of the section was modeled to simulate desert, complete with dunes, cactus, and stone mesas. The desert merged with what appeared to be a swamp; water drained into lagoons, which in turn fed a large lake. There was even what might be termed an ocean. The top leg of the F, barely visible through the condensed mist which had collected on the plastic, was a model rain forest, with condensation coils, battery powered in the model, set into the plastic over it. Even as I watched, it began to "rain" in the jungle section under the dome; water dripped from the ceiling, ran down hillsides to collect in streams and lagoons, which in turn emptied into the "lake" and the "ocean."

The middle leg of the F comprised living quarters for the inhabitants. There was a "Main Street" lined on both sides with small cottages, tilled fields, an orchard, and cutaway models of buildings that appeared to be a laboratory, a library, and an amphitheater. At the end of Main Street was a white church topped by the group's swastika-cross.

I stared down into the biosphere, trying to understand the point of this thing that was Henry Blaisdel's fantasy and obsession; since part of his religious fantasy had been that all true believers would be "Raptured" up to heaven in the early stages of the coming Tribulation, there wouldn't seem any need for this oversized goldfish bowl on earth.

It appeared that he and his fellow believers had been hedging their bets, so to speak, preparing something he conceived of as a refuge for those of his group who, for one reason or another—perhaps overcrowding in heaven—might not be Raptured in the Final Days. But then, I thought, it probably made no sense for me to try to make sense of the thinking of a bunch of murderous schizoids, or to understand what there was about Eden that Blaisdel had thought made it demon-proof.

It wasn't demons I was worried about. If Eden had, somehow, already been built to the scale represented by the model, it covered several acres—and it was certainly nowhere in the New York metropolitan region. Tanker Thompson had said as much. To be constructed in secret, and its gargantuan presence kept a secret, it would have to be located somewhere where there were vast, empty spaces—and, even then, it might be camouflaged. With all of Nuvironment's records destroyed and its personnel decimated at their own hands or Tanker Thompson's, I might never find Eden.

Then again, Eden might exist only in this model; there might never have been a shipment of a hundred tons of rain forest soil, but only the cubic yard or so I estimated to be in the model—and that could have been brought into the country with little difficulty. Perhaps Vicky Brown had been here, getting her hands dirty as she'd played with the soil while the model was being built.

But that was not the gospel according to Tanker Thompson, who'd said he'd carried the letter in his pocket from somewhere else. I could think of no reason why the man should have lied to me. Also, even if Vicky Brown had been up in this penthouse, she certainly wasn't now. And I was no closer to finding out what had happened to Garth, and where he was being held.

I was thinking these thoughts, feeling thoroughly frustrated and sorry for myself, when the chair was abruptly pulled from under me. I pitched forward, banging my face against the hard plastic of the dome. An instant later something very hard hit me at the base of the skull. I imagined I passed like a ghost through the barrier of plastic; I was falling, as if pushed from a plane, through the sky, down toward the jungle, swamp, desert, ocean, lagoons, and lakes. I finally landed on a blood-red carpet that swallowed me up in darkness.

12.

I awoke to some bad news, some good news, and some more bad news. The bad news was that I was up on a wooden platform, hands securely strapped over my head to some kind of skeletal metal frame; since I didn't recognize anything in my surroundings, I assumed I was in another room on the third floor of the triplex.

The good news was that Garth was there beside me, alive.

The bad news was that he was also strapped to the frame. Judging from the dried blood on his wrists around the leather thongs that cut into his flesh, he'd spent a good deal of time trying—unsuccessfully, obviously—to free himself. It didn't bode well.

"Hey, Mongo," Garth said to me when he saw that I was conscious. "You okay?"

"Is that a rhetorical question?"

"You've got a hell of a bump on your forehead, and two black eyes. Are you hurting?"

"I'm betting I've got an even bigger bump on the back of my head, but it's nothing that a couple of aspirin won't fix. You?"

"I'm all right—but the situation kind of sucks, doesn't it?"

"Yeah."

"Shit," my brother said with a thin smile. "You can't rescue anybody. What the hell good are you?"

"I didn't even know you were here, brother," I said tightly. Now that I saw that Garth was alive, my relief at finding him was being rapidly supplanted by anger—and I didn't care if it showed. "I didn't know where you were, or whether you were dead or alive, and for some reason that bothered me just a tad—especially when I recalled what William Kenecky looked like when he finally turned up. I was on my way up here to confront the old man."

"Blaisdel's dead, you know. Probably has been for years."

"Yeah; I saw the mummy downstairs. And by the way, I checked through all the files in your office, and couldn't find even a teeny-weeny clue as to what you were up to, or where you were going. That's a procedure we're definitely going to have to change, even if it's in the next life. Where the hell did they catch you?"

Garth studied me for a few moments with his limpid brown eyes, then looked away. "Here," he replied evenly. "I figured Blaisdel would certainly know where the girl was, and I wanted to go right at him; I was tired of all the complications and bullshit.''

"You'd already made your decision the last time we talked, hadn't you? Even then, you knew Goddamn well that you were going to try to break in here.''

Now Garth looked at me again, nodded. "Yeah," he said quietly. "I thought I'd figured out a way to bypass the security system, and I figured that if I could get close enough to Blaisdel to put a gun to his head, we'd find out fast enough where Vicky Brown is. Obviously, I missed a circuit somewhere; those two ballplayers, Velazian and Rokan, got me on the way in.''

"*Damn* you, Garth!" I snapped. "Why the *hell* didn't you tell me what you planned to do?!''

"Because I didn't want you to know," he replied matter-of-factly. "I was planning a forced entry, trespassing, and assault on one of the richest and most powerful men in the world. After we found Vicky Brown and made certain she was going to be all right, I didn't care what happened to me; I did care what happened to you. Just by telling you what I was going to do, I'd have made you an accessory to a series of major crimes. You'd have lost your license and your business. Considering that, I couldn't see the sense in involving you in what I considered to be a one-man job.''

"Let me tell you something, brother," I said tightly. "You're lucky I'm tied up, because if I wasn't I'd sure as hell go to work on your nose again. How do you know I wouldn't have agreed with you? What the hell do you think I'm doing here now? It's true that I came looking for information on you, but why did you assume I wouldn't have done the same for Vicky Brown?''

"You would have. That's my point. You'd have agreed, and you'd have insisted on coming along. I wanted to keep you out of this particular little venture.''

"If you weren't my brother, and if I didn't love you, I think I'd call you a shithead. Sometimes you really piss me off.''

"How tight are those straps of yours, Mongo?"

I wriggled a bit, wriggled harder, then started really heaving myself around. The leather straps on my wrists and ankles held tight, and I could easily understand how Garth had cut himself trying to get away. "Tight," I said.

"Anything in your bag of tricks that might get us off this frame?"

"Not that I can think of at the moment."

"Then we've got a real problem, Mongo."

"No shit?"

"You don't understand."

"I understand that I don't like being tied up here. But if they just mean to leave us here to die of thirst and starvation, why didn't they simply off us and be done with it?"

"Probably because they're getting their jollies out of letting us think about what's going to happen; with these guys, it's anybody's guess what they're thinking."

"Uh, what's going to happen?"

"Look behind you."

I was spread-eagled to the frame in such a way that it was hard for me to turn my head, but by arching my back and craning my neck it was possible for me to catch a glimpse of what was being supported by the skeletal, boxlike apparatus: it looked like a massive steel cannister, perhaps twelve feet high and more than a yard in diameter, bristling with red, yellow, and blue wires. I swallowed hard, found that my mouth was dry.

"A bomb?" I croaked, looking back at my brother.

"Not just any old bomb, Mongo," Garth replied softly. "What we've got at our backs is the guts of a B-53—a hydrogen bomb, with a built-in nuclear device to set it off. It has a yield of nine megatons—the equivalent of seven hundred and fifty of the atomic bombs that were dropped on Hiroshima. If that thing goes off, Manhattan will be vaporized, and all of the other boroughs will be flattened. Millions of people are going to die, Mongo—not only here, but in Detroit, and Israel, and maybe a few other sites. What happens after that will depend, I suppose, on who the various world leaders think is responsible. Blaisdel—when he was alive—Kenecky, and Peter Patton believed that the explosions would trigger a nuclear war with Russia, because the Bible told them so. I don't know where they found that in the Bible, but they may have been on to something. This bomb, and the others like it, will be triggered by a radio signal beamed by satellite at exactly midnight, New Year's Eve, unless we can find a way to stop it.''

Numb with horror, I moved my lips—but no sound came out. Then I realized that I really had nothing to say. I started desperately jerking my body around on the frame; I stopped and let my body sag when I felt blood begin to ooze from the cuts on my wrists and flow down my forearms. ''Jesus Christ,'' I groaned.

''That's who they think ordered this all up,'' Garth said softly.

''How the hell could they get hold of hydrogen bombs?''

''It probably wasn't nearly as difficult for somebody like Blaisdel as we'd all like to think it should be. For decades, he had his fingers in just about every military production pie there was. He owned a number of bomb production plants that operated under the aegis of the Department of Energy. In the sixties he was building some components of hydrogen bombs—B-53s—for them. They used to be fitted on the Strategic Air Command's B-52 Stratofortresses, but SAC mothballed them in 1983 and went to smaller bombs and Cruise missiles. Then, a while back, the Pentagon made a rather quiet decision to start taking them out of mothballs— probably because the generals are a little concerned that all the newer gadgets aren't nearly as reliable as they're supposed to be; they wanted some serious, proven firepower on hand. That much is for certain. My guess is that if we had access to classified information we'd find out that Blaisdel's facilities were used to store the bombs; he had access, and he somehow managed—or made it possible for his lieutenants to manage—to spirit away three or more of them. Considering all the talent he had working for him, it's even conceivable that he had his own built.''

"How do you know all this?"

"I spent a lot of time in the library checking up on Blaisdel, remember? That's where I found out about the defense contract work. When I found myself tied up here with that thing behind me for company, I put the rest together. What I didn't know, Velazian, Rokan, and the big guy who was originally driving the car that was tailing me were happy to provide. They're all higher than a kite on this religious ecstasy kick of theirs, and they like to talk about what's going to happen. They were really quite chatty.''

I licked my lips, which were now dry and cracked, as I felt a chill go through me. "When was Tanker Thompson around here?''

"Oh, not too long before you got here. When I saw he was missing his ears, I assumed you had something to do with it. What did you do to him, and while you were at it why didn't you kill the son-of-a-bitch?''

"Oh, Jesus, Garth,''I said in a haunted voice that sounded like a stranger's. "I thought I had.''

"Yeah?'' Garth said dryly. "Well, not quite. I must say, though, that he didn't look too chipper, and he sounded like he had a bad cold.'' He paused, studied me. "So do you, as a matter of fact.''

"The man's a great advertisement for resurrection, and that's for sure,'' I said, still unable to comprehend how Tanker Thompson could be not only alive, but walking around. In a way, I was as afraid of Thompson as I was of the bomb at my back; the pain, death, and inexorable force he represented was more personal. "I ambushed him—or thought I ambushed him—Sunday morning; I was going to force him to tell me where you were being held. We both took a dunking in the Hudson. The last time I saw him, he looked at most a minute or two away from freezing to death.''

"How'd you take his ears off?''

"Krazy Glue; he took them off himself.''

Garth shook his head. "He's insane."

"Sure; they all are. Incidentally, Thompson killed Kenecky, and as an afterthought he killed Patton. I don't think there's anybody left in charge of this operation."

Garth grunted. "Blaisdel and Kenecky found each other under some rock years ago. Both heard voices, and both agreed that God was urging them to join forces to bring on Armageddon. This New Year's Eve was the date that was chosen."

"Thompson told you all this?"

"The three of them took turns. I told you, they were all really chatty. They can't wait to die—or for just about everybody else to die—because they think they're going to wake up in a world containing nothing but white, born-again Christians, with Jesus as a kind of kindly Big Brother who'll make sure the trains run on time. There are more Jews in New York than there are in Israel, so that's how we get to be tied to this particular bomb. The bomb in or near Israel is to nail those Jews they don't nail here."

"And the one in Detroit is for the blacks they don't nail here?"

Garth nodded. "Thompson wasn't sure exactly how many bombs there are around the world. Blaisdel and Kenecky were working on this little project for a lot of years."

"Where the hell did Thompson, Velazian, and Rokan go to? They hung around here long enough to form a reception committee for me."

"You were the last bit of business to be taken care of, if you'll pardon the expression. I can't say I'm an expert on their theology, but it seems that not everyone who deserves to be Raptured can be, so God told Blaisdel to build a biosphere to house those deserving few—Blaisdel's and Kenecky's people, naturally—until Armageddon blows over. They believe that radiation and demons can't get in because it's been blessed by God. That's where they are now, I suppose."

"Eden? I saw the model downstairs. So something like that actually does exist, life-size?"

"Yeah. According to my informants, it's somewhere in the desert west of Boise, Idaho. That's where Vicky Brown is; her father's part of the caretaking staff."

"And the signal that will set off the bombs . . . ?"

"Blaisdel Industries has its own satellite—two of them, as a matter of fact. The radio signal that will trigger all the bombs will be relayed from one of those satellites, and the transmitter that will send the signal is somewhere inside Eden, which is better than ten acres."

"Somewhere?"

"Somewhere. None of those ex-jocks knew where it was, and they didn't seem to care. It's set to automatically transmit at the appropriate time."

"Maybe it won't work."

"Right; maybe it won't work."

Again, I started flopping around on the steel frame, desperately trying to free myself, but I managed only to irritate the chafed, cut flesh on my wrists and ankles even more. I glanced around, looking for something—anything—that at least might give me some *idea* for how we might get loose. There was nothing—and if there had been, I wouldn't have been able to reach it. Except for the raised platform which we shared with a hydrogen bomb, the large room was empty. A single door, which I assumed opened on to the central corridor on the third floor, was directly across from me. To our left, perhaps fifteen yards away, heavy gray floor-to-ceiling drapes across the windows blocked out any light except for the faint, ghostly illumination radiated by small, recessed lights in the ceiling. It was impossible to tell whether it was day or night.

"What day is it?" I asked, gasping for breath.

"I'm not sure. I was kept in another room until they nabbed you, and there were no windows. I've lost track of time."

"It was a little before noon on Monday when I started up here. How long was I out?"

Garth thought about it, shrugged slightly. "Not too long—I

think; you were already strapped up here when they brought me in. It's probably Monday night, maybe Tuesday morning.''

"Then, at the outside, we've got three days to find the transmitter and deactivate it.''

Garth didn't say anything. He didn't have to. If we couldn't find a way to get free, we weren't going to have to worry about deactivating the transmitter. We didn't even have to worry about being vaporized by the exploding bomb, because it was going to take a lot less than seventy-two hours for us to die of suffocation or heart attacks induced by our hanging, crucifixion-style positions; before too many more hours had passed, the blood would begin to pool in our legs and refuse to be pumped back up to our lungs, hearts, brains. There would be a lot of initial discomfort, then unconsciousness, and finally death. Already, It was becoming increasingly difficult to breathe.

"Garth?'' I continued hoarsely. "What are we going to do?''

My brother was silent for some time, and I didn't think he was going to answer. When he did finally speak, I was almost sorry he had.

"I don't think there's anything we can do, Mongo,'' Garth said in a matter-of-fact tone. His voice was growing weaker. "I can't break or slip out of these straps, and we've seen that you can't; we'll only break our bones trying. For a time, I thought I'd broken my left wrist; now I think it's only sprained. As long as you were still free . . .''

"I'm sorry, Garth.''

"Don't be ridiculous. What could you have done differently?''

"Not got caught.''

"They were waiting for you. And if you hadn't come up here, they'd have probably hunted you down and killed you anyway. Alone, there was just nothing you could do.''

"You're saying we're just going to hang around here, alive or dead, until this bomb goes off and kills a few million people?''

Garth looked away. "We gave it our best shot, Mongo,'' he said in a voice so low I could hardly hear him.

"I've never known you to give up hope, Garth."

When Garth turned his head back toward me, I could see that there were tears in his eyes—but the tears were not for himself. "You asked me what I thought, Mongo, and I told you. You think I've given up hope? I haven't. But hope and a dollar will get you a cup of coffee in Times Square. There are times when hope is irrelevant, and this is one of them."

I went into a fit of coughing that was punctuated by a sneeze. It occurred to me, not without some amusement, that I could be coming down with something serious. "That fucking McCloskey," I wheezed. "He cut us loose on this thing, and he's been dragging his feet from day one because he's worried about his pension, which goes into effect at precisely the time this thing is supposed to go off. He's certainly going to start off his retirement with a bang, isn't he?"

"That's terrible, Mongo," Garth said, and grinned. "Really terrible."

"My sense of humor is rapidly deteriorating."

"It's not his fault," Garth said seriously. "He turns out to be a better man than I gave him credit for. After all, he stayed in the department after I turned him in, took the heat and his demotion, and then worked his way back up."

"Oh, terrific. It's just too bad that he never got around to working his way up here."

"He was afraid, Mongo—and probably with good reason. If he had tried to make any kind of serious move on investigating Nuvironment, Patton would have crushed him. In the end, he probably would have lost his pension—and for nothing. He couldn't have cracked this thing."

I was beginning to feel dizzy and nauseous, and I closed my eyes. "We did give it our best shot, didn't we?" I said, and groaned. It was becoming painful to talk.

"Yes."

As if sensing that before long neither of us would be able to talk at all, we changed the subject of our helplessness in the face of our impending deaths, and the deaths of millions of others. We reminisced about the past, our growing up together, past perils, our good times together, and finally, our love for each other. Then I slept, or passed out. I woke up, or dreamed that I woke up, then slept, or dreamed that I slept, or passed out again. Occasionally I would hear Garth's voice calling to me, as if from a great distance, but I couldn't respond, and I knew I was dying.

13.

THEN I woke up again—and I knew it wasn't a dream. Thick mucus was clogging my nostrils, running down my chin, dripping down the back of my throat and choking me. I was sucking in meager amounts of air in great, labored breaths. The muscles in my arms and legs were rapidly twitching in spasms, and felt like they were on fire. All of me felt on fire, and I knew it was fever raging in me. I was very conscious of my heart, which felt like a small, hard thing about the size of a golf ball pumping and burning in the center of my chest.

Something had woken me up.

I turned my head to look at Garth. He was very pale, his face knotted in pain, but he was conscious. He licked his dry lips, swallowed hard. "There's someone downstairs," he croaked. "Hang in there, Mongo. Don't die on me."

Garth had certainly piqued my interest enough to make me straighten up and take notice, at least in my head. But I didn't hear anything but the pounding of my own heart in my ears. I decided that Garth was delirious, and I was about to let myself slip back into the merciful oblivion of unconsciousness when the door across the room slammed open and Patrolman Frank Palorino, in full riot gear, burst through at an angle to his right, dropped to one knee, and swept his semiautomatic rifle around the room as another patrolman, similarly outfitted, darted in and dropped to a similar stance at Palorino's left flank. Seeing that Garth and I were the only occupants in the room, Palorino abruptly stood, shouted something that I couldn't understand into his walkie-talkie, then hurried across the room to me as the second patrolman went to Garth.

"You have another little accident, Mongo?" the stubble-faced policeman said wryly as, supporting me with his left arm around my waist, he proceeded to undo the buckles on the straps binding my wrists. I collapsed over his shoulder, and he went to work freeing my ankles. "Shit, buddy, you're burning up with fever. But you're going to be all right. We'll get you to a hospital just as soon as this fucking blizzard lets up."

Palorino gently laid me down on the floor, next to my brother, just as a team of three paramedics rushed into the room, knelt down beside us, and began unpacking their leather bags. Everything above me was a blur of hands and faces. I felt my feet being raised and propped up, and, mercifully, my pounding heartbeat began to slow. I kept wanting to close my eyes and go to sleep, but knew that I couldn't until either Garth or I had told the police what we knew. Malachy McCloskey, dressed in a blue parka over a bulletproof vest, drifted in and out of focus as he hovered over us. His pockmarked face was gray, his brows knitted in concern. Somebody raised my head, and I gulped greedily at a cup of tepid water that tasted slightly salty. This was followed by another liquid that also tasted salty, but was more substantial, like chicken noodle soup with a kick. One of the paramedics rolled up my sleeve and started to slide a needle into a vein. I winced and tried to pull away, but the woman held me tightly. Then a hand which I recognized as my brother's came into my field of vision, gripped the woman's wrist, and pulled the needle away. Then Garth was on his knees beside me, talking to the startled paramedic.

"Don't give either of us anything that will put us to

sleep," Garth said in a weak but clear voice. "Get me to a phone. I have to call somebody in Washington right away. It's very important."

"You can't call next door, much less Washington," Frank Palorino said, shaking his head. "The phones went out three hours ago, and New York Telephone has no idea when they're going to be working again. But don't you worry about—"

"You don't understand," Garth said curtly, his voice already growing stronger.

My brother held out his hand to me. I gripped it and pulled myself up to a sitting position. From there we both got to our feet, and I was vaguely surprised when I managed to stay up on mine. I wasn't quite ready to run any marathons, but I was feeling better, despite the fever in me. The paramedic who'd tried to give me a needle held out another cup. I took it and drank; more of the chicken noodle soup with a kick. I cleared my throat, managed a weak, "Thank you."

McCloskey stepped up to us. Now that we were up and about, the furrow in his brow was gone, and there was just the trace of a smirk on his face. "Well, well, well," he said in the tone of voice of a man who was savoring a triumph. "It looks like the famous Fredericksons needed a little help to get out of this scrape, doesn't it? We found what was left of those two cars down by the river. When Frank told me what had happened, and when we couldn't find the two of you, I figured it was time to exert a little individual initiative. When I found out Nuvironment's phone had been disconnected, I figured that was sufficient reason to go up there; when we found Patton's body, I figured that was sufficient reason, despite the weather, to hustle up here and take a look around. To tell you the truth, it really surprised me how much I was worried about you two." He paused, and his smirk became full blown. "That was kind of lucky for the famous Fredericksons, huh?"

"You misread the situation, Lieutenant," I wheezed. "We were just getting ready to escape when you all came in and spoiled it." I paused to drink some more chicken soup, continued, "Thanks, McCloskey. Now, we've got us a big prob—"

"What the hell is that?" McCloskey interrupted, pointing to the apparatus up on the platform behind us.

"A hydrogen bomb," Garth said. "What's the day and time?"

"A what?"

"A hydrogen bomb," Garth repeated evenly. "You'll need specialists to deactivate it, probably federal people. Make damn sure they know what they're doing, because if they don't, and they make a mistake, Manhattan and most of the other boroughs are going to end up nothing more than one very large hole in the ground."

Palorino, the other policeman, and the three paramedics took a step backward, but McCloskey seemed rooted to the ground, staring up at the steel frame and enclosed cylinder with eyes wide and mouth open.

"Lieutenant," I said, looking around in vain for some sign of my sneakers, "what's the day and time?"

"Holy shit," McCloskey said. "Are you kidding me?"

"No, Lieutenant," I replied, and wearily sank back down on the floor.

Garth stepped up to the police detective, gently shook his shoulder. "What's the day and time, McCloskey?"

McCloskey, face pale and eyes even wider, turned to look at Garth. "That really is a—?"

"Yes, damn it! What's the—?!"

"It's Thursday, about three in the morning," McCloskey said in a hollow voice.

Less than twenty-four hours. That got me back up on my feet. Frank Palorino reached for my arm, but I shook him off. "We can't wait on the telephone company," I said, looking at Garth, who nodded in agreement. "And you can't wait for the feds to deactivate that thing. Have your best people get up here to look at it; it may be just a radio receiving antenna that has to be disconnected."

"We have people who can do that," Palorino said tightly. "When is it set to go off, Mongo?"

"Midnight—tonight. None of you guys saw or picked up a pair of sneakers on your way up here, did you?"

"Huh?"

"Never mind. Lieutenant, if the phones aren't working, then we have to start right now thinking of how we're going to get to the outskirts of Boise, Idaho. That's where the radio transmitter is located. Unless we can destroy that transmitter, at midnight tonight a signal is going to be relayed from a satellite and at least two other bombs like this one, and maybe more, are going to go off."

McCloskey, recovered from his initial shock but somehow looking even more stricken, strode stiffly to the end of the room. He grabbed a section of the heavy gray drapes with both hands and yanked. The material tore loose from its fastenings and billowed like a parachute as it fell to the floor. In the faint light spilling from the room out into the night it was possible to see huge flakes of snow swirling in a maelstrom of wind, which could now clearly be heard through the section of thick glass where the drapes had been torn away. The lights in the triplex, I realized, had to be powered by an emergency generator which had automatically kicked in when city power had gone off, for out in the night there was nothing, not a single light to be seen.

"This started yesterday, around six in the evening," McCloskey said in a tortured voice. "It's a freak storm that none of the meteorologists predicted; it's only been getting worse, and nobody is really sure when it's going to let up. The last I heard, some of the experts were predicting that it could last another day. People are saying it's the worst blizzard in a century—maybe the worst blizzard we've ever had. It's blanketed the whole east coast. We're under four feet of snow so far, and Washington has five. Nothing's moving, and all communications are out."

"And yet you came up here looking for us," Garth said quietly.

McCloskey shrugged, and seemed slightly embarrassed. "We came over on snowmobiles. I had a notion. I'd tried to call Nuvironment before the storm hit, so you might say that I had the two of you on my mind." He paused, looked hard at me, continued, "You're not the only one who was haunted by what was done to Kenecky, Frederickson. I admit I dragged my feet at the beginning; I was afraid of what could happen to me. But then I realized that what I was doing to myself was worse; I was letting you guys do my job for me, and I found I couldn't live with that. I was ashamed—and I wasn't about to keep being ashamed. After all the things you'd said to me, there was no way I was going to pass into retirement with the deaths of the Fredericksons on my conscience. I had to try to make up for lost time. Frank and the others volunteered to come with me."

"You came up here on your own hook?"

Again, McCloskey shrugged. "Kind of."

"Well, Lieutenant, now there's even more to be afraid of. We have to get to the airport—JFK, not La Guardia."

McCloskey stared at me in disbelief. "That's impossible," he said at last. "Even if there was enough gas in the snow-mobiles to get us there—"

Garth said, "We'll siphon the gas we need from stalled cars along the way."

"Jesus Christ, Frederickson. Even if we could get out there, what good do you think it would do? Nothing—*nothing* —can fly out of there. I heard what you said about the transmitter and the other bombs, but making some insane gesture is no answer." He paused, shook his head in consternation, then pointed to me. "Your brother could *die* out there, Frederickson. Look at him; he hasn't even got any fucking shoes!"

Garth moved closer to me and draped an arm across my shoulders. "I know I can't stop him, McCloskey," he said evenly, "and I'm not going to waste my time trying."

"My brother's right, Lieutenant," I said, drawing myself up straight. I was glad Garth was next to me, because I felt very faint. "I'm not going to die of a cold, but a whole lot of people are going to die in nuclear blasts if somebody doesn't shut down that transmitter."

"But you can't go anywhere, Frederickson. Don't you understand? Nothing can fly in this blizzard. We have no choice but to wait until communications are restored. Then you can make your call to Washington."

One of the paramedics handed each of us a blanket. Garth draped his over his arm. My teeth had begun to chatter, and I wrapped my blanket around me. I had the distinct impression from the look on Garth's face that he was about to walk out, commandeer a snowmobile, and be on his way. But I felt we needed McCloskey, needed the official power he represented.

"You're the one who doesn't understand, Lieutenant," I said, deciding that it was up to me to explain Garth's perfectly correct point. "Do you know when the phones are going to come back on line? You said you didn't. We have about twenty hours to work at getting that transmitter deactivated. It's essential that we keep moving, at all costs, toward that goal; when there's nothing else to be done, that movement has to be physical. We can keep checking on our way. If and when communications are restored in the city, and between here and Washington, then either Garth or I will make two calls. We can make direct contact with the president of the United States, probably, or with the Director of the Defense Intelligence Agency, for sure. Okay? You'll agree that nobody can get things moving faster than either one of those two gentlemen. As much force as is needed will be immediately directed at that site in Idaho, and the transmitter is long gone. But we need a second option in case the storm doesn't let up and we can't make those calls. If we can make it to the airport, and there's a break in the storm, it just might be possible to get into the air. Then *somebody*, at least, will be on the way to Idaho. The bombs are going off at midnight, Lieutenant. If there's even a *chance* that we—and maybe only we—can get to the transmitter, can you refuse to try? We've got to be on the move. Time is all-important. Would you like to be five seconds late? One second?"

"Mongo and Garth are right, sir," Frank Palorino said quietly. "We've got to go for it, even if it does seem impossible. You coordinate the bomb deactivation here, and Harry and I will take off with these two guys to JFK. Mongo's right about JFK too; if we can get off the ground, we'll need the biggest, fastest plane we can find.''

"I'm going," McCloskey said tersely.

"You're needed here, Lieutenant," Garth said. "If this thing behind us isn't defused properly, New York City and all the people in it, as well as most of the people in the surrounding counties, are gone. Your badge and rank may be needed to get people listening and moving.''

"You'll need my badge and rank at the airport, Frederickson —that is, unless you think you can commandeer and fly an airplane out of there on your own.'' He paused, turned to the second patrolman, a very young man who had been listening to our conversation intently with a pale face but firmly set jaw. "Harry, can you take care of business here?''

The young patrolman named Harry swallowed hard, then took his walkie-talkie from his belt and gripped it so hard that his knuckles turned white. "I certainly can, sir," he said in a strong voice. "I guarantee you I'll get people listening and moving. I've got a wife and two kids living here.''

"Then get to it.''

As the patrolman hurried out of the room, I turned to the female paramedic. "I need something that will keep me on my feet, maybe for as long as twenty hours. After that, it doesn't matter how hard I crash; I can spend as much time as I need to in a hospital. But now I need to keep moving. Do you understand?''

"Me, too," Garth said.

The paramedic looked at McCloskey, who nodded. The woman reached into her satchel, removed a hypodermic needle and a transparent plastic bottle filled with large green pills. "This will reduce your fever for a time," she said to me, indicating the needle. "The pills are for both of you.''

"Amphetamines?" I asked.

The woman nodded. "I'll give you the bottle—but you really have to be careful with them. We use them with some heart attack and shock victims; they're fast-acting, and very potent. The usual dosage is one—not to be followed by another for four to six hours. They'll keep you on your feet, all right—but you're going to pay a heavy price if you take too much of this stuff, or use it for too long.''

"Got it," I said, taking the bottle from her. I popped open the cap, shook out one of the green pills, and swallowed it as the paramedic rolled up my sleeve, daubed my shoulder with alcohol, then gave me an injection of what I assumed was some antibiotic.

"I'm all right for now," Garth said, shaking his head when I offered him the bottle. "I'll take one later if I need it."

I put the bottle of pills in the pocket of my jeans. Another paramedic had removed two packets from his valise; he gave one to Garth, one to me. I ripped open the plastic and found myself holding what I recognized as one of the silver-colored heat wraps developed by NASA—it was very lightweight, but would have astounding insulating properties.

"These should help keep you warm," the man said. "Just wrap them around yourselves, and keep them closed as much as possible."

Garth and I nodded our thanks, then hurried out the door after McCloskey and Frank Palorino. The amphetamine was already starting to kick in; it was putting strength in my legs, but I felt giddy, with a strong metallic taste in the back of my mouth.

"How are you feeling?" Garth asked as we followed the two policemen down a corridor I hadn't had time to explore.

"Don't ask—but the answer is probably no worse than you."

Garth grunted. "I didn't take a dunking through the ice in the Hudson," he said in a low voice. "Maybe you should take a pass on this, brother. It's not going to do anybody any good if you fall off a snowmobile in our travels. You know I'm not going to leave you behind; but if you agree to stay here, you'd be in a position to get right through to Kevin Shannon or Mr. Lippitt as soon as the telephones come back on line."

"No. You had it right the first time. Either of us can call Shannon or Mr. Lippitt anywhere along the line. I won't fall off any snowmobile—and I won't slow us down; if I do think I'm slowing us down, then I'll bail out the first chance I get. There must be emergency shelters all over the place. In the meantime, all I have to do is keep truckin' along for a few hours. After that, it won't make much difference, will it? At least not for millions of other people."

"Okay," Garth replied simply.

I'd hoped to have time to look for my sneakers and my Seecamp, but we were going out another way and, as I myself had pointed out, at the end seconds could count. I, at least, was wearing heavy wool socks, and I knew I was just going to have to make do.

There was another elevator at the end of the corridor, and it took us express all the way down to street level. It opened into a wood-paneled vestibule; three doors—smashed in by McCloskey on his way to our rescue—later, we were out on Fifth Avenue, which I barely recognized.

Wind screamed all around us, and in the whipping, swirling gusts of snow we could barely see each other. Garth wrapped the silver, life-preserving shroud tightly around me, then lifted me up in his arms in order to keep my stocking-clad feet out of the snow. We might have been somewhere in a blizzard-whipped Arctic, except for the huge, towering black shapes of surrounding buildings which occasionally came into view when the wind shifted. Off to our right, McCloskey and Palorino were conferring with three parka-clad policemen. When they had finished, the three men nodded, then walked away, quickly disappearing into the blinding snow. A few moments later we heard an approaching roar, and then we were surrounded by men on snowmobiles. McCloskey and Palorino replaced two of the drivers. At McCloskey's signal, Garth sat me down on the seat behind Palorino; I pulled my feet up as far as possible, adjusted my silver shroud, then wrapped my arms tightly around his waist, burying my bare hands in the deep pockets of his down-filled parka. Garth climbed on behind McCloskey, and then we were off in a roar of unmuffled engines.

Speeding, bumping, sliding, carving through the Arctic night that had somehow descended over New York City, I was completely disoriented. I knew where we had to go, and how to get there, but it was as if the world had been turned upside down, and the swirling white made it impossible—for me, at least—to tell direction. But McCloskey and Palorino somehow managed to keep going. Occasionally we swerved sharply, or flew through the air; after a few of these tricky ground and aerial maneuvers, I realized that we were running an obstacle course of abandoned cars that were three-quarters buried in the snow. With my cheek pressed tightly against Frank Palorino's back, I could see only to my right, and, although we were making our way through midtown Manhattan, I could not make out a single landmark through the slit in my silver wrapping. I wasn't exactly warm; but, with Palorino's body acting as a wind screen, I wasn't exactly cold, either, and I knew that I would be all right as long as I kept the foillike material wrapped around me. I felt like a candy bar. Oddly enough, my feet were giving me the most problems—not from cold, but from the heat from the manifold on which I was resting them; I kept pulling them up and trying to lock my knees against the front of the carriage rack.

The amphetamine and antibiotic injection notwithstanding, I kept passing out for brief but dangerous periods; wrapped in my thin cocoon in a world of darkness, I kept segueing in and out of semiconsciousness. Every once in a while I was conscious of Palorino's hand on my hip or thigh as he reached back to make certain I was still centered on the seat behind him. Once I woke up to find that we had stopped, and we were surrounded by a number of National Guardsmen who were talking to us excitedly—nodding, gesturing, pointing. There was the acrid smell of gasoline, and then the delicious aroma of coffee right under my nose. I grabbed at the Styrofoam container and drank greedily, burning my tongue and the roof of my mouth and not caring. Then came the deafening roar of the motors, and we were once again on our way.

Sometimes I dreamed fever dreams, and in one of my dreams I glimpsed a great silver object in the snow, white on white, a potential weapon in our thus far decidedly one-sided battle against insane men and mindless nature. "SST!" I shouted against the thick material of Frank Palorino's parka. "SST!"

But Palorino couldn't hear me over the roar of the engine, or maybe I was only dreaming that I was shouting, because there was no response. Time lost meaning, and I just focused all my attention on the need to hang on to my driver. Once when I woke up, my surroundings seemed clearer, and I realized that it was dawn. I drifted back to sleep.

14.

I awoke with a start, started to sit up, and grabbed at my head as a sharp pain shot through my skull. For a moment I couldn't figure out where I was or what had happened—and then I remembered. I sat up straight, ignoring the pain in my head, and looked around me. It took me a few moments to orient myself, and then I realized that I was alone on the backseat of an olive-drab-colored National Guard Sno-Cat, which had been left with the motor running and the heater turned on full blast. Above the steady, throaty growl of the Sno-Cat's engine, I could hear wind screaming outside the frosted Plexiglas windows. The storm had not let up, but the milky light pouring in through the windows told me that it was day. I glanced at my watch, then realized that it had been thoroughly disabled during my tussle and dousing with Tanker Thompson.

Cursing under my breath, I yanked on the door handle and pushed open the door with my shoulder; the door was promptly caught and yanked back off its hinges by a powerful gust of wind. I stuck out my head, squinted against the swirling snow; the Sno-Cat, along with the two snowmobiles we had been riding on, was parked atop a massive snowdrift near the entrance to the control tower at John F. Kennedy International Airport. Still cursing Garth for leaving me behind, I eased back into the interior of the Sno-Cat to take stock of myself. I felt groggy, to be sure, but I thought that my fever might be down. I took the plastic bottle of amphetamines out of my pocket, shook out one of the green pills, and swallowed it. Then I rewrapped myself in my foil shroud, slid back across the seat, and fell out into the snow. I slid down the face of the drift on my back, got up, hippety-hopped and waded through the snow in my stocking feet to the entrance to the control tower. I went through the door, paused long enough to brush as much snow as I could off my socks, then hurried up the stairs.

I found Garth, McCloskey, Palorino, and two National Guardsmen up in the glass dome at the top of the control tower talking to two unshaven, obviously exhausted air traffic controllers who kept shaking their heads and gesturing out the windows.

Garth turned and saw me as I came through the door. "Mongo!"

"What time is it?"

"Four o'clock," Garth said quietly.

Eight hours left.

"Are the telephones working?"

Garth shook his head.

"We can't wait."

"Mongo, there's nothing we can do but wait and hope," McCloskey replied in a weary voice. His eyes were bloodshot, and there were dark circles around them. "Nothing can get out of here; even if it could, it's debatable whether we could get to Idaho in time to do anything. Our only hope is that we'll get telephone communications back in time for the Air Force to send planes to find and destroy the place."

"There's at least one child in there, McCloskey," Garth said evenly, "and probably more. If you bomb Eden, you'll kill children."

The muscles in McCloskey's jaw clenched, and he looked away. "I know that—but it won't be my decision. That's certainly what they'll have to do. It's the only course of action that makes sense. You said you don't know exactly where Eden is, and you don't even know where the transmitter is inside Eden. The Air Force certainly isn't going to want to waste time looking for it; there's too much risk, and too little time."

"There's already too little time for us to waste any of it standing around here and having this conversation," I said. "The place to establish communications is in the air, away from this storm. There'll at least be military planes in the air. We can communicate with them, and they'll find a way to get through to Shannon or Mr. Lippitt."

"For Christ's sake, Frederickson, you've got eyes! Can't you see what's going on out there?!"

I turned to one of the air traffic controllers, a slight, blue-eyed man with blond hair that was now greasy and plastered to his forehead. "The Concorde. Does Air France or British Airways have one parked here now?"

The blue-eyed man looked at his equally disheveled companion, who nodded. "Yes," he said, turning back to me. "British Airways—it was the last plane in before we closed down the airport. But I don't see how . . . Even if the captain agreed to make the attempt, it would be suicidal to try to take off in this storm. The wind shear factors alone would be almost beyond belief, and—"

"Where are the captain and his crew staying?!" I snapped, grabbing Garth's wrist and bending it around in order to look at his watch. It was 4:28.

"The International Hotel, up the way."

"I know where it is," I replied, turning to the senior

National Guardsman. "Captain, do you suppose you could round up some of your men and plow out a corridor of sorts in front of the British Airways hangar?"

The guardsman looked at McCloskey, who nodded. "I can try," the guardsman replied tersely.

I said, "I don't want it plowed right down to the tarmac; it would only drift in again. See if you can level off the drifts and leave a cushion of, say, two or three feet. The path should be at least as wide as the hangar doors, and as long as you can make it. And make sure there are no buried planes or machinery out there. Okay?"

"I'll do my best, Frederickson. Good luck to you guys."

"And to you." I turned back to the blue-eyed air traffic controller. "Can I borrow your watch?"

Without a word, the man removed the stainless steel watch from his wrist, handed it to me. I put it on.

"Let's get going," Garth said. "We've got to get up the road to the hotel."

Leaving the two stunned air traffic controllers staring after us, the two policemen, Garth, and I hurried back down the stairs. Once again Garth picked me up and carried me up the side of the drift to one of the two snowmobiles. It was almost completely dark now, and I huddled in my silver wrap behind Frank Palorino as the snowmobile engines roared to life and we raced ahead through the blizzard.

The International Hotel was bathed in a dim, eerie glow, the power supplied by emergency generators which I was vaguely surprised to see were still working. We drove right up to the entrance, got off, and walked into a lobby that was overflowing with men, women, and children huddled in over-coats, blankets supplied by the Red Cross, whatever they could find. We went to the front desk, where McCloskey showed his shield to a weary-looking middle-aged man who looked about to fall asleep on his feet. McCloskey asked what room the British Airways captain was staying in, and after some fumbling through file cards the desk clerk found the information. The elevators had been shut down to conserve emergency power; we hurried up the stairs to the third floor, where Garth knocked on the door to Room 315.

I glanced at the loose-fitting watch the air traffic controller had given me; it was 5:30.

Six and a half hours.

The door was opened by a bleary-eyed, unshaven man in a thoroughly rumpled flight attendant's uniform. McCloskey showed the man his shield. The man turned on the light, and we stepped into the first of what was actually a suite of rooms in which all of the dozen or so crew and flight attendants of the British Airways Concorde were sleeping on beds, couches, in chairs, or on the floor. The attendant stepped over three snoring men on the floor, shook the shoulder of a man who was sleeping in a chair with a yellow blanket wrapped around him. He stirred; the attendant whispered something in his ear, and he sat up quickly, then stood up.

The man was about six feet tall, with sharp features, deep brown eyes, and a firm set to his jaw and mouth. Even dressed only in boxer shorts and an undershirt, he had the bearing of a man used to command.

"I'm Captain Jack Holloway," the man said as he came across the room to us. "Which of you is the police lieutenant?"

"I am," McCloskey said, and then proceeded to tell Captain Jack Holloway the purpose of our visit.

McCloskey spoke unhurriedly, but in a firm, clear voice as he related the events that had occurred in the past few days, concluding with his description of finding us strapped to a B-53 hydrogen bomb—which, by now, we hoped had been deactivated—in a penthouse suite at the top of a skyscraper in the middle of Manhattan, and the existence of at least two other such bombs, on opposite sides of the world, that would explode unless a way was found to destroy the transmitter that would send the signal to set them off.

By the time McCloskey had finished, all of the people in the suite were awake. Female crew members who had been sleeping in the other room were huddled just inside the doorway, eyes wide with shock and faces pale. One of the women suddenly began to sob uncontrollably.

"Captain," I said when McCloskey had finished, "the whole idea is to somehow find a way to get up in the air—high enough and far enough away from the storm so that Garth—my brother here—and I can make contact with certain powerful people we know in Washington; even if the phones there are still out—and we don't know that they are—there should still be lines of military communication that can be used. If we can get through to them, either of the two men will act as quickly as humanly possible to mobilize forces to infiltrate the structure that houses the transmitter, which is somewhere outside Boise, Idaho. But it's going to take time for us to get them the message, and it will take them time to get planes into the air, and then find the place. Time is something we're rapidly running out of."

"Are you sure of your information?" Holloway asked in a firm voice.

"Yes," Garth replied in an equally firm voice. "We all saw the bomb in Manhattan, and there's absolutely no reason to doubt the existence of at least two others—in Detroit, and near Israel."

I said, "Captain, right now there are men plowing snow in front of the hangar where your Concorde is parked. Not all of the snow—they're trying to plow it down to a level of two or three feet, enough to belly-slide on if that's what has to be done. My thinking is that if there's one plane that's sleek and powerful enough to slice its way up and out of this blizzard, it's the SST—if we can only get it going, and off the ground."

"And you think we might be able to do that by sliding the plane on its belly in the snow?" Holloway asked evenly.

"You're the only man who can answer that."

"It's impossible, Captain," a very thin, tall man standing over in a corner said in a tense voice. "Even if you could gain enough speed to lift off the ground, which is unlikely, the wind shear out there would certainly tip your wings, or even slam you right back into the ground. It would be suicide to even try."

I swallowed hard, licked my cracked lips. "Is that right, Captain?"

Jack Holloway drew back his shoulders and adjusted his boxer shorts. "Frankly," he announced in his clipped British accent, "the odds of us even getting off the ground before we tip over and explode are not at all favorable."

"Captain," I said with a heavy sigh, "naturally, we have no right to—"

"But we must attempt it, of course," Holloway continued as if I hadn't spoken. "After all, the lives of millions of people depend on us, no?"

"Yes," Garth said softly. "You're a good man, Captain."

"Captain Holloway," one of the women in the doorway said, "I'll go."

There was a chorus of murmured assents as every member of the British crew started forward and pressed around us.

Holloway held up his hand, and everyone fell silent. "That won't be necessary, Evelyn," he said in an even voice. "After all, we're not carrying the Queen, are we? None of you will be going on this trip."

"I will be going, sir," the tall, thin man who had described the attempt as impossible said. "Although it's possible for you to pilot the plane alone, that certainly won't increase your odds, will it? I suggest you could use a copilot and navigator."

Holloway's brows knit slightly as he thought about it. Finally he nodded. "Very well, Nigel," he said. "I do believe you're right. Gentlemen, this is Lieutenant Nigel Fickley, my copilot and navigator."

We all exchanged nods. Crew members brought the two men their uniforms, and they began to dress.

"Captain, what's your fuel situation?" I asked. "I understand yours was the last flight in before the airport shut down, so you didn't have time to refuel."

"That's correct," Holloway said as he carefully adjusted

his tie and brushed a speck of lint off his jacket. "But we have sufficient fuel to get up—if that's possible—and ride beyond the radius of the storm."

"Do you have enough fuel to get us to Idaho? It's about two thousand miles."

Holloway turned to his slim navigator, who gave a noncommittal shrug of his shoulders. "Perhaps we can scrape up some fuel somewhere in the terminal."

"Captain," Garth said, "I know it's asking a lot when you've already agreed to risk your life, but Mongo and I have to get to Boise, if we can. There's no telling how close a margin the Army and Air Force will be working on by the time we can get our message out and they can get mobilized. The logic of choosing the greatest good for the greatest number of people dictates that they'll just fly in and bomb the biosphere to bits if the time margin is too close. There's at least one innocent in there—a little girl. Mongo and I would like to try to get her out before the bombs fall, if that's what's going to happen."

"Even if the bombs end by falling on you?"

Garth's silence, our answer, was most eloquent.

"Well, then," Holloway said as he slipped on a fur-lined parka and zipped it up, "I guess we'll just have to find fuel, or coax sufficient mileage out of the aircraft, to get you to Idaho. We certainly won't have enough to get back, but I'm sure Her Majesty will understand. Shall we go and see how the plowing is coming along?"

"Just one more thing, Captain," Garth said. "We know you can fly an SST—probably by yourself, if you had to. Can you drive a snowmobile?"

Ah. I thought I had a pretty good idea why my brother had asked the question; I caught his eye, gave a curt nod of approval.

Holloway looked slightly taken aback. "Actually, we don't get that much snow in England."

"I can handle it, Garth," I said as I walked quickly to a

desk set against the opposite wall. I opened a drawer, took out a pad and a ballpoint pen.

"You can hardly stand up."

"I believe I can drive a snowmobile," Nigel Fickley announced. "I'm somewhat of a winter sports enthusiast, you might say."

"Hey, wait just a minute," Malachy McCloskey said, seeming slightly bewildered as he looked back and forth between Garth and me. "What the hell's the matter with the chauffeurs you've got? We can fit—"

That was all he managed to say before Garth hit him on the point of the jaw with his fist. It was a pretty good pop—what I estimated to be a half-hour punch.

"The man's scheduled to retire in a few hours," Garth said to a startled Frank Palorino as he caught the unconscious McCloskey and eased him down onto the floor. "He's got children and grandchildren. We could die in the plane—or in Idaho. There's no way he'd stay behind if we gave him the choice, but there's no reason for either of you to come along. Your jurisdiction ends if and when we get in the air, and it's better that the two of you stay here—first, to follow through to make sure they've deactivated that bomb back in Manhattan, and second, to make the necessary calls if we crash and explode. Don't think about it, Frank, because we know you want to come too. But you'd just be excess baggage."

"Here," I said, handing Palorino a slip of paper on which I had written two telephone numbers. "These are direct lines to the Director of the Defense Intelligence Agency and President Kevin Shannon. I've also written down a code word you use to make sure you get no hassle from anyone who may be answering the phones for them."

Palorino looked at the paper, shook his head. "Valhalla?"

"Tell whoever answers that this is a Valhalla priority."

"This will get me through to the president of the United States?" The policeman seemed stunned.

"Actually, the Director—Mr. Lippitt—is harder to get

hold of than Shannon, but that's neither here nor there.'' I paused, smiled thinly. "Have McCloskey tell them you got the numbers from the famous Fredericksons.''

"Let's go, Mongo,'' Garth said from where he, Holloway, and Fickley were standing by the door. "Schmooze later.''

Frank Palorino quickly unholstered his service revolver and gave it to me. Then he slipped McCloskey's automatic out of the unconscious detective's shoulder holster, handed it to Garth. "Take these,'' he said. "You may need them where you're going.''

"Mongo,'' Garth said tersely, "let's go.''

"Be right with you,'' I said, and turned to the flight attendant who had first volunteered to go up with us. She looked like she had the right size feet. "Evelyn, I don't suppose you have a pair of sneakers you could lend me, do you?''

Shod in a pair of pink sneakers that were only a tad too small for me, I hurried back out into the storm with Garth and the two British Airways pilots. Garth got on one of the snowmobiles, with Jack Holloway behind him, and I got on the second snowmobile behind Nigel Fickley, pulling the silver wrap tightly around me. Throughout the long night and day I'd been running on adrenaline and amphetamines, and I had almost forgotten just how weak I was. Now my mind and body reminded me. I suddenly experienced a wave of dizziness, and I came close to falling off the snowmobile. Garth seemed to be holding up just fine without stimulants, but I knew that I was perilously close to not being able to hang on unless I got a little chemical help. As Fickley fumbled with the starter switch, I groped in my pocket for the bottle of amphetamines, found it. I shook out two pills and swallowed them both. I'd just managed to get the bottle back into my pocket when the engines of both snowmobiles roared to life and we shot off into the gelid, snow-swept darkness.

The two pills hit me fast and hard. One thing was certain, I thought; I wasn't cold anymore. Nor was I hot with fever. I was alternately numb from head to toe, and then tingling. I wanted to throw up, but I didn't want to soil myself, and I was afraid that I'd fall off the snowmobile if I leaned out too far. Swallowing bitter bile, taking deep breaths of the frigid air through my nostrils, I cursed myself for taking two of the pills. In my desperate desire to be on stage at the final act, I'd placed myself in danger of falling into an empty orchestra pit where—because Garth would be concerned and distracted by my condition—I'd be worse than useless. I kept sucking in deep breaths, tried to will myself to remain conscious.

But the double dose of greenies was coursing through my system, addling my brain.

My world of darkness, driving snow, and wind rolled around a few times, and for a moment I thought the snowmobile had tipped over. But it was only my brains rolling around, and I somehow managed to keep my grip on the navigator's jacket and my pink sneaker–clad feet on the riding bar. Suddenly, without warning, the snowmobile ran up the side of a huge snowbank, flew through the air, then came down with a teeth-rattling jolt into a field of intense white light in which the rumble, clank, and grinding of gears of heavy machinery was even louder than the roar of the wind. We swooped across a wide swath of relatively flat, hard-packed snow, came to a stop in front of a soaring structure that, in my blurred field of vision, looked as high as a mountain, but was only a hangar. I rolled off the back of the snowmobile, fell into a mound of snow. I stuck my face into the icy powder, trying to clear my vision and my thoughts.

Strong hands gripped the back of my shirt and pulled me to my feet. I turned, found myself looking up into my brother's face.

"Mongo!" Garth cried in alarm. "What's the matter with you?! You're cross-eyed!"

I managed to mumble, "If you think my eyes are crossed, you should see the circuitry inside my head. What time is it? I can't see my watch."

"You lost your watch. It's six fifteen."

I hoped the fact that I couldn't keep a working watch on my wrist wasn't a bad omen. I stepped to the side, raised my hands to shield my eyes from the driving snow, looked out over the area in front of the hangar, and felt my heart constrict. The National Guardsmen had done a good job in mobilizing equipment and personnel, because I estimated that there were at least a dozen pieces of heavy machinery rumbling around in an attempt to clear a path in the snow. But it wasn't enough. I had no idea how long a runway an SST needed to take off, but it was certainly more than the hundred yards or so that the snow movers were operating in. And as soon as the plows moved farther out, snow blew and drifted back in behind them, accumulating at an alarming rate. Just in the few minutes I'd been standing in front of the hangar, huge flakes had collected on my hair, lashes, shoulders, and sneakers.

Less than six hours to Armageddon, and it was looking more and more like the second horseman out of Eden was going to be riding forth, killing untold millions in the initial explosion of his appearance and more untold millions in the radioactive wake of his passing. I clenched my fists in frustration, choked back a sob of grief and rage.

"We're not going to make it, Garth," I murmured, and immediately hated myself for saying it.

"Let's get you out of the cold, brother," Garth said, and started to haul me up the side of the snowbank.

I angrily shook off his grip—and promptly fell on my face in the snow. He grabbed me again, and half-pulled, half-carried me to the top of the mound of snow. We slid down the other side, found a door, went into the hangar. As soon as the steel door was shut, there was an almost eerie silence inside the cavernous space, which was filled with a ghostly, yellowish glow cast by spotlights powered by emergency generators.

In the center of the glow sat a magnificent, sleek airplane, its metal skin glistening in the light, its needle nose almost touching the closed hangar door. Even as I watched, two men in maintenance uniforms came around from the opposite side of the plane; they opened hatches under the rear of the fuselage, shone flashlights up into the compartments, checked hoses and dials.

Garth grabbed me as I started to sag, picked me up and carted me over to a corner, set me down on top of a pile of folded blue tarpaulins. I started to get up, but he put a hand on my chest and shoved me back down, covering me with a flap of the top tarpaulin.

"Rest, Mongo," Garth said in a low, firm voice. "You're going to need it. I've got a nose for other things besides evil, and it tells me that we're going to get up. I know it."

"It would take a miracle, Garth."

"We're going to make it."

"Garth, don't leave me behind."

"I won't, Mongo."

"Promise me."

"I promise."

"You know I have to be there, the same as you."

"I know."

"Promise again that you won't leave me behind."

"I promise again."

My brother didn't lie—not usually. But I didn't trust him; not this time, since he was certainly capable of lying—and leaving me on the ground—if he thought it would save my life. Consequently, I struggled to stay awake. The result was a kind of surreal semiconsciousness in which blurred images moved about, accompanied by the muffled howl of wind and roar of machinery.

Segueing in and out of consciousness, I suddenly heard something begin to whine; the whine quickly grew in volume until it became a roar of sound cascading against my senses. I came fully awake, panicky, afraid that the plane was about to take off without me. I sat bolt upright—and saw Garth hurrying across the hangar toward me. He looked exhausted, his brown eyes glassy and sunken deep in their sockets. At the same time, there was an almost eerie serenity reflected in his features.

"Ready to roll, brother?" he said softly, smiling down at me as he brushed a thin, greasy strand of wheat-colored hair back from his eyes.

"Oh, yeah." I struggled to get to my feet, fell off the pile of tarpaulins onto the concrete floor. I was feverish again, bone-deep exhausted, and still nauseated from the amphetamine overdose. "I'm sorry, Garth. Help me, please."

He did, pulling me to my feet and supporting me with one arm as we walked toward the ramp that was extended from the center of the SST's fuselage. I glanced at his watch; it was 9:00.

"The phones . . . ?"

"Still out."

"Did they manage to plow . . . ?"

"No. But we're going anyway."

With Garth supporting me by the back of my shirt, I managed to walk up the ramp and into the plane. Garth steered me left, through a thick steel door that Nigel Fickley was holding open for us, into a spacious cockpit that was in semidarkness except for the light cast by a glittering array of instrumentation that seemed to be all around me. Jack Holloway was strapped into the pilot's seat, and he gave a thumbs-up sign to me as we entered.

"Strap yourselves in, gentlemen," Holloway said in his clipped tones. "And please allow me to apologize in advance for what may be a slightly bumpy takeoff."

Garth and I sat down in two seats at the rear of the cockpit, on either side of the steel door, and strapped ourselves in. Nigel Fickley eased his lanky frame down into the copilot's seat, buckled himself in.

Holloway tilted his head back. "Ready, gentlemen?"

"Hit it, Captain," Garth replied evenly.

Holloway signaled to someone below him, and a few moments later the huge hangar door opened—onto a nightmare. In the glare carved out of the darkness by the plane's lights I could see that the snow-removing equipment had been removed—but it was almost as if nothing had changed; snow was everywhere, and I knew that in the darkness beyond the light there were huge drifts. Also, undoubtedly, there were trucks, perhaps even stalled planes—dozens of snowbound, buried obstacles that could kill us.

Holloway pushed the wide handle of the throttle forward, and I could feel as well as hear the power surging through the plane. But we didn't move.

"Release the brakes on my mark, Lieutenant, and raise the landing gear on my second mark."

"Yes, sir," Fickley said easily. "Luck."

"Luck."

Holloway eased the throttle even further forward, and the roar of the engines grew in volume; the plane began to vibrate as tens of thousands of horsepower howled in a kind of mechanical dismay and outrage, demanding that their awesome power be unleashed.

"Mark!"

"Aye!"

The screaming, gargantuan silver bullet that was the Concorde shot out of the mouth of the hangar into the maelstrom of night, wind, and snow.

"Mark!"

"Aye!"

For the first few seconds, before the landing gear came up into the belly of the plane, there was tremendous drag on the plane as the wheels ground through the snow. The muscles in Holloway's forearms bunched and stood out as he pulled back on a control. Then the wheels were up and the SST became an improbable ballistic sled catapulting us out across unknown territory.

Suddenly I suffered another dizzy spell; my vision blurred, and the cockpit began to spin. I screwed my eyes shut, opened them again just as the plane began to sideslip, its tail yawing over to the left. Holloway, his hands virtually flying from one control to another, struggled for control. I felt as if

I were hurtling down a roller coaster, and I was afraid I would vomit. The plane yawed sharply in the opposite direction, shuddered, then finally straightened out and shot forward with even greater speed; but now I was certain it was heading in a different direction, toward—whatever. Dark, terrifying black shapes that I was certain were planes or trucks or hangars flashed by, and great waves of snow splashed like water against the windows as we sliced through huge snow drifts. Again the plane yawed from side to side, again Holloway managed to correct.

Again, everything began to spin—but this time I was certain it was the plane itself, and not my head. We were out of control. The last thought in my head before everything exploded in brilliant flashes of red, black, and green was that this time Garth's nose had been wrong. We were about to die, only a couple of hours ahead of millions of other people.

15.

''HEY, Mongo. Wake up.''

Somebody, undoubtedly Garth, had unbuckled my seat belt, and I sat upright. My brother pushed me back into the seat, handed me a plastic cup filled with something that was redolent with the delicious aroma of, of all things, fresh coffee.

''What—?! Garth, what—?!''

''It's all right. Just sit back, relax, and think of me as your happy steward. I was a bit worried about you; your face was the color of those pills when you passed out. I do believe you're looking better now.''

''I feel better,'' I said, sipping at the steaming coffee. It hit my stomach, spreading a warm, tingling glow throughout my body. The coffee was very sweet. ''You look terrible.''

"Now I'm ready for one of those pills. You got the bottle?"

I dug the bottle out of my pocket, handed it to him. He shook out one of the amphetamines, swallowed it with his coffee. When he proffered the bottle back to me, I shook my head. I'd had enough of the greenies, and would now settle for whatever energy I could get out of the sugar in the coffee. For however long we had left.

"What time is it?"

"Ten thirty."

"Could you get through to Lippitt or Shannon?"

"Yes. You passed out on us, so you missed the takeoff. Once we got off the ground, our good captain here took us right out over the ocean, and up. We cleared the storm in minutes. It was quite a ride."

"I'm just as happy I slept through it, because I certainly didn't care for the first part. But you did get through?"

Garth smiled. "I said I did. To both of them."

"And?"

"They're working on it."

"What the hell does that mean?"

"Lippitt brought up a good point, Mongo. We may have a problem."

I pushed Garth's hand aside, sat up on the edge of my seat. "What would that be?"

"First, he pointed out that the signal could be sent out manually—before midnight, Eastern Time—if the people inside that biosphere get wind that somebody's trying to interfere with their plans."

"You said Thompson and the other two ex-jocks told you they didn't know where the transmitter was."

"Other people will. Vicky Brown's father is a caretaker; he knows. A lot of people could know. We have to assume that every single person in there is as loony as the creeps we've run into, and just as dedicated to their Armageddon fantasy. Lippitt argues—and I agree with him—that somebody in there might just traipse off and trip off the transmitter prematurely if an Army battalion comes knocking at their door."

"Oh, Christ, you mean they're just going to go ahead and bomb the place with everybody in it?"

"No—not yet. He also pointed out that there's no guarantee that the initial bomb run would destroy everyone, or the transmitter. Assuming the transmitter can be manually operated, and somebody gets to it, that's the ball game. Ten acres is a lot of area; if the first bombs don't destroy the transmitter, the shocks might trip it."

I licked my lips, swallowed hard. "What about . . . something nuclear?"

Garth shook his head. "I didn't even ask, and Lippitt didn't bring it up. If that's an option, he'll be talking it over with Shannon. Eden may be too close to Boise."

"So it's up to us."

"Right. Lippitt is counting on us to get in there, find the transmitter, and shut it down. It means we have a chance to save the girl."

I thought about it, shook my head. "Shit, Garth. That's too much responsibility. What if we can't find the transmitter?"

"The bombers start their run at five minutes to midnight, Eastern Time. If we're not out of there by then, we've celebrated our last New Year's Eve."

"What did you tell him?"

Again, Garth smiled. "I told him we'd take care of it, naturally, and that he should have somebody bring along a bottle of bourbon and a bottle of Scotch."

"That's cute, brother," I said tersely as I grabbed his wrist and twisted it around in order to glance at his watch. It was 10:40. "How long before we get to Idaho?"

"The captain tells me we're there—have been for the last ten minutes. That's why I woke you up. It seems we're sort of circling around the borders of the state. This is an SST, remember? They're trying to find the place, which isn't the easiest thing to do from this high in the sky, at night."

"Come here, Mongo—if I may call you Mongo," Jack

Holloway called over his shoulder. "I have something to show you."

"You can call me anything you want, Captain," I said, rising and walking to the front of the cockpit, where I squeezed the shoulders of Holloway and Nigel Fickley. "Damn, you guys are good. Thank you both."

Holloway made a self-deprecating gesture with his right hand, then indicated a small scope that the copilot and navigator was hunched over. "Show them, Nigel."

"That's a satellite tracking beacon," the lanky copilot said, placing his finger on the green, flickering screen directly over a thin pencil line of light that was just barely discernible among a cluster of specks and lines of light. "It's possible that we're wrong, but the captain and I think that's a reference beam from the biosphere to the satellite. There are a number of military installations in this general area, but their reference beams have a particular 'signature' that isn't evident here."

"You get all that from that screen you're looking at?" I asked the navigator, making no effort to mask the awe—and a touch of disbelief—I felt.

"That, and certain other instrumentation. Anyway, the signal is emanating from a site a few miles outside of Boise. We've checked, and there are no broadcast stations, military installations, or commercial ventures that might use satellite facilities. That, and the fact that the satellite the beam is locked onto belongs to a private company, lead us to believe that the signal may be coming from the biosphere you say is down there."

"Who owns the satellite?" I asked tightly.

"Blaisdel Industries," Garth said quietly from behind me. "We checked it out with the F.C.C."

"Jesus Christ. That's the one."

"Let us hope so," Jack Holloway said dryly, "because that's the signal we're homing in on, and we're almost out of fuel. We're way below safety regulations, really."

"When are we going down?"

"Now," Holloway said, and banked to the left as he eased up on the throttle. The horizon line on the screen directly in front of him began to rise slightly. "You have a decision to make. With that signal to home in on, we can virtually land on top of the facility. But we need considerable runway space—"

"Are you going to be able to bring this down in the desert?"

"You're assuming that's desert down there, and that there are no trees or rock outcroppings to run into. That's impossible to tell at this point. In any case, we'll just have to do our best. But you must tell us how close you want to be taxied in. I understood from the conversation Garth had with your friends in Washington that there's concern over our presence being noted."

"How much noise does this plane make when it's taxiing, Captain?"

"There'll be a high-pitched whine, but there are steps we can take to minimize it. Depending on the terrain, we may be able to coast a quarter mile or so with the power off; it will require timing, and good visibility on the ground."

I felt a large, familiar hand on my shoulder, and then Garth leaned over me to speak to Holloway. "I realize it's dangerous, Captain, but I think it would be best to try to land some distance away, then slowly taxi in as close as you can without any lights. Mongo and I just don't have the time or energy to jog too far on the ground."

"You've got it," Holloway replied evenly as he banked the plane even more and began a steeper descent. "Buckle up, then lean forward as far as you can and brace yourselves."

"How long, Captain?" Garth asked.

"About a minute—and I have no idea how rough it's going to be."

As Garth and I sat down and buckled our seat belts, I glanced out the windows and saw nothing but darkness. "Where the hell is it? They must have lights in the place."

"There's still a thin layer of cloud cover below us," Nigel

Fickley replied over his shoulder. "When we pass through the clouds, it will be about a hundred miles to the west—your right."

"We'll go subsonic in a few moments so as not to warn them with a sonic boom," Jack Holloway said. "About . . . now."

There was no indication inside the cockpit that we had slowed below the speed of sound, but a few seconds later we emerged from the clouds and, far in the distance, I could see a cluster of lights that I assumed was Boise. Slightly closer, appearing just off the plane's wingtip, a faint, greenish-yellow blob stood out from the blackness of the desert. The blob vanished beneath the body of the plane as Holloway banked and made another sharp turn, then came back once again. Now the blob was clearly visible—much larger—through the front windshield. I was astonished at how far we had traveled in only seconds, and how close we were to the ground; even from where I was sitting, I could see that the guidelines on the horizon indicator were only a fraction of an inch apart.

"Brace!" Holloway barked.

The landing gear touched ground; we bounced slightly, landed again, and the plane began to vibrate. Just before Holloway cut off the power and the lights I could see apparently open desert, its seeming flatness belied by the clatter of the Concorde as we rolled over it. The greenish-yellow light kept coming closer, and gradually became a mammoth dome that reminded me of nothing so much as a huge fluorescent light bulb. Finally the plane shuddered, and came to a stop. As far as I was concerned, Jack Holloway and Nigel Fickley were magicians; I estimated that we were no more than three or four hundred yards from the sickly green plastic hemisphere that was Eden.

"Christ," Fickley murmured, wiping sweat from his forehead with his forearm, "I wouldn't have thought it possible to do that; we take off in a blizzard, than land virtually blind on an unknown surface. I can't believe we're not dead."

Jack Holloway slowly unclenched his fingers from the controls, sucked in a deep breath as he leaned back in his seat, slowly exhaled. "Well, I think this is as close as I can get you," he announced in his clipped accent. "Sorry I couldn't get you to the door."

"This is as good as the door," Garth said as we both took out the guns Frank Palorino had given us, checked the magazines and chambers. I noted that he had found the time to tape his sprained left wrist, and it didn't seem to be bothering him.

"I'm going with you," Holloway said, and started to get out of his seat.

"No," Garth said softly but firmly as he laid a hand on the pilot's shoulder. "There's nothing either you or Nigel can do that Mongo and I can't handle. It will take both of you to get this thing off the ground if the bombs do start falling. Also, we need you here to establish communications with those fighter-bombers if and when they have to come in."

"Frederickson, I can't let the two of you go in there by yourselves. It just isn't done!"

"The captain's correct," Nigel Fickley said, and started to unbuckle his seat belt. "We're both—"

Something in Garth's face—or perhaps the memory of how Garth had arranged for Malachy McCloskey to miss the trip—caused the slender copilot abruptly to stop speaking and slowly sink back into his seat.

"The fewer of us there are in there," Garth said in the same firm voice, "the fewer people there are for those lunatics to spot. The two of you stay here, get back up in the air if we're not back by, say, five minutes to midnight. Make it ten; leave at ten minutes to the hour, and provide a tracking beacon for the bombers. Mongo and I have done this kind of thing before, and you'd only be in the way. Captain, can you find us a crowbar, or something else that we can cut or smash with?"

"Just a minute," Fickley said as he rose from his seat and hurried out of the cabin. He was back in a few moments with a small but heavy fire extinguisher. "Will this do for smashing?"

"It will have to," Garth said, taking the fire extinguisher. "Jack, let us out of here."

The captain flicked two switches on the console to his left. I heard a door open behind me, and then a *whomp* as an emergency escape chute was deployed and inflated. I glanced at Garth's watch as we hurried back to the exit: it was 11:03. As I jumped onto the air bag and slid to the ground behind my brother, I found that my head and vision were clear; the cold night air in my face was invigorating. I no longer felt feverish, and now, at least for the time being, my legs felt strong.

Perhaps, I thought as I hit the ground and, with Garth beside me, came up running toward the massive, glowing structure, my heightened sense of concentration and newfound energy might somehow be connected to the fact that Garth and I could have less than an hour left in our lives.

The assault on Eden had begun. Santa Claus and helper were coming to town.

16.

IN moments we had reached the base of Eden, which was a wall of concrete five feet high. We crouched in the darkness, just below the eerie green, chemically or solar-cell produced light that seeped out of the translucent plastic dome that covered the vast expanse of the biosphere.

"How are you holding up?" Garth asked.

"Okay. You?"

"Okay. Decision time."

"I know. If this thing was built to the same scale and

design as the model I saw, we should be just outside the desert region. The living quarters will be in the first arm, which is a good way up. Where do we go in?''

"What do you say, Mongo?"

I thought about it, said: "It's too risky to try to break right into the living quarters. Hell, we could end up falling in through Tanker Thompson's window and into his lap, which is grief we don't need. Besides, I doubt that the transmitter is anywhere in the living quarters section, or Thompson would have known where it was. If the transmitter is someplace else, then it doesn't make any difference where we break in and start looking, because one place is as good as another. I say we go in here, and check out the terrain as we make our way toward the living quarters."

"Agreed," Garth said, and swung the fire extinguisher full force at the plastic material that rose from the concrete wall.

The steel cylinder struck the plastic and rebounded like a tumbler on a trampoline, almost pulling Garth off his feet.

"Shit," I said. "That's reinforced Plexiglas. It's going to be a bitch to break."

Garth took a deep breath, gripped the handle of the fire extinguisher with both hands, and swung again—with the same results. I grabbed his wrist, looked at his watch: it was 11:11.

"Come on," I said, tugging at my brother's sleeve. "We don't have time for this. We're going to have to look for the front door."

"No," Garth replied curtly as he took McCloskey's automatic out of his pocket and slipped off the safety catch. "We could waste time looking, make just as much noise going in there as here, and possibly warn them. Let me see if I can't weaken the shield with a bullet or two."

Garth fired two bullets, spaced closely together, into the Plexiglas. I knew that the thickness of the shield would undoubtedly muffle the sound, but I still winced each time the gun went off. Again he smashed the steel cylinder into the plastic, just below the two holes; and again. A slight crack had appeared, but the material still held firm.

His watch read 11:13.

Garth raised his gun again, but I grabbed his arm and shoved Frank Palorino's revolver at him. "Here, use two from mine. We don't have any spare ammunition, and neither one of us can afford to have an empty gun."

Garth nodded, pocketed his automatic, and used the revolver to fire two more shots into the Plexiglas, just below the first two. Then he banged the end of the fire extinguisher into the center of the rectangle formed by the four holes. The material cracked further—and parted. Three more whacks, and there was a hole big enough for a man to crawl through.

"Up, up, and away," Garth said, crouching slightly and cupping his hands together at the level of his knees.

I tucked the revolver, which Garth had given back to me, in the waistband of my jeans, took two steps backward, then ran forward, jumped, and planted my right foot in Garth's cupped hands. He gave me a moderate heave, and I sailed head first through the opening in the Plexiglas, prepared for the shock of landing on what I assumed would be hard-packed sand.

Wrong.

So much for relying on scale models, I thought as I landed in foul-smelling muck that almost immediately closed over my head as it began sucking me down. I fought against the slime, struggling to right myself, and finally felt my feet touch bottom. I stood up, found myself in blackish-brown mire that came up to my shoulders, gagged when I sucked in a breath. It seemed I had landed in the swamp—which was virtually a cesspool.

Something was definitely rotten in Eden; or it was Eden itself that was rotting. Blaisdel, Peter Patton and Company had missed an equation somewhere.

I checked my waistband to make certain the revolver was still there. It was—not that it was going to be much use, except maybe as a club; the firing mechanism would be hopelessly fouled with the lumpy slime.

"Watch out!" I called through cupped hands, shuddering

as I felt—or imagined I felt—something large, cold, and slimy slither across my back. "Forget the floor plan! It's a fucking swamp!"

Garth's head and shoulders appeared above me in the opening. He looked down at me, frowned. "You all right?"

"I'm all right, but my gun has to be fouled. Watch out for yours."

Garth nodded, then raised the automatic over his head and jumped into the mire beside me. Taller, and with more leverage, Garth was able to wade more easily through the muck, and I didn't object when he grabbed my arm and dragged me after him across the surface toward higher ground seventy-five yards or so away.

Blaisdel and his people had dreamed of building themselves the ultimate greenhouse, I thought as I gazed into the distance, and my first impression was that they'd wound up with the ultimate shithouse. I wondered how the people living there could stand it. The fetid air hanging over the swamp could not be that much better anywhere else in the biosphere; it was humid and cloying, and felt like wet wool in the lungs. The "sky" above Eden—the same sickly, dim green glow we had seen outside—was, I presumed, supposed to give some psychological satisfaction so that Eden's inhabitants would not be depressed by utter darkness in the absence of the sun, moon, and stars; I would have preferred darkness. It was hot—too hot—and I suspected that the inevitable greenhouse effect induced by the coated Plexiglas was considerably greater than the designers had anticipated, and would eventually become unbearable. Eden was no place to hang out during any Tribulation; Eden itself was a tribulation.

Perhaps a half mile away, the "sky" seemed to lighten and ripple slightly, and I suspected this might be a reflection from Eden's "ocean." Unless the whole biosphere had been redesigned, the living quarters would be in a separate arm or wing constructed on higher ground near the shore of the ocean.

Further in the distance, barely visible, there was what

appeared to be a heavy mist hanging like a diaphanous curtain from the ceiling to the ground. That would be the rain forest.

Somewhere in this vast, artificial, rotting world a machine was ticking away, preparing to send a signal that would trigger explosions that would kill tens of millions of people. Eden, indeed. Leaders like Blaisdel, William Kenecky, and Peter Patton, abetted by followers like Tanker Thompson, the Small brothers, Hector Velazian, Billy Dale Rokan, and Craig Valley, had always suffered their patently insane obsessions and superstitions, along with a desperate need to inflict their obsessions and superstitions on everyone else. I had always believed that at the bottom of every political and religious zealot's heart was a death wish. They were, in every sense of the word, enemies of humanity, creators of hell on earth, infecting generation after generation down through the centuries, their lineage of paranoia, hatred, and terrorism going all the way back to the dawn of humankind's tenure on earth. Henry Blaisdel and William Kenecky had presumed to go to the head of the class, and Garth and I had only minutes left to stop them.

We reached the edge of the swamp, scrambled up a bank of mushy ground that rose at a sharp angle, squatted down on the crest of a hill, and looked around us. The transmitter was obviously not in the swamp area we had just come through, and the light was too dim for us to see anything but large, general features on the ground. There was no time to search randomly through the biosphere, which meant that we were going to need help—and we needed it right away. Covered with slime, we began to jog at a fairly good clip in the direction of the living quarters. There were a number of filthy streams draining into the swamp; most we could jump over, but one we had to ford. Garth took care to hold his automatic high over his head, keeping it dry.

As we ran, we constantly scanned our surroundings; there was no sign of anything that resembled a transmitter.

The ground gradually rose and became firmer as we approached the area where the light above us was paler and shimmering. And then we reached the shore of the "ocean"—a sizable expanse of water that was perhaps a half to three-quarters of a mile wide, and about as long. Here the air was even heavier, and sweat ran in thick rivulets down our bodies as we gasped for breath. We took only moments to try to catch our breath, then headed along a narrow pathway by the retaining wall, toward a soaring archway that—we hoped—would be the entrance to the arm containing the group's living quarters.

At the edge of the arch we stopped, bent over double, and struggled to suck air into our lungs.

"What time is it?" I gasped.

"What difference does it make?" my brother replied, shaking his head. "Let's go."

We stepped around the edge of the archway and, keeping low, sprinted twenty yards to the edge of an orchard of sere, withering trees with remnants of fruit on them that was, like everything else in Eden, rotting; here, too, the air was tainted, sickly sweet. We hurried through the orchard, stopped when we came to the edge of a wide dirt road that ran the length of the area. Across the road were a number of cottages, all a uniform color that might once have been white, but was now gray.

In front of the cottage almost directly across from us was a red tricycle.

We could have only a few minutes left.

Millions of people . . .

And in, on, Eden, at any moment, bombs would start to fall . . .

But there was nothing to do but keep going.

Again keeping low, we sprinted across the road and into the shadows between two cabins, pressed up against the side of the cabin with the red tricycle in front of it. Once again we were gasping for air in the tainted atmosphere of Eden.

As we crossed the road I had caught a glimpse of Eden's place of worship—a church, or an obscene parody of a church, with a gray-white gabled front and a twisted swastika for a cross. The sight of the structure, placed here as it had been in the model, gave me a perverse sense of hope.

Houses of worship were the places where worshipers placed effigies of their gods, and the only real god these people worshiped was death.

"Did you . . . see . . . the church?"

Garth nodded, and from the expression on his face I could tell that he was thinking the same thoughts I was: the bombs would have to start falling at any moment. Indeed, I could hardly believe that the bombing run had not begun already. The alternative—that the planes had not been able to get into the air, and that at that very moment a radio signal was being sent that could ignite nuclear holocausts—was almost unthinkable.

I continued, "Do you suppose the transmitter could be in there?"

"I'm going to check it out."

"I'll go with you."

"No. At least you may be able to save the girl. You try to find her, then get her to someplace safe, if you can."

"Garth—"

"There's no time to argue, Mongo. Go get the child—and be safe."

And then he was gone, his running, mud-covered figure disappearing into the darkness of the shadows surrounding the cottages as he headed toward the swastika-crowned church down the road.

I sidled along the edge of the house, darted around the corner, went up the single step, and tried the front door. It was open. I eased myself into the darkened living room, quietly closed the door behind me until only a sliver of light was coming through, then looked around—and started.

Across the room, on a table set next to a half-closed door from which flickering candlelight emanated, the luminous dial of a clock radio glowed.

It was 10:10 in Idaho, Mountain Time.

In New York, the new year had already begun.

Mr. Lippitt's planes were too late.

Unless the radio transmitter was keyed to Mountain Time, and Lippitt had somehow found that out. But how could he?

All moot questions, I thought as I moved to the doorway, mud-filled revolver in my hand. I paused to clean some of the slime off the metal, hoping to make it at least look threatening, then peered around the edge of the door.

In the center of the room a young couple was kneeling in front of a small, makeshift altar on which a swastika-cross was flanked by two crimson candles. Both the man and woman were dressed in hooded white terry-cloth robes. I put the gun back in the waistband of my jeans, next to my spine, then stepped into the room.

"Excuse me, Mr. and Mrs. Brown," I said quietly. "I have to talk to you."

Both the man and woman whipped their head and shoulders around. They were young, fresh-faced, and attractive, probably in their mid-twenties. The man had close-cropped brown hair, and the woman's hair was a reddish-blond. Their eyes were filled with shock, fear, and alarm.

"Who are you?!" the man shouted as he leaped to his feet. "*What* are you?!"

"My name is Robert Fred—"

"Demon!" the man screamed as he leaped at me "You're a demon!"

So much for the easygoing approach. I hit him in the stomach as he reached down for me, then followed up with the barrel of my gun against the side of his head. He went down, and stayed down.

"Mrs. Brown," I said quickly, "please listen to me! If I meant harm, I could have killed your husband just now. But I didn't. I didn't even hit him that hard; he'll be all right. I'm not going to hurt you. I just want you to listen to me."

I paused, put the gun back in my waistband and smiled tentatively—but the woman's almost childlike face remained frozen in shock and horror that I felt almost as a physical blow. She was, I realized, thoroughly terrified of me—not because I was a mud-covered intruder who had startled her, or even because I had cold-cocked her husband with a very large and nasty-looking gun.

The woman was speechless with horror because she believed me to be a demon.

"I'm just a man, Mrs. Brown," I continued in a quiet voice that I hoped she would find soothing. "You are Mrs. Brown, aren't you? Vicky's mother?"

"You're one of them," the green-eyed woman said in a weak, quavering voice. Then she closed her eyes, threw back her head, and raised her arms in supplication. "Oh, Jesus, please take me to you now. Please take me now."

"Mrs. Brown, your daughter wrote a letter to Santa Claus. The letter was mailed in New York City by Thomas Thompson, and my brother and I wound up with it because of a certain Christmas tradition that's followed in New York. I'm no demon; I'm a private investigator who just happens to be a dwarf, and right now my brother and I are trying to save a few lives. Did you know that your daughter wrote a letter to Santa Claus a few weeks ago?"

The woman stopped her mumbling, lowered her head, opened her eyes, and stared at me. Then, for my efforts, I got a tentative nod.

"Did you read it?" I continued.

She shook her head.

"Your daughter was being sexually abused by William Kenecky. He was raping her, and he was doing it frequently. Did you know that?"

The green eyes clouded, and the color drained from the woman's face. "What . . . ? What are you saying?"

"All right, you didn't know. Kenecky was molesting Vicky, Mrs. Brown—raping her, and worse. She was afraid to tell either you or your husband because Kenecky had her convinced that she wouldn't go to heaven with you if she did."

"It's a lie," the woman breathed. "Reverend Kenecky has

gone on ahead, so he's not here to confront you. What you say can't be true.''

"Mrs. Brown, just how do you think Reverend Kenecky 'went on ahead,' as you put it?''

"God took him in a blinding flash of light. Mr. Thompson told us about it. Reverend Kenecky was Raptured ahead of all the others. It's a very great honor.''

"Thompson killed him, Mrs. Brown. He killed him because *he* knew Kenecky was a child raper, and because he thought that by killing Kenecky he could keep my brother and me from finding this place—which, by the way, doesn't seem to have worked out so well. The air here smells poisonous.''

The woman slowly, reluctantly, nodded. "Eden is wrong; it was not meant to be. I don't understand why the reverend said we should be here. If we are not to be Raptured, then it must mean that we were meant to die, to go to God now to wait for the end of the Tribulation. You're right when you say that Eden is poisoned. It is another sign. We do not want to suffer at the hands of the demons, so we're all going to God in a little while.''

"Huh?''

"Please let us be.''

"What do you mean, you're 'going to God in a little while'? Who's going to God?''

"All of us. It's been agreed that we should all die by our own hands. It doesn't make any difference, because we'll all be resurrected when Jesus comes to establish His kingdom on earth. That's only seven years away. In the meantime, God will take us to His bosom and we will be spared the agonies of the Tribulation.''

"You're all going to commit suicide?''

The woman's silence was her answer. A chill went through me, and I shuddered.

"Are you going to kill Vicky, too?''

The woman tilted her head slightly and stared at me. She seemed genuinely puzzled. "Of course,'' she said at last.

"Do you think I would leave my own daughter behind to suffer seven years of Tribulation, to be torn by the claws of demons? Armageddon is about to begin."

"Please listen to me very carefully, Mrs. Brown. Armageddon *could* begin in a little while—not because God or Jesus wants it, but because Kenecky and a man by the name of Henry Blaisdel wanted it. There are hydrogen bombs, and—"

"It's God's will. All but white, born-again Christians will be sent to hell anyway. What difference does it make if kikes, niggers, and mud people die now or later?"

Hearing the words from the young, attractive, innocent-looking woman shook me, and I involuntarily took a step backward. I wondered if she sensed how afraid I was of her, of the poison in her mind that had, in a few short years, corroded her rationality and morality.

"I'm no demon, Mrs. Brown," I said, struggling to keep my voice even. "There aren't any demons outside now, and there aren't going to be any demons outside after midnight. What there's going to be is a whole lot of death and destruction if we don't stop what's been set in motion. But we are going to stop it. You know about the radio transmitter, and you know where it is; if you don't, your husband does, because he's been looking after the place. One of you is going to tell me where it is, and then we're going to shut it down. Then we'll see if we can't talk some sense into the rest of the people in here. If you kill yourself, it will be for nothing. Armageddon isn't coming, Mrs. Brown; just a new year."

"Lie," she hissed, and suddenly hatred glinted in her green eyes. "You *are* a demon! Satan sent you!"

"Lady, those hydrogen bombs aren't going to go off in any event, because this place is going to be leveled to the ground before the signal is sent. So let's do us all a favor and—"

"*Demon!*" she screamed. It was her last intelligible word, as she suddenly threw her head back again and began to babble at the top of her lungs. Saliva flew from her lips, dripped down her chin.

There'd already been a good deal too much shouting, as far as I was concerned, and the woman's sudden, very loud fit of glossolalia wasn't helpful to either my nerves or the situation. "Sorry, ma'am," I said as I stepped quickly across the room and clipped her on the chin. The speaking in tongues stopped, and she collapsed to the floor.

I went back into the other room, walked over to the clock radio, which now read 10:50; I reached out with a trembling hand, turned it on.

The radio was tuned to a country radio station, which was playing a Hank Williams tune. I slowly turned the dial, got light classical music, a talk show, a New Year's Eve party, a news report on local weather conditions.

It was almost one in the morning in New York, but the bombs had not exploded—yet; it had to mean that the transmitter was set to Mountain Time. We still had a little more than an hour. I heaved a deep sigh of relief, shut the radio off.

Where the hell was Garth?

But I didn't have time to worry about my brother, and I didn't think it was a good strategy to follow in his footsteps. I had to assume that he was taking care of business. While it was true that the transmitter might be somewhere in the church, and while there was always the possibility that Garth had been captured, I didn't think I should go there until I had explored other possibilities. Eden was a big place.

I was going to have to have a serious talk with Vicky Brown's father.

Suddenly a hot flush spread over my body, and I felt faint. Sweat popped out on my forehead, rolled down my face. My vision blurred. Just what I needed.

There was a small bathroom off the living room. I went into it and splashed cold water over my face. Then I took out the bottle of green pills. I shook one out, started to put it in my mouth, then thought better of it. I was very sick, to be sure, and feverish once again. I was probably hanging by my toenails over the edge of exhaustion—but I remembered the reaction I had suffered earlier, and I didn't want to risk having that happen to me again; if I passed out at any time in the next hour, I could well wake up in a world that had been forever changed, one with a few million fewer people in it and clouds of deadly radiation circling the planet. I tossed the pill in the toilet.

I pulled down the shower curtain and grabbed a towel, intending to use the items to bind the couple and gag the woman before I had my chat with Mr. Brown. I walked into the other room, stopped abruptly when I saw the child, dressed in a white terry-cloth robe like her parents, standing at the bottom of the staircase, which I assumed led to her upstairs bedroom. Considering all the commotion, I supposed it was surprising she hadn't come down before, and I knew I was lucky someone hadn't come to investigate.

The girl, rubbing her knuckles into eyes that were puffy with sleep, was staring at her parents on the floor, perhaps thinking that they were asleep. She was a beautiful child, with the same light, Nordic features as her parents. When she took her hands away from her eyes I could see that they were a pale blue. As I watched her I felt my boundless rage at the dead William Kenecky rekindled. I wondered how much damage, physically and emotionally, he'd done to her, and if it could ever be repaired.

"Vicky?" I said softly.

The child looked at me, then back at her parents—and perhaps saw the blood trickling from the gash I'd put into her father's left temple. She looked at me again, and her cherubic features twisted with anger at the same time as tears welled in her eyes.

"What have you done to my mommy and daddy?!" she screamed, and then came running across the room, tiny fists raised in the air. She reached me, began pounding my chest and face. "You hurt my mommy and daddy! You're a demon! I won't let you hurt my mommy and daddy anymore! Go away and leave us alone, you demon!"

As the tiny fists flailed at me I felt tears well in my own

eyes; I was struck by the incredible courage of this child who would attack a demon with her bare hands in order to protect her mother and father. I decided that she'd survive her trauma at the hands and penis of William Kenecky—and possibly, with some good professional help, the poisonous spiritual growth undoubtedly already growing in her mind from seeds planted by her parents and the other lunatics she'd been living around might be uprooted.

"Vicky, listen to me," I said in an urgent whisper as I reached through the pounding fists, gently grasped the child, and pulled her to me. "Shhh. I've come from Santa."

"You're a demon!" she shouted as she pulled her hands free and began to pound at my head again.

"No. I'm one of Santa's helpers. Look at me. Don't I look like one of Santa's helpers?"

That got her attention; she stopped pounding, carefully looked me up and down. "You're all dirty," she announced. "And you smell terrible."

"That's because I fell in the mud on my way here. You have to listen to me, Vicky, and don't shout anymore. Santa got your letter asking for a puppy and telling him how Reverend Bill was hurting you and doing other bad things. Santa has a puppy for you, but it was even more important to him to make sure you weren't hurt any more. Santa can't stand it when children are hurt, and so he sent me to make things right for you."

Vicky Brown's tiny brow wrinkled in a puzzled frown, and there seemed to be a newfound—if tentative—respect in her pale blue eyes. "You really are one of Santa's helpers?" she said in a small voice. "It's the truth?"

"Santa's helpers never lie," I answered, and cast a quick glance over at the girl's parents. They were both beginning to stir, and that didn't bode well; I thought it might be a little difficult to explain to the girl why one of Santa's helpers had been bashing her parents around. "Can't you see that I'm an elf?"

"What's your name?" she asked, eyes narrowed suspiciously.

"Mr. Mongo. I'm one of Santa's helpers who takes care of heavy duty . . . uh, Santa sends me out to take care of people who hurt little girls and boys. I'm his toughest helper."

Mr. Brown moaned, then fell silent again. Mrs. Brown, however, was starting to come around. One leg twitched, and she started to raise her head.

"You sure you're not a demon?"

"Yes, Vicky. Uh, why don't you go into the bathroom and spla—"

"How come you have on pink sneakers?" she asked in an accusatory tone as she pointed a tiny finger at my unusual footgear, which the streams I'd waded through on my way from the swamp had washed clean. I decided that her interrogation techniques were as good as, probably better than, Malachy McCloskey's. "Elves don't wear pink sneakers. They wear shoes with pointy toes."

"Only the elves who make toys in Santa's workshop wear shoes with pointy toes," I said tightly, keeping my eye on the woman, who was now pushing herself up from the floor with her hands, shaking her head. The child's back was to her parents, but in another few seconds I was going to have to make some kind of move, and it looked like it was going to have to be an unpleasant one. "Tough elves like me who are sent out to help little girls wear pink sneakers."

"I have to go to the bathroom, Mr. Mongo."

Ah. "You go right ahead, Vicky. I'll be right here when you come back. We'll talk about your puppy."

She'd no sooner stepped into the other room than I was across the floor. I stepped in front of the woman, once again clipped her on the chin—this time more gently, using the heel of my hand. I caught her head, eased it down to the floor, put the towel under it. Then I checked the man's pulse and breathing. I'd apparently hit him harder than I'd intended, but I decided that he'd be all right as soon as he slept a little longer.

Next I checked on the clock radio in the other room. It read 11:05. I returned to the unconscious couple, made a show of covering the woman with an afghan from a sofa set against the wall. The child had become the key, and I couldn't rush.

The child, still looking sleepy, entered the room. Now apparently trusting me completely, she came over to where I knelt beside her mother, wrapped her arms around my neck, and rested her head on my chest.

"What's wrong with Mommy and Daddy, Mr. Mongo?"

"I . . . I had to make them go to sleep, Vicky."

"Why?"

"For two reasons, Vicky. First, they might not understand that I have to find something and shut it off before it hurts other little girls and boys like you. Second, because they might want to hurt themselves—and you—if I didn't make them go to sleep."

"Why would Mommy and Daddy want to hurt me, Mr. Mongo?"

"They wouldn't know they were hurting you. They believe wrong things. They believe they have to take themselves and you off to God. That's wrong. If God wants you, He'll take you in His own good time."

"We're all supposed to go to God in a little while, Mr. Mongo. There are going to be demons all around outside. We were supposed to stay here until Jesus came down to drive away all the demons and take care of us, but now everything here smells like poo-poo. Mr. Thompson says it's a sign that we're supposed to go to God now, before the demons come. He's made us stuff to drink that will make us sleep while God takes us."

"Vicky, do you like Mr. Thompson?"

She made a small grimace. "I guess he's all right, but he looks real funny now that he doesn't have any ears. Some demon hurt him and took away his ears. Now he kind of scares me sometimes, and I know he scares my mommy and daddy. When he came around here and told us we have to drink that stuff, Mommy and Daddy tried to argue with him. He made them be quiet. I think he scared them."

"Vicky, Mr. Thompson is wrong. He believes wrong things about what God wants. Santa knows what God wants, and Santa doesn't want you or anyone else to drink that stuff and go to sleep like Mr. Thompson wants you to. If you do, you'll never wake up again, and then you won't be able to play with your puppy. That's why Santa sent me here to stop Mr. Thompson from doing those bad things. Do you believe me, Vicky?"

Her answer was a small nod of her head.

"I have to tie your parents up, Vicky, but it will only be for a little while. It's so they won't hurt themselves or try to stop me. After I find what I'm looking for, we'll come back and untie them. Okay?"

She thought about it, finally nodded. "Okay, Mr. Mongo. But please don't tie them too tight."

"I won't. Is there any rope in the house, Vicky?"

"I don't know. I don't think so."

"It's okay," I said, quickly getting to my feet, hurrying across the room, and sticking my head around the door to glance at the clock radio.

11:19.

I went back, quickly rolled the shower curtain lengthways, and started to tie the man's hands. "Vicky," I said tentatively, feeling the breath catch in my throat, "your father's been working here at Eden for a long time, hasn't he? He takes care of things, right?"

"Yes. But it's not his fault that things here smell like poo. He told me that they weren't building it right, and that they were putting too many people in here."

"Did he ever take you around Eden with him?"

"Oh, yes," she said, and smiled. "He used to take me with him all the time, and he let me help him take care of things. It was a lot of fun before everything started to smell like poo."

"Do you know what a radio transmitter is?"

She shook her head, and I swallowed a grunt of frustration as I tried to think how to describe something when I didn't even know what it looked like.

I continued, "Did your daddy ever talk about a machine, or anything, that was going to send everybody to God just before the demons came?"

"You mean the thing that's going to kill all the niggers, kikes, mud people, and burnoose-heads?"

"Where is it, Vicky?"

"Across the ocean, up on the shore just before the place where the jungle begins. Daddy never did anything to it. He told me it takes care of itself, and that it's all set. But he used to show it to me. It's going to help Jesus when He comes to fight the demons."

"How can we get to it, Vicky?"

"We can get there in a cart by going around the ocean, but it's more fun to go across in a boat."

"Where do they keep the carts, Vicky?"

"They're parked down by—" The girl suddenly stopped speaking, and her eyes suddenly went wide as she looked at something behind me. "What are you going to do with that ax, Mr. Thompson?"

I pushed Vicky to one side, then leaped away just as the heavy head of a fire ax buried itself with a loud *thunk* into the floor on the spot where I had been kneeling a moment before. Tanker Thompson cursed loudly as he struggled to free the ax head.

First I threw a pillow from the sofa at him, because it was the only thing at hand. He didn't seem even to notice as it bounced off his face. But he noticed when I threw a side kick into his left thigh, just above the spot where I had pumped a bullet into his leg. The seemingly indestructible giant screamed, grabbed with both hands at his thigh, and began hopping around on his right foot. I hopped after him, drawing my revolver and aiming it directly at the hole on the right side of his head where one of his ears had been before he'd pulled it off. I pulled the trigger; just as I feared, I was rewarded for my efforts with nothing more than a dull click. As he roared with pain and rage and reached for me, I ducked under his arms and brought the end of the barrel up hard into his groin.

His roar went up two or three octaves, and his torso came down. I brought the butt of the gun down with all the strength I could muster onto the top of his shaved head, and that sent him crashing to the floor.

From past experience, I estimated that it would take me at least a week to beat Tanker Thompson to death, and I had neither the inclination nor the time to hang around to see if he was going to stay on the floor. "Let's go, Vicky!" I shouted, grabbing the child's hand and pulling her after me out of the room.

We ran through the living room, and out the front door. When Vicky tripped, I swept her up in my arms and carried her, staggering drunkenly as I tried to run on legs that felt like rotten rubber. Sweat was pouring into my eyes, blinding me. Gasping for breath, I weaved my way down the center of the road back the way we had come, toward the shores of Eden's ocean.

I suffered two serious stumbles, but I managed to catch myself each time before I fell with the child in my arms. After what seemed an eternity of breathlessness and pain, I reached the shore of the ocean—which, now that I looked closer in the shimmering, pale green light, appeared to be covered with lumps of what looked suspiciously like unprocessed human excrement. I set Vicky down, looked up and down the shoreline. Twenty-five yards to my right, barely visible in the eerie chemical glow, were a rowboat and a kayak with portals for two people. In the distance, in what seemed to me at least a lifetime away across the ocean, the green, misty mass of the rain forest rose up, filling the entire end of the dome.

And I was about to pass out. I reached into my pocket with a violently shaking hand, took out the bottle of pills. I shook one out, popped it in my mouth, and swallowed it.

"He's coming, Mr. Mongo!" Vicky screamed.

I spun around and was astonished to see Tanker Thompson, blood running down over his bruise-colored face, hobbling up the road toward us, dragging his left leg along behind him. He was holding the fire ax firmly in his hands, occasionally using it as a crutch.

Although the amphetamine certainly couldn't have had time to work its way into my bloodstream, the sight of the ax-wielding Tanker Thompson making his way up the road had a near-miraculous effect on my nervous system and energy level. It was motivational. Vicky ran on ahead of me as, pumping my arms and gasping in the fetid air, I managed to shuffle along at a pretty good pace across the feces-covered sand to the boats. There was a two-bladed paddle next to the kayak. I gave the rowboat a shove with my foot, sending it out into the water, then sat Vicky down in the front portal of the kayak. I slid into the back, pushed against the sand with my paddle, and we glided out over the greenish-brown water.

I grabbed the two-bladed paddle in the center, with my hands about two feet apart, then began paddling, stroking first on one side, then the other. I tried to concentrate on keeping my pace steady, for it seemed an impossibly long distance across the polluted body of water, and I knew I was very near the edge of my energy reserves. I'd needed the pill, because I'd been close to collapsing, but now I was having a reaction. I wasn't having the near-hallucinations I'd experienced before, but it felt like there was a ball of fire in my stomach—and the ball was gradually growing hotter as it expanded, sending tongues of flame throughout the rest of my body. I didn't like the sensation at all.

"Vicky," I said to the child in a stranger's voice that shocked me with its raw hoarseness. "You have to point out to me where we have to go."

"I . . . I'm not sure, Mr. Mongo. Daddy never took me over there when it was dark like this."

"Do the best you can, sweetheart. We have to land as close to the machine as possible."

Vicky hesitated, then pointed off to the right at a forty-five-degree angle. "I think it's over there, Mr. Mongo."

I stroked twice, hard, on my left, waited while the nose of

the kayak swung around to the desired direction, then resumed my steady windmill paddling, trying to concentrate on taking deep, steady breaths. The air was growing even fouler as we crossed the water toward the far shore with its infernal machine, and the rain forest beyond.

"He's coming, Mr. Mongo!" Vicky cried out in a small, frightened voice as she pointed back over my shoulder.

Although I knew it would disrupt my rhythm, fear made me stop paddling and glance back behind me. I wished I hadn't. We were perhaps a quarter of the way across Eden's ocean; yet, despite the fact that Tanker Thompson had to be suffering a giant headache, and despite the fact that he'd had to wade or swim out into the water to retrieve the rowboat, he was no more than twenty-five or thirty yards behind me. Like the monsters of nightmares that keep coming at you, he was rowing the boat with steady, powerful strokes generated by his bulk and the bulging muscles in his broad back and thick arms. Even with his back to me, I could see that he was covered with offal from the fouled waters; he glistened in the pale green light like some giant slug turned into human form.

As I stared back at him, momentarily paralyzed with horror, he slowed his pace slightly, turned around, and met my gaze. He was close enough so that I could clearly see his features; his small eyes were filled with hate, and his lips were twisted in a grimace of fierce determination. The main outrider of the second horseman out of Eden was threatening to ride me down—or sink me. I wondered if he still had his fire ax with him.

I wondered what time it was, and if it was going to make any difference.

And then Tanker Thompson turned back, leaned far forward, dipped his oars in the water, and gave a mighty pull. His boat seemed to surge through the water; with that one pull, it seemed to me that he had almost halved the distance between us.

His performance was tremendously inspiring to me.

"Are we still heading in the right direction, Vicky?!" I

shouted as I turned my head forward and began to paddle furiously.

"That way a little, Mr. Mongo!" she shouted back, pointing a few more degrees to the right. "Please don't let him catch us! I'm scared!"

Me too. Escaping from Tanker Thompson had become a moot point. He was definitely going to catch us—or at least me; I was resigned to the fact that I was a dead man, even though I didn't much care for the idea. The only question that remained was whether I was going to be able to wreck the transmitter before Tanker Thompson wrecked me.

And I had to find a way to save Vicky Brown. The child Garth and I had pledged to help must not die.

"Vicky! Is there a way to get out of Eden on the other side?!"

"No, Mr. Mongo!"

Pull! Pull! Pull!

"How do you get out?!"

"There's a door back there behind the church! But it's locked to keep the demons out!"

Pull! Pull! Pull!

"Vicky!" *Pull! Pull!* "The moment we reach the shore, you must jump out and run away just as fast as you can! Don't look back! Just run! Run into the jungle and hide! Try to get as close to the wall as you can and curl up into a ball! Bombs are going to be falling on this place, but you'll be all right if you stay close to the wall! Then nice men will come and find you! Do you understand?!"

"What about my mommy and daddy?!"

I tried to think of something reassuring to say to the little girl, but I had no more lies left in me, and precious little wind. "I hope they'll be all right, too. By now, your mommy and daddy will be with the others."

"But they could be hurt by the bombs."

"I'm . . . sorry, Vicky."

The girl began to cry, but I could think of nothing else to say. The fire that had started in my belly was now blazing in my arms and thighs, and I noted with alarm that it was burning away much of my remaining strength and resolve. There was a terrible temptation simply to stop paddling, lean forward, and wait for Tanker Thompson to come up and split my head open. I wondered if my heart would rupture when the fire in me reached it, but I tried to put that thought out of my mind.

Pull! Pull! Pull!
Pull! Pull! Pull!

There seemed no point in trying to see what progress I was making, and no point at all in looking behind, and so I screwed my eyes shut, sucked in a deep breath, then opened them to slits and concentrated only on trying to keep the kayak pointed in the right direction. The only point was somehow to keep going. I tried not to think of the pain and fire in me, and tried to find solace in the fact that Tanker Thompson, despite his seemingly superhuman endurance and tolerance for pain, also had to be hurting; if I could suddenly collapse with a heart attack, or simply run out of gas and pass out, then—damn it—so could he.

I hoped. I certainly had to admit that Tanker Thompson was the closest thing to a flesh and blood demon I had ever come across, a terrifying creature that kept popping up, back, from death by freezing, bludgeoning, and bullets like some malevolent jack-in-the-box from hell.

That's the kind of thinking an oxygen-starved brain will give you, I mused, and might have smiled if I'd had the energy.

In any case, I just didn't think Tanker Thompson was going to do me any favors by having a heart attack or passing out. Just as I was operating far over the edge, discovering reserves of energy and determination inside myself I wouldn't have imagined I had, because I was driven by the need to save one child in particular and millions of people in general, so, too, was Thompson operating far over his edge, driven by his equally fervent desire—implanted, he fully believed, by God—to see this child and those millions of people die.

Pull! Pull! Pull!

I knew I was now in danger of completely losing it; the fire in me had spread up to my neck, down to my toes, and my head felt like it was ready to explode. I was breathing in a series of small, tortured gasps, and my windpipe felt like it would seize up and close at any moment.

Pull! Pull! Pull!

Desperately, I tried to concentrate on images of scorched earth, flattened buildings, craters in the ground—and bodies; millions of bodies. That was what was going to happen if I couldn't reach and destroy the transmitter.

I wondered what time it was.

Pull! Pull . . .

A universe of pain, a world without air, heart and lungs that felt ready to burst at any moment. I tried to recall what I was doing, why I was suffering, where I was going, and what it was I was supposed to do when I got there.

Pull . . .

Somewhere, sometime soon, something horrible was going to happen unless . . .

Unless . . .

"Mr. Mongo, wake up! Wake up!"

Oh-oh. I snapped awake to find myself slumped forward in the portal of the kayak. My hands were empty, the paddle having slipped from my fingers. I was wondering how long I'd been out, then realized that it could only have been seconds; I could see the paddle ten yards or so to my right, just beginning to float out of sight.

"Mr. Mongo—!"

I spun around and looked up just in time to see Tanker Thompson rear up in the prow of the rowboat, fire ax raised over his head . . .

And then the prow of the kayak bumped the shore at the same time as the fire ax came swinging down, narrowly missing my head, crushing the stern of the kayak. I rolled to my left, out of the portal and into the water, put my feet down and touched bottom. I plucked Vicky out of the front portal, staggered up on the shore, and set her down.

A metal structure perhaps three feet high, enclosed in what looked like an inverted test tube with an enormous aerial atop it, rose out of the sand perhaps twenty yards up a slope, slightly to my left, clearly visible in the green light of the artificial world.

"Run, Vicky!" I shouted hoarsely as I struggled up the slope that suddenly seemed as steep as Mount Everest, feet plowing in the dirty sand. "Run!"

"*No!*" Tanker Thompson's deep voice, equally hoarse, boomed from behind me. "Don't you dare run away, Vicky! You belong to your parents and to God, not this man!"

To my horror, Vicky Brown, clearly terrified, suddenly stopped at the crest of the slope, beside the transmitter, and slowly turned back. Her small body was trembling all over.

I glanced over my shoulder, saw that Tanker Thompson was out of the water and onto the shore—but he was obviously hurting pretty good, too. Dragging his injured leg behind him, leaning on the fire ax, he lurched forward, then stumbled, did a pirouette, and fell on his face. I turned back to the child, struggled to yell, but could no longer make any sounds come out of my swollen throat. I mouthed the words.

Run! You'll be killed!

But the child remained frozen in place. In the ghostly light, her tiny body was framed by a soaring, greenish-black mass that almost seemed to be flowing behind her. What remained of the rain forest was clearly now nothing but melting biomass rotting and running down to accelerate the pollution of Eden.

Behind me, Tanker Thompson was using the handle of the fire ax to haul himself to his feet.

Once again able to suck air into my lungs after my brief rest stop, I resumed my labored struggle up the side of the slope. I reached the top, grabbed the revolver from the waistband of my jeans, and used the butt of the ruined weapon to smash the glass case over the transmitter. I tore wires from the terminals of the huge storage batteries powering it, then smashed the butt against the transmitter itself—once, twice, three times. The LED lights on a panel in front went out. I grabbed the antenna and snapped it off before slumping to the ground, quite thoroughly exhausted. I raised my head, still more than mildly curious to see what kind of progress Tanker Thompson was making.

I estimated that I had about six feet of life left—the distance between Thompson and his fire ax and me. And then even that was gone as he loomed over me, his earless, blood-covered skull appearing decidedly otherworldly as he stared down at me with his raisin eyes that now seemed virtually lifeless.

". . . Over," I croaked. "It's over. Please . . . please don't kill the girl."

"I won't kill her," Thompson mumbled through lips that I could now see were covered with froth. "She will go to God with her parents, as God wants her to."

"No . . . no sense. No . . ."

He staggered slightly, then planted his feet wider apart and used both hands to lift the ax over his head. The ax head simply kept arcing backward as his hands released their grip on the handle. A bullet hole had appeared in his temple, just above a ragged piece of flesh that had once been his ear. Still, he didn't go down. Even with a bullet in his brain, he continued to stagger around like some grotesque chicken. He finally collapsed when a second shot rang out, and his right earhole widened.

I wearily turned my head to the right, the direction the shots had come from, to see who my savior might be, and was not at all surprised to see my brother, standing in a green-striped golf cart, slowly lowering his automatic to his side.

The meanest Santa's helper of all.

Garth stuck the automatic into his back pocket, climbed out of the golf cart, and walked steadily but unhurriedly toward us. On his face, in his soft brown eyes, was an expression of incredible gentleness, and I could see tears running down his cheeks. He was looking at Vicky, and when I glanced into the face of the child standing beside me I saw that she was staring back at him with open joy, as if he were a favorite uncle she had known all her life. As he approached, she unhesitatingly ran to him, arms extended, and Garth swept her up in his arms and held her tight.

"It's all right now, Vicky," Garth murmured in her ear. "It's all right."

"Uh . . . dear brother of mine?"

Slowly, one of Garth's hands came down and rested itself gently on my shoulder. "You do good work, Mongo," he said softly, in a voice choked with emotion.

"So do you," I replied, grabbing the hand and pulling myself to my feet. I was quite amazed that I was able to stand; I was still reflecting on my amazing recuperative powers when my legs gave out under me and I sat down hard on the sand. I stayed there, drawing my knees up and resting my forearms on them. "Do we have time to try to get her parents?"

Garth kissed Vicky on the forehead, then set her down. He glanced at his watch, then at me. "Yeah," he said, once more pulling me to my feet and holding me under the arm as he steered me toward the golf cart.

"Uh, how much time *do* we have?"

"Just about enough for a very quick chat with a bunch of fools."

17.

I sat against the passenger's door of the golf cart, which was equipped with bicycle pedals, my arm wrapped tightly around Vicky as Garth, his powerful legs pumping furiously, guided the surprisingly speedy cart along a narrow pathway that circled the inner perimeter of the biosphere. To our left, the rotting biomass of Eden's rain forest resembled nothing so much as a giant bowl of green Jell-O that had been tipped over.

"They're planning to hold a Jim Jones–Guyana remembrance party back there," Garth said as he deftly steered the cart around something lumpy in the middle of the path. "They want to poison themselves."

"I know. What are they planning to use?"

"I got close enough to a bowl of the stuff to smell it, and it doesn't smell like Kool-Aid."

"It was Tanker Thompson's idea."

"Well, my guess is that they've mixed together gasoline, battery acid, and maybe a few other things to give it color. If they want to check out of this shithole by killing themselves, that stuff will certainly do the trick. But it's going to be ugly."

"Where are they?"

"They were gathering in the sanctuary of their church when I saw them; they've got the poison and a lot of paper cups up on the altar." Garth whipped the steering wheel to the right, and we sped along the path next to the concrete wall, toward the glow spilling out of the archway leading to the living quarters. "I snuck in through a back door. Incidentally, there's a door in the wall behind the church that looks like it must lead to the outside."

"It does. What time is it, Garth?"

"What difference does it make?" Garth replied evenly. "We have to go in this direction anyway."

"We're running a little late, aren't we?"

Garth looked over at me, laughed. "I love the way you put things. Actually, we're running a lot late."

"But—"

"Mr. Mongo," Vicky said, tugging at my sleeve, "will my mommy and daddy be all right?"

"We're on our way to get them now, Vicky."

Again, Garth glanced in my direction, frowned. "Jesus, Mongo, you look green."

"So do you; it must be the color of the month. At least I don't have to do the driving. How are your legs holding up?"

"Legs? What legs? You had to mention them, right? By the way, if my calculations are correct, that business back there puts me one up on you in the rescue department. You botched your chance in the Blaisdel Building."

"Bull—nonsense. That doesn't count as a rescue."

"It doesn't? I could have sworn I saw Thompson standing over you with an ax, and it looked to me like he was getting ready to split you right down the middle."

"I was just sitting down to get my second wind. But I won't deny that I was happy to see you; I could tell that you were all right, and it meant that I didn't have to rush back to rescue you after I took care of Tanker Thompson. How *did* you manage to get over there when you did?"

"While I was in the church, I debated whether or not to jump somebody and try to get the information we needed, but they all stayed together. I'd determined that the transmitter wasn't there, and I figured that my best move was to go back to the cottage and work with you to get the information out of one of Vicky's parents." He took one hand off the steering wheel to rub his thighs, which had to be beginning to cramp, then reached out and pressed my shoulder. "The bottom line was that if we were going to die, I wanted us to be together. I hadn't seen Thompson inside the church, and that made me uneasy. I wanted to make sure you were all right."

"Thanks, Garth," I said seriously. "I may give you rescue credit after all."

"Anyway, I was on my way back to the cottage when I caught sight of Thompson lurching up the road with that ax. I had a pretty good idea who he was chasing, so I took off after him. I was looking to get a good shot at him, but he had too much of a lead. By the time I caught up, you were all out paddling on that oversize cesspool. I couldn't fire at him without risk of hitting you or Vicky, and I didn't want to waste any bullets. I'd seen some of these golf carts back by the church, so I ran back and got this. By the time I made it back to the water, you were out of sight. But I knew you had to be trying to make it to the other side, so I just pedaled around on this path." He paused and, despite the pain evident in his body and his shortness of breath, chuckled. "If I'd known you were just sitting there resting, I wouldn't have been so quick on the trigger; I'd have just stood there and waited for you to stick that ax up his—"

"We have young ears among us, brother."

"—nose."

At the arched entranceway to the living quarters, Garth turned sharply and headed straight down the center of the road toward the swastika-crowned church at the end.

"Hold it!" I said as we came abreast of the Browns' cottage. "Vicky's parents may have stayed in their cottage; we have to check."

Garth braked to a halt, then grabbed the back of my shirt just as I'd been about to topple out of the cart onto my face. "You stay here," he said curtly. "I'm still a paler green than you are."

Garth got out of the cart, paused for a few seconds to catch his breath and knead the muscles in his legs, then hurried into the cottage. I held Vicky very close, waited. He reappeared a few moments later, hurried back to the cart. There was a strange expression on his face.

"They're gone?" I asked.

Garth nodded absently, got back into the cart, and resumed his pedaling.

"What's the matter?"

His reply was to show me the watch on his left wrist. He had reset it to local time.

It read 12:07.

"Maybe it's wrong," I continued tightly.

Garth shook his head. "It's not wrong; I checked the time when we were up in the plane."

"As much as Lippitt cares for us, I can't believe that he'd take a chance with the lives of millions of people and risk a world war just to spare the Fredericksons. And he's had plenty of time; even if his people somehow missed the Eastern Time deadline, they couldn't have missed this one. And he can't know that I managed to smash the transmitter."

"I agree."

"Then why the hell are we still alive? Where are the bombs?"

"I don't know," Garth said as he braked to a halt in front of the church. He quickly got out, pointed to a path leading around behind the church. "Get Vicky out of here. That path leads right to the door that will let you out of here."

But the child was having none of it. "I want my mommy and daddy!" she cried as she struggled out of my grasp, jumped over the side of the cart, and hurried after Garth.

I caught up with her on the steps, swept her up in my arms. I walked through the open door into the sanctuary, stopped beside my brother, and almost cried out. I quickly reached up and pushed Vicky's face into my shoulder, shielding her eyes from the horror.

There were upwards of three dozen people in the sanctuary, the population of Eden. Twenty of them were still on their feet, all dressed in white terry-cloth robes, lined up in the center aisle before their altar of death on which had been placed the large bowl of poison and a stack of paper cups.

The rest were dead or dying. Hector Velazian was crumpled in a heap at the foot of the altar, his once-handsome Latin features now almost unrecognizable in a face knotted in horrible agony. The ex–major league ballplayer's head lay in a pool of vomit. Billy Dale Rokan, the other ex-ballplayer who had served on Nuvironment's security staff, had lifted a cup to his lips, but was apparently having second thoughts as he gazed in horror at his dying friend.

Whatever Tanker Thompson had mixed into the brew was obviously doing the trick—perhaps too well; a number of the others were looking at one another uncertainly, while a few were exhorting the man at the head of the line to get on with it and drink up. Vicky's parents were standing just behind Rokan.

"Mommy!" Vicky called as she struggled to get out of my arms. I held her firmly. "Daddy!"

The people on line turned, saw us standing at the other end of the aisle. There were gasps, cries of alarm. Both of the Browns started toward us, but Billy Dale Rokan grabbed their arms and pulled them back.

"I want my baby!" the woman shouted.

"The demons have her," Rokan said in a trembling voice as he set aside the paper cup filled with poison. "If you go to them, they'll have you."

"Shut up, Rokan," Garth said in an even voice that nevertheless carried throughout the chamber. "Stop being a horse's ass."

Billy Dale Rokan looked back and forth between Garth and the cup he had placed back on the altar.

"Now, all of you listen to me," Garth continued in the tone of voice of a stern parent, "and you listen good. We don't have a hell of a lot of time. You've all been duped—first by William Kenecky and Peter Patton, and then by Thomas Thompson. The world isn't ending tonight, and there aren't any demons outside. You'll find the world outside just the same as it's always been, except that it will be missing those poor fools on the floor who've burned their guts out."

"*Please*," Vicky's mother pleaded as she struggled to break free of Rokan's grip. "Have mercy! We can't live here any longer. We want to go to God now. Please let me take my baby with me!"

"Why be in such a hurry to die, Mrs. Brown?" I asked as I stroked Vicky's hair. The child had relaxed slightly, and had buried her face in my shoulder, apparently content now to remain in the arms of her Santa's helper. I could not know what the child was thinking and could only hope that her mind was numbed by shock; she'd already had far too much horror inflicted on her.

"Because it's the end of the world! The Final Days are here!"

"No, Mrs. Brown," Garth said firmly. "There are no demons outside. If there were, they'd already be in here by now, because my brother and I put a pretty good hole in your dome when we let ourselves in. You have three choices: drink that stuff and die like your friends have died, stay here and wait for bombs to start dropping on your heads, or come out with the three of us. There's nothing outside to be afraid of; it's all in your minds. Come and see."

I said, "You've all been listening to people like Kenecky and hopping each other up for so long that you can't tell truth from fantasy. Now's the time to listen to my brother. For once in your lives, give reality a chance."

Billy Dale Rokan slowly blinked. "Bombs?"

"You heard right," I replied. "By rights, this place should be rubble right now. I don't know why it's not, but the bombs could start dropping at any moment." I paused, looked hard at Vicky's mother. "Come out with us, Mrs. Brown. Take your husband's hand, and come out with us and your daughter. Look at the corpses in front of you. Do you really think God wants Vicky to suffer like that? Take a chance on life."

Vicky turned her face toward her parents—but she did not try to get out of my arms. Instead, she brought her hands up and gestured to her parents, beckoning them in a way that brought tears to my eyes. "Please, Mommy," she said in her small child's voice. "Daddy? I don't want to go to God now, and I don't want you to go. I want to play with my puppy. Please listen to Mr. Mongo and Garth. Please come away."

"Let her go, Rokan," I said. "Let them both go. If you want to drink that stuff and burn away your insides, go ahead. But let the Browns make their own decision."

Billy Dale Rokan hesitated, then released his grip on the arms of the man and woman. The Browns came rushing up the aisle to us. I set Vicky down to allow her to embrace her mother—but I kept a firm grip on one small hand.

"If the rest of you don't come out with us now, you'll be committing suicide, one way or another, for nothing," Garth announced coldly, then abruptly turned and started for the entrance. Mrs. Brown, with Vicky between us, walked with me, with Vicky's father just behind. When I glanced over my shoulder, I saw Billy Dale Rokan and the other robed figures hurrying up the aisle after us.

When I came abreast of Garth, I glanced at his watch. It read 12:26. I could not understand how Lippitt could have failed to level the place before midnight—but I was certainly glad that he had.

By the time we reached the path leading to the door cut into the retaining wall, all of the residents of Eden had caught up to us and were close behind. I again glanced over my shoulder, saw in their faces a mixture of hope and anxiety. Despite all I had seen and experienced in connection with bizarre human belief systems over the years, I was astonished anew at the insane and murderous self-delusions our species is capable of; these people, I kept reminding myself, really were still worried about the possibility that beyond the door they would find themselves face to face with demons who had risen from the depths of hell to shred their flesh with tooth and claw. It made me sick. I turned back, stumbled, but caught myself and kept walking. Garth, still leading, was a blur to me. I could have called to him for help, but I didn't want to let go of Vicky, and I was determined to walk out of this rotting hell humans had made on my own.

Garth reached the door, kicked at the lock bar across it. Nothing happened. He kicked again; the bar snapped forward, and the door swung open to let in a draft of cool, sweet-smelling desert air that wafted over my feverish skin like a balm. I opened my mouth wide, drew the clean air into my lungs in great, heaving gulps.

Mrs. Brown, Vicky, and I had just followed Garth through the door when suddenly the night was pierced by powerful searchlights that hit me square in the face, blinding me. I winced, turned away, and lifted my free hand to shield my eyes.

The people behind me began screaming in terror. I felt Vicky being tugged away from me, and I tightened my grip, sensing that something horrible would happen if I let go. But the sudden movement had caught me by surprise, and I felt the small fingers being pulled from my hand as she was tugged back in the direction of Eden.

Everything was spinning around me. I dropped to my knees, desperately reached for the girl with my other hand, couldn't reach her.

"Garth!" I shouted—or tried to shout. The screams of the panicked, terrified people behind me were blocking out all other sounds. The night was filled with horrified shrieking, then screams of pain, the sounds of bodies colliding with each other, and then the sickening crunch and crackle of breaking bones.

"Demons! Demons!"

The little fingers kept slipping away.

"Garth, help me!"

Billy Dale Rokan's voice momentarily rose above the screams. *"Go back! It's a trap! The demons are here!"*

And then the child was pulled from me. I collapsed on my face, struggled not to sink down into the hot mist that was swirling all around me. Then my vision cleared for a few moments—just long enough for me to see that Garth was

using his body to block the entrance to Eden. I could see that
he was standing on top of bodies, and between his out-
stretched legs I could see the bodies of other white-robed
people who, in their blind panic to escape from the "demons" with their white lights, had crushed one another
against the ground or the concrete wall.

As I watched, my mouth opening and closing in horror,
the Browns, with Vicky being dragged between them on the
ground, rushed up to him. Garth hit the man with a right
cross to the chin, knocking him, unconscious, to the ground.
Then he grabbed the woman's arm as she tried to slip past
him, pushed her hard to one side at the same time as he
scooped up the child in his arms.

The last thing I heard before falling down into the hot mist
was the sound of more distant screaming coming from inside
Eden.

18.

THE screams of the doomed, poisoned men and women
who had "escaped" back into Eden kept echoing through my
dreams, along with visions of the people crushed in and
around the doorway. I thought I had seen Garth stop the
Browns, and rescue Vicky—but I wasn't sure it hadn't been
an hallucination. To escape the screams and visions, and to
satisfy a terrible need in me to make sure the child was safe,
I struggled back up through the hot mist that still cloaked me.

I opened my eyes to find myself looking up into a very
familiar face that was brightened by a most unfamiliar smile.
Mr. Lippitt, our ancient, totally bald, seemingly ageless friend
who was the Director of the Defense Intelligence Agency and
with whom we had shared so many adventures, hardly ever

smiled. But now his smile was a veritable grin, and his large, soulful brown eyes gleamed with warmth.

Behind him and slightly to his left, at the opposite side of what appeared to be the hold of a cargo plane outfitted as a hospital emergency room, my brother, wearing slippers and wrapped up in a heavy gray woolen blanket, was watching as an Air Force medic gently applied a sling to Vicky Brown's injured left arm. A few feet away, a very sheepish-looking Mr. and Mrs. Brown stood by themselves, trembling slightly, arms wrapped around one another, also watching the daughter they would have killed to save from an end of the world that hadn't come, and demons that didn't exist. They looked not only sheepish, but also bewildered and lost—as if, for them, their world really had ended, and they had no idea how they would cope with the one they found themselves in. Despite the infectious pus I knew their thoughts to be, and despite what they had tried to do, I found I felt deep pity for them.

"Don't bother asking me how I feel, Lippitt," I croaked, trying and failing to sit up in the bed. "I feel like shit."

"Considering the fact that you have double pneumonia and are suffering the effects of amphetamine overdose, I don't really find that too surprising," the D.I.A. Director replied, still grinning. "Actually, what I was thinking is how cute you look in pink sneakers. They go quite well with your slightly greenish pallor. It's really quite festive."

"You and your warped sense of humor can go to hell, Lippitt," I said as I finally managed to sit up.

"Lie back, Mongo," the old man said seriously, gently gripping my shoulders and trying to push me back down onto the bed. "You're going to be all right, but you're a very sick man."

"It's all right, Lippitt," Garth said as he came across the hold of the plane, put one arm across the Director's shoulders and used the other to support my back. "He's not going to be able to really rest until he's checked out the situation. Everything's fine, brother. You see Vicky and her parents over there, and none of the bombs exploded. It's all over."

I turned, looked out one of the plane's windows. Search-lights had been set up on the desert, and emergency and police vehicles were everywhere. There were reporters and photographers with sick expressions on their faces as they watched teams of gauze-masked paramedics carting plastic-shrouded corpses out of Eden.

"The others?" I asked in a small voice.

"A couple who got mashed in the doorway will survive," Lippitt replied, shaking his head slightly. "The rest are all dead—either trampled, or as a result of the poison they drank after running back in there." He paused, sighed, added softly, "Crazy bastards."

"Crazy bastards is right," I said, glancing over at the Browns, who, shamefaced, were studying us and listening to our conversation. "Christ, Lippitt, they panicked when the searchlights came on. They thought you were demons."

"I thought they might be chasing you, Garth, and the child. We'd been waiting outside for more than two and a half hours, worrying about you and wondering if you were all right. We were all a bit on edge. The moment the door opened, my first concern was to see just what was going on. I never dreamed the lights would cause them to try to run back in and poison themselves."

"There's no way you could have known. You've been out here since ten?"

Lippitt nodded. "Ten here, midnight New York time."

"But—"

"In all likelihood, that was when the signal was supposed to be sent to detonate the bombs. But there was no need to bomb this place, Mongo—especially since you, Garth, and the others were still inside. The National Security Agency managed to identify and scramble the signal from here to the satellite; in fact, I think they might even have found a way to destroy the satellite itself, although they don't want to con-firm that, even to me. The point is that the thermonuclear bombs weren't going off once the signal had been disrupted; we confirmed that from the bomb that was dismantled in

New York. Our next concern was the welfare of the Frederickson brothers, the child, and the rest of the people in this cursed place. We had no way of knowing how those inside would react to our forced entry, and virtually no chance of getting in without announcing our presence. Considering the forces and technology the planners of this thing had at their disposal, it was even conceivable to some people, including me, that they might have some sort of doomsday device—say, another hydrogen bomb—inside that they could set off if they were attacked. We just didn't know. You can't see it from here, but we did manage to attach a listening device to the section of the dome over the living quarters. We obviously couldn't hear everything, but we heard enough to know that the two of you were still on the loose and taking care of business, so to speak." Lippitt paused, looked back and forth between Garth and me, smiled wryly. "Past experience with you two has taught me never to underestimate the ability of the Fredericksons to take care of business, and themselves. If we'd heard anything to indicate that you'd been captured, then we'd have gone in. As it was, I felt the best course of action was to wait and see what happened. As I said, the situation was uncertain when the door was finally opened, which is why I ordered the lights turned on."

A khaki-clad angel of mercy appeared beside me with a china cup filled with what turned out to be chicken broth. It seared the roof of my mouth when I sipped it, but I couldn't remember anything ever tasting so good. Then the female medic held up a little paper cup with two purple pills in it. Garth took the cup from her, set it down on the bed next to me.

"Thanks, Lippitt," I said between more sips of the steaming broth. I was almost ready for sleep—lots and lots of it. "Thanks for taking care of business at your end, and thanks for caring about the kid and us. You do good work."

"No, my friends," Lippitt said. Then he really surprised me by hugging Garth, and then me. "You are the ones who do the good work. Because of your willingness to risk everything, including your lives, to help one child, the lives of millions of other people have been saved from a singular act of evil and insanity. The entire world owes you a tremendous debt of gratitude. And who knows? When the parts of this story that won't be classified come out, perhaps people will come to listen to deranged hatemongers like William Kenecky with just a bit less credulity and tolerance. Incidentally, our mutual acquaintance, the president, would like to speak to both of you on the phone when you feel up to it. He'd have been here in person, but he felt that his place was in the White House situation room until this matter had been resolved. I agreed, of course.''

I looked at Garth. "You want to talk to Shannon?"

He shook his head. "Not at the moment."

Lippitt smiled thinly. "You're still angry with him over the Archangel business, aren't you?"

Garth said, "Mongo and I are still angry with a lot of people over the Archangel business, Lippitt. But not you."

"Hmm. Well, anyway, he wants to mount a very big White House dinner to honor the two of you with the Medal of Freedom; your second, I believe. But these won't be awarded in secret. There'll be a lot of publicity. I suggested to him that he consult with you before he starts making a lot of plans for your futures—he sometimes neglects these little niceties, as you're aware. And so he delegated me to ask if you would accept the honor, and agree to the publicity. My opinion is that it would be good for you to accept. I know you don't much care for the president, but he likes and respects the two of you very much. I also know that you think he's amoral, but in this case I think much benefit could come from the publicity surrounding the story; perhaps it could serve as a warning to others about the kinds of religious charlatans and zealots exemplified by the people who built Eden.''

I thought about it, and almost laughed when a most diabolical thought occurred to me. I looked at Garth—and could tell by the look on his face that the same thought had occurred to him. He raised his eyebrows mischievously, grinned, and nodded to me.

"You tell him, Mongo."

"Garth and I accept, Lippitt—but there are conditions."

"And what would they be?"

"There are two other men who have to be similarly honored—one in particular."

"Who are they?"

"One is Lieutenant Malachy McCloskey of the NYPD, now retired. The other is Frank Palorino, another cop. If it weren't for McCloskey, Garth and I would have been vaporized hours ago—along with New York City and those millions of people you mentioned. We'll tell you all about it when we're feeling a bit more chipper."

"I'll look forward to it," Lippitt said evenly, his eyes, if not his voice, mirroring his interest. "And I don't see that there would be a problem in honoring the other two. In fact, I suspect the president might feel it would be to his political advantage to honor the common man, so to speak."

"Another thing, Lippitt," my brother said.

"What is it, Garth?"

"Palorino will advance very quickly in the department. It's McCloskey we want really taken care of—the full treatment; that's as it should be. We want him to get the full honors and publicity treatment. Like Mongo said, he's retired now, and he'll be looking for a decent job to while away his retirement years."

"In short, Lippitt," I said, "Garth and I want Malachy McCloskey to suddenly find himself very famous and very rich."

Mr. Lippitt narrowed his eyes as he looked back and forth between my brother and me. "Somehow, I get the impression that there are things you're not telling me."

"We'll tell you all about it, Lippitt," I said. "Later. There are also two pilots from British Airways—"

"Of course."

"For now, you give Shannon the message about our conditions. If he wants our help in getting political mileage out of the Eden business, he has to take care of those other people—

especially McCloskey. And McCloskey can't know that we had anything to do with it.''

Lippitt merely shrugged. "Politics, patronage, and influence aren't within my jurisdiction. But if I tell the president that the Frederickson brothers would like to see a retired police lieutenant become rich and famous, I wouldn't be at all surprised if such a thing came to pass.''

"Hot damn,'' I said.

"I love it,'' Garth said, grinning at me.

A soldier wearing general's stars came up to Lippitt and whispered something in his ear. Lippitt nodded.

"Excuse me,'' the old man said. "I have to take care of some matters. Mongo, take your medicine.''

I took the purple pills Garth handed me, washed them down with the last of the chicken broth. As far as I was concerned, it was time to go to sleep. I lay back on the bed, sighed, closed my eyes—and felt Garth gently nudge me.

"One more thing, Mongo,'' Garth said in an oddly stern tone of voice.

"Mm.''

"Did you tell Vicky you were one of Santa's helpers?''

Thoroughly puzzled by such a question, I opened one eye—and was startled to see that Garth was, if not angry, at least upset. "Yeah. As a matter of fact, I did.''

"Why did you do that?''

"Because it seemed like a good idea at the time, that's why. What's the problem, Garth?''

Garth raised his arm over me and pointed out the window to the bright lights, the emergency vehicles, the dense, poisonous mist oozing out of Eden's door and rising into the night sky. "*That's* the problem. Human superstition is the problem, and feeding little kids all that shit about Santa Claus sows the first seeds. You start off by filling kids' heads with fantasies, no matter how harmless they may seem, don't be surprised if a lot of them grow up with some very twisted fantasies about God, death, and you name it.''

"You're putting me on, right?''

"I want you to tell her the truth. She's already got enough shit in her head that's going to have to be flushed out. She doesn't need any more."

I said nothing. Garth abruptly turned, walked across the hold to where the medic had just finished adjusting the sling on Vicky's arm and was rewarding her with a large red lollipop. My brother spoke to the man, who nodded. Then he bent over, whispered something in the little girl's ear, took her hand, and led her back to my bedside.

"Tell her, Mongo."

"Hey, brother," I mumbled, now desperately wanting nothing more than to sleep for a very long time, "you want to be Scrooge, you tell her."

"Tell her the truth, Mongo."

"You tell her."

"Sweetheart," Garth said, kneeling down next to the girl, "I have some things to say to you." I turned my head, looked down, and saw that his features had softened; his eyes glowed with a degree of gentleness and kindness I saw only when he spoke to children, or those in great need. "First, I'm certain that other people who care a lot about little kids won't want you to live with your mommy and daddy until they go to doctors who will make them feel better so they'll never try to hurt themselves again. If that happens, would you like to live with Mongo and me until they get well?"

The child looked across the hold at her forlorn parents, then back at Garth. "I love my mommy and daddy, Garth."

"And they love you," my brother answered. Tears had begun to roll down his cheeks, and he made no move to brush them away. "It's because they love you that I think they'll want to go for treatment so that they'll be better able to take care of themselves and you."

The child thought about it, nodded. "Then I'd like to live with you and Mr. Mongo until they're better. Are we going to live at the North Pole?"

Garth slowly but firmly shook his head. "No, Vicky. We don't live at the North Pole. You'll be getting your puppy, but it won't be coming from any Santa Claus. Mongo and I are going to give you a puppy, because we love you and we want you to be happy. But Mongo isn't Santa Claus's helper. He's a fine man with a lot of love in his heart, but he doesn't work for Santa Claus. There is no such person as Santa Claus. Children should learn to have love for all other people in their hearts, but they shouldn't be told things that aren't true. Do you understand what I'm saying?''

The child was silent for some time, sucking thoughtfully on her lollipop. Finally she nodded. Garth kissed her forehead, then straightened up, realigned me on the bed and pulled the covers up to my chin.

"Sleep well, my brother," Garth said softly. "You've earned it."

I heard Garth walk away, then felt a child's hand patting my forearm.

"I still believe you, Mr. Mongo," Vicky Brown whispered.